# SEAGULLS DANCE

# Seagulls Dance

Larry Tracey

Corryann Ltd

First published in Great Britain by Corryann Ltd in 2005

Corryann Ltd
1 Horseshoe Park
Pangbourne
Berks
RG8 7JW

www.corryann.com

Edited by
Lynne Summers

*British Library Cataloguing-in Publication data*
A catalogue record for this book is available from the British Library

ISBN 0-9551610-0-2

The moral right of the author has been asserted

Typeset and Printed in Great Britain by Antony Rowe Ltd,
Bumpers Farm, Chippenham, Wiltshire

*. . . to my family and friends who have helped me
in this endeavour.*

# Part One

Part One

# Chapter 1

THE Irish village of Corryann, the First of September, 1794.

Connor Macken lay gazing at the sky, the white seagulls above dancing against the azure canvas in time with nature's orchestra. The scent of his wife Kathleen and the freshly crushed grass mingled with the salty taste of the air. The fingertips of Connor's right hand gently tickled the small hairs on the nape of Kathleen's neck. Her slender fingers were at once pressing and pulling the button on her blouse 'til her modesty was recovered.

Absorbed in contemplation, Connor lay some six paces from the cliff's edge, his back compressing the turf beneath him. The soles of his bare feet pressed down upon the grass, his breeches re-fastened at the waist by a knotted leather belt. He wore no shirt; this garment lay squashed beneath his head allowing his eyes to gaze through his toes at the headland and the sea beyond. The sunlight warmed his chest and face, minute droplets of water gathering on his torso like early morning dew. It was certain from his complexion and exposed toes that the sun had, for many summers, bathed him in its warmth. Connor's eyelids were slipping, resting on the brown lashes beneath. His mind was massaged by the steady rhythmic shush of the waves caressing the sand on the beach below. The intermittent whisper of the wind traversed the nearby field of ripened corn. The cymbals clashed from the ocean as the waves from the sea battered the rocks impeding their progress. Recollections of the past floated leisurely, impassively cerebral.

It was six years to the day since Kathleen and he had pledged themselves to each other before the villagers of Corryann. The images of that time, his feelings as he walked to the small church remained fresh in his head even today, especially today... It had been his nineteenth birthday. His feet, as he strode out towards the church were inhibited by the novelty of wearing boots which he'd borrowed for the occasion; his heart swelled, pressing out his chest against the freshly laundered, grey, collarless shirt. Cock of the village he felt as he led his three friends towards his matrimony, David and Mark jostling him, Mark's foot set out to trip him. The yell when Connor's boot made contact with his ankle brought smiles and grins from the others as Mark hopped on one leg, clasping the suffering ankle as if to stop the pain escaping, his upper teeth exposed, gripping his lower lip to contain his anguish.

"You'll not be wearing the boots in a few hours. It'll be her who'll be doing the kicking," laughed David.

"Not just the boots, she'll have your trousers too," quipped Mark releasing his ankle. "She's a fine spirited woman is Kathleen. She'll be sure to have the measure of you," he continued, his face contorted now in glee at his own wit.

"Pay no heed to them," Christopher, the third and closest of his friends rejoined. "You're the best match for each other there ever was," he concluded in support of Kathleen and Connor.

Connor nodded in agreement at his best friend's wise words. Wasn't he the luckiest of men to have a girl such as Kathleen love him above all other suitors? Indeed, love him so much that she was prepared to marry him, live out the rest of their lives in each other's company. For sure, the date, the first of September, would forever after be a special day in his calendar.

Connor remembered they were the first to arrive at the church. His friends had tried to persuade him to tarry longer at the inn, to slake his thirst with a tankard of ale they beguiled but the only thirst that he had that day, was to be married to Kathleen. His friends understood.

"It's through no fault of your own," consoled David. "It's a sickness you have and ale's not the remedy," he smirked.

"Women seem to have that effect on some fellows," rejoined Mark, winking at David. "Thank God it's not contagious."

With nearly an hour to go before the ceremony, Connor

pushed on the heavy, wooden door. He entered the church, the stillness inside calming his pulsing heart. His three friends stayed outside in the sunshine, "to give you time alone to re-think this folly," joked David, addressing Connor's back.

Sitting in the first right-hand pew available for common folk, Connor was five benches from the altar. All seats in front were marked with the name of the local notable who had bought the right to sit closer to God. Connor bade his mind ignore the slight for he knew none of the notables were likely to attend this day.

The thought of those who would not witness his day caused tears to well from his eyes, streaking the day's dust on his face, dripping from his chin to wet his clasped hands. No, Sarah Macken, his mother, she had gone to God before Connor's sixth birthday. She died soon after the birth of his sister Veronica, herself an angel within two days. They lay buried together outside this church. Connor prayed hard to God that they could see him now. His body ached that they should share his joy. Gerard Macken, his father, sailed to Spain to fight for the coin, driven to leave Corryann for the crops had been poor for two seasons. Landlord's rent and churchman's tithes were still payable on pain of eviction from land and home. He remained like so many other young men of Ireland, finished on a foreign field in search of a means to live on their own land. It was five years since the tidings of his death. Connor's sadness increased by the lack of a grave to mourn over. His hands now clasped so tight in prayer, his knuckles seemed close to breaking through the skin. The effort of prayer quelled Connor's aching. Comfort came from his belief that his family would be looking down with pride when Kathleen and he pledged each to the other.

Kathleen...ah...Kathleen...melancholy melted from Connor's mind at the thought of her. In a short while she'd be beside him. They had known each other all their lives save for the fact that Connor was eighteen months the elder. For the past fifteen months and three days they had been walking out together. It was nine months to the day since Connor had called on Seamus McDonagh, Kathleen's uncle and guardian. Seamus' consent was willingly given.

Connor had then undertaken all manner of tasks from dawn 'til well past dusk to gather the five shillings required by the local churchman, Fitzpatrick, for the wedding.

Christopher, a broad grin on his face, had knelt beside Connor, touching his arm with a gentle squeeze of encouragement, Connor returning his smile. Shuffling noises came from behind as the villagers arrived. He awaited Kathleen, his stomach tightening, his mouth parched – what if she'd changed her mind? Then Kathleen was beside him, standing, talking, Fitzpatrick, Seamus, Christopher, villagers smiling, the bright sunlight, as he walked out of the church, Mrs Kathleen Macken on his arm. For all he tried, Connor could not replay the church ceremony in his mind. All that went before, most of what came after, were clear in his memory, the event itself presenting only abstract imagery in his head.

"What amuses you so?" asked Kathleen, tickling Connor's left nostril with a blade of grass.

Connor awakened from his reverie and, itching the spot with the knuckle of his forefinger, replied, "I was reliving our wedding day." He rolled over, pinning Kathleen to the ground.

"And I'll bet I know which part of the day made you smile so," she wheezed with the weight upon her, twinkling blue eyes signalling her own interpretation.

"Is it more you're after, you wanton woman?" rejoined Connor, "For if it is, I'm the man for it!" His lips closed in on hers.

As the passion of the embrace hardened, Kathleen rolled, pushing Connor onto his back, she now atop, astride his stomach.

"We've our son, Liam, to go to!" she mockingly admonished. "There's been enough babymaking for one day. We've to tend to the one we already have. Yomi will expect us to collect him soon," she said as she pushed her palms against his chest to regain her feet.

"It's for the want of a daughter that I put my body through all this strain," laughed Connor as he rose to his feet, plucking his shirt from the turf.

Kathleen and Connor stood facing the blue of the sea, his

6

left arm thrown across her shoulders, her right arm about his waist, her hand resting upon his hip.

"What a wondrous place it is," sighed Kathleen.

"We surely have been blessed," replied Connor as his eyes followed the line of seaweed meandering along the sand below, the warmth of the sun drying patches from black to bottle green. The vivid, golden colour of the sand below the straggling seaweed path lay in contrast with the dusty fawn of the shore above the tideline.

"Look at the way the sea makes its lather," he pointed out to Kathleen as bubbles of air at the water's edge fought to escape the embrace of the sea, only to be recaptured as fresh waves broke upon the shore in the rhythmic ocean flow.

"That's not much of a lather!" Kathleen retorted. "Sure, look at the ocean there, now. That's a lather!" she stated, turning her gaze to her left. Connor followed her eyes. A fine mist of salty dew bathed their faces. He nodded in agreement. A few paces to their left, the cliff face had subsided. Some sixty feet below, the wreckage was strewn across the beach, tumbling into the sea. The ocean, in defence of its territorial rights, sent waves crashing, clashing with the obstinate rocks too large to dislodge, creating a spray of brine carried ashore on the breeze.

"This is my favourite place in the whole of Corryann," said Kathleen. "It's here that I listen to the messages from the sea, hark the tales of the gulls above." She breathed deeply, "In times of trouble and moments of joy, I find solace here," she concluded, looking into Connor's eyes. Connor's brown eyes locked onto Kathleen in support of her words.

"I don't understand why but I do know what you mean."

The sun was close to touching the ocean on the horizon as they turned from the headland. They paused. Sails of a ship had gathered their attention. Some eight miles distant, it entered Clay harbour.

"I wonder if it's bringing in new cotton?" queried Kathleen. "The last time I went to Clay there was little to be had," she said.

"We can go to Clay in a few weeks, once harvesting has finished," Connor replied as they turned towards their cottage and the village of Corryann some one mile distant. Kathleen playfully pushed Connor who, unbalanced, landed on the seat of his trousers. She ran giggling at the mischief she had caused. It was some four hundred yards down the track before Kathleen's laughter was cut short, replaced by a girlish shriek as Connor caught her by the waist. They were now alongside the ripened fields of corn which covered much of the ground between themselves and the village. The two-acre field to their right was their crop, the land rented, as was their cottage, from the cleric, Fitzpatrick.

"It's a fine harvest," said Connor still holding Kathleen by the waist as they stopped to survey the ripened ears. "There will be enough to provide food 'til this time next year," he continued.

"Even after we've paid Fitzpatrick his rent and church tithes?" interrupted Kathleen.

"For sure, for sure. Some of our obligations are already met from my unpaid labour on his land," Connor stated emphatically, aware of his wife's concern.

Moving his hands from her waist to hold her hands, Connor stared intently into Kathleen's face, "This I promise you Kathleen, we will never want for food, not you, not Liam, not any of us. I will always stay here beside you to provide for you, I swear. I'll never be driven to leave for the want of coin," he promised. Kathleen squeezed his fingers between her own in acceptance of his words.

Hands clasped, they continued down the track that led to their one-roomed cottage on the outskirts of Corryann.

# Chapter 2

THE old man sat on a round topped, four-legged stool. The seat was broad enough to readily accommodate his scrawny haunches, the legs of the stool slightly longer than his heel to his knee. His unshod heel rested on the earth floor, the spindly bones of his feet projecting forwards, easily discernible beneath the brown skin which lacked the support of any noticeable flesh. His wizened hands were a pair with his feet. One held a small, white, clay pipe, the other a tankard of ale. The thinness of his upper body was evident through the woollen shirt as his right arm raised the tankard to his lips. He supped his ale though a shrivelled mouth unencumbered by teeth. Above was a narrow beak-like nose; nasal hair peeking from his nostrils ebbed and flowed with each heave of his meagre chest. His eyes were set back deep in their sockets, a pale, shy blue with pinprick black centres; the outer regions a mixture, white overlaid with red, they appeared to be continually weeping. Yet, for all his physical frailty, Seamus was probably the most popular man in the village, a carpenter by trade. His woodworking skills, although sought after, were not the cause of his popularity, rather the results of the use of such talents. As a young man he had crafted a fiddle. The intervening forty or so years had refined both the construction of the instrument and his fingers' ability to converse with it. He was an honoured guest at all weddings, funerals and caelighs; as important, more important to the tavern than the ale. He could lift the peoples' spirits and hearts above their travail, Seamus, the Joymaker.

Seamus transferred the unlit pipe to the side of his mouth, clamped it between his gums and downed the remnants of the tankard of ale still clenching his clay. His was a fairy tankard, a possessor of special properties. In the thirty years

9

it had rested in the tavern for his exclusive use, he had never had to refill it, yet he was always able to drink his fill from it. He reached for his fiddle and stick and, as he struck up his first tune, behold his tankard was again brimming. As the melodies bounced off the walls, the gathering in the tavern became infected with gaiety, Eoin on the pipes, Shaun with the drum, vocals, solos, duets, chorus, bass, alto, soprano, a cacophony of aural delights to dispel all thoughts save pleasure. For some, the tap of foot on ground was an itch that needed to be scratched. To their feet they leapt, swirling and twirling across the floor, flashing toes stitching a pattern on the earth as they passed.

Through the open tavern doorway tumbled a small, redheaded boy, his feet unable to keep pace with his headlong rush towards the sounds of merriment. As the four-year-old Liam picked himself off the floor, Kathleen and Connor strolled in, smiling at their son's exuberance.

As the evening rolled happily on, Connor was immersed in discourse with four other men. He sat at a table next to Seamus on his own hand-crafted stool. Liam was outside, playing with the other children. Kathleen had joined a group of women who sat listening to Yomi's ideas on dance.

"From the land where I was born, our dance came from the birds with wings, beaks, flappin', dippin', little import given to the feet." She then demonstrated her point, bending and rising from the waist, articulating her shoulders with her hand to her breasts.

"In this land, the dance comes from the gazelle, the fleet of foot. Most of the actions are below the waist," she concluded. As her audience quietened to absorb her description, one listener, Colette, pleaded with wide-eyed countenance, "Tell us the tale of the land from whence you came and how your journey brought you to here."

Yomi had lived amongst these people for nine winters; she particularly marked the cold seasons! Many times she had recounted the tale that brought her to these shores. She felt a deep inner contentment and pride in herself that this tribe, once strangers to her, held her in such esteem. Her knowledge of remedies for illness (learned by observing her father) and her ability to deliver babies (from assisting her mother) had made her a strong and valued individual in the community. Now Yomi's pride was rooted in her ability to relate her own history, held in her head, in the tongue of her adopted land.'

"I lived in a place much warmer than here. I have heard it called Africa but this was not the name we used for our land. My tribe numbered perhaps six hundred people. We lived from the land, from our crops. At certain seasons, the men would go hunting to return with fresh meat. In my family were three sisters, five brothers. Of the girls, I was the eldest; two of my brothers were older. It was in my fifteenth dry season that I was taken along with eight other maidens from our village. We were at a water hole, a little way from the settlement. A group of strange men from another tribe leapt upon us from the bush. Tying our hands and binding our mouths, they forced us to trek for many days. The bindings to our mouths were removed on the first night and, although we had little food, they gave us ample water. We were taken to their village. Many people lived in this settlement. None were kind to us. We were put to work in the fields during the day, beaten by the men with sticks if we stood erect to stretch our aching muscles. In the evenings, the women made us fetch the water in great pots which we had to carry from the river. The women needed no reason to prod us with pointed sticks or slash at our legs.

"At night," Yomi paused, she had never yet revealed the night-time terrors, being woken and taken from their cages quietly by the men, into the bush; the bad things that had been done to them; she was too embarrassed.

"Go on," encouraged Colette, "What happened at night?"

"At night," Yomi continued, "we were shut in cages. This was our daily routine until, after one season, we were sold to very dark-skinned strangers who came and took us away. Our hands were bound as we were led through long grass for days on end. Then we spent even more days walking through bush-covered hills until we reached the coast. This was the first time I had seen the ocean. We were taken to a compound housing many more like us and there we were well-nourished. I believe that we were sold again because our captors left without us.

"After seven nights, some white men, much like those that live here, came and bought many of the captives, four from our tribe. We were taken onto a ship that lay waiting. It was dark, stale, rotten in the belly of the ship. After three days, with more and more captives being squashed amongst us, I began to imagine I had died. My mistake became known to me when the ship moved. The air became less choking as the boat picked up speed, the hold in which we were stored becoming fresher.

"It was some days into the voyage that I first met O'Rourke. He was helping to pass out food to the captives. Having caught his attention with my eyes, I felt emboldened to smile. My reward was swift in coming as he returned the smile with an extra chunk of bread. As friendship developed, I was moved to his quarters. There I helped with his duties as medical officer. He was kind to me; I, in turn, was kind to him. The ship reached its destination some weeks later. I and a few other fortunate women were secreted in the crew's quarters. The cargo manifest recorded us as having been amongst the many that died, being buried at sea. Having unloaded its human cargo, the boat was laden with tobacco bound for Bristol. It was during my time at sea with O'Rourke that I learned your tongue, speaking it readily by the time we arrived here, at his homeland."

"Do you think you will ever see O'Rourke or your village again?" questioned Colette, gently.

"For now, I'll work O'Rourke's land in case he returns from the wars. I've waited eight years," Yomi responded. "As for my village, now that I have seen the scale of the earth, I cannot foresee how I might find my own tribe's land," she finished wistfully, moisture gathering in the well of her eyes. She sniffed, clearing the tear before it could trickle down the side of her nose as so many had before when she remembered her homeland.

# Chapter 3

THE wooden cart bounced as the wheels rolled over a rut in the track. Liam sat on its floor, wobbling to the rhythm, his small hands clutching the basket containing his own and his father's lunch. Although still low in the sky, the sun had been rising long enough to evaporate the dew from the corn. At the southernmost edge of the cornfield, Connor lay down the handle of the cart upon the earth. Liam slid towards the inclined handle until stopped by the wall of the cart.

With the sweeping motion of his long-handled scythe, the stalks, yielding to the sharpened blade, fell to the ground alongside as Connor traversed the field of ripened corn. On arriving at the opposite side, he lay down his scythe, picked up two stalks, knotted them and gathered an armful of corn, tying it into a bundle. He carried the bundles to the cart, placing them tightly bunched in the bottom. The sun increased its warmth as it climbed higher in the sky. Connor had removed his shirt, his torso glistening from his exertions. He worked the scythe, first with his right hand, on the next trip with his left, bending, bundling, carrying, the soft ache in his muscles reward for his toil.

The vertical slats of the cart had been extended above the sides to trap the sheaves of corn. With two-thirds of the crop already gathered in and the sun now directly overhead, Connor sat down beside his bounty. Liam lay close by, his head propped up by his hands as he gazed in wonderment at a pastel blue butterfly which flitted from leaf to leaf on a nearby plant. The cutting of the corn had disturbed the insects which had settled there. As the bewildered creatures took to the air, the swallows swooped to feast on their dismay. The elegant, graceful movements of these birds beguiled the labourer, his eyes picking up the rhythm of their dance, blinking in time with it. A tug on his trousers broke the spell as Liam handed him the lunch basket. Father and son ate in contented companionship.

Connor returned to his labours, harvesting the crop which he relied on to provide for his family for the next twelve months at least. He used his sharpening stone to hone the blade of the scythe. As he felt its improved keenness, he nicked his finger. The trickle of blood seeped into the deep callouses which covered his hands. He rubbed some earth on the cut. The bleeding stopped.

With the field cleared, the cart full to overflowing, twenty sheaves were left on the ground. Connor cast around for a suitable place to store the twenty sheaves. On the far side of the track, forming a right-angle with it, ran a dry ditch grown over with hawthorn bushes. He determined to place them there and cover them with bracken, away from prying eyes. He placed the sheaves some thirty paces from the track, camouflaging them well enough that a person walking by would remain ignorant of their presence. The sun had now fallen halfway between its zenith and the horizon. Connor picked up the handle of the heavily laden cart. His hands gripped the wooden bar in front of his chest as his feet drove the whole ensemble forward. Liam walked at his side. Though his legs were short, he sometimes had to cut his stride as his father's progress was slower.

As he trudged homeward, Connor considered the likely demands on his crop from the churchman, both in rent, for he was his landlord, and in taxes as the church was entitled to levy tithes on the peasantry. It was as well, he thought, that he had hidden a part so that the full extent of the crop did not whet the cleric's avarice.

# Chapter 4

PLOP...plop...plop... The surface of the thick corn soup erupted like molten lava from a volcano as bubbles of air escaped. Then the walls of the craters subsided. Kathleen, with a cloth wrapped around the handle, took the pot from the fire to the table. Placing it in the centre, she ladled the broth into three wooden bowls. Connor sat facing her, Liam at his side on the bench. A loaf of bread lay broken on the table, the dark brown crown atop the lighter brown crust of the sides, the ivory interior exposed. Liam pulled at the soft interior, dropping small pieces onto the top of his soup. He squashed them beneath the surface with the underside of the spoon, then recovered the corn-covered bread, dipping the spoon beneath it and placing the laden spoon into his small mouth which had travelled down to shorten the journey of the food betwixt bowl and satisfaction. Kathleen ate the crusts left over from Liam's efforts. She spooned the soup to her mouth to lubricate the passage of the drier bread which preceded the broth.

Connor exercised a different technique. He held the crust of bread between thumb and forefinger, plunging the soft dough beneath the surface of the soup, then, raising his arm and tilting back his head, he placed the dripping food in his open mouth, clamping his teeth to incise below the crust. Connor manipulated the remaining crust so that the end was pinched between thumb and finger. This was then dashed into the soup which stuck to the crust as well as the tips of his gripping fingers. A sweep of his left arm, a toss of his head, the food was placed through his open mouth onto his waiting tongue. The ends of thumb and finger rested on his parted teeth, lips closing to remove soup from the tips of his fingers, his tongue cleaning the broth from lips. Connor used his

15

bread to carry all of the broth to his mouth and to clean his bowl; the spoon lay idle.

Kathleen smiled from deep within herself as the food was consumed to the obvious quiet satisfaction of her family. With all bowls empty, a few crumbs on the table silent witness to the passing of the bread, the conversation absent throughout the meal, restarted.

"Will you play the pipes a while?" asked Kathleen as she moved the bowls from the table.

"I'll do all and everything I can for you but I ask reward in return," responded Connor as he moved the cooking pot from the table.

"Oh, and what reward might that be?" said Kathleen, twirling away from Connor's grab for her waist, laughter in her voice.

Liam looked on at his parents' merriment, bathed in the comfort that their joy brought him, small head resting in small hands, small bottom on bench, small elbows on table.

"My pipe can yield but a plaintive tune if all alone it sings. Without the voice of a girl with wings to draw it ever upward, down in the depths will my music be; so, come my angel, accompany me. My pipe will trill, my fingers dance, if your words you'll add to the tune I play," waxed Connor looking into the eyes of Kathleen, the palms of her hands resting lightly on his.

Connor and Kathleen shared their music. Liam delighted in it until the weight of pleasure descended upon his eyelids. Kathleen tucked him beneath the covers of his bed and Connor kissed his head. Kathleen placed her lips gently upon his face. The pipe began a melody; the voice began a lullaby. The soft sounds washed over Liam, caressing his body 'til his ears heard no more. The pace and depth of his breathing subsided. Though recognising his slumber, his parents continued lest he wake and because they enjoyed the tune.

The door of the cottage burst open.

# Chapter 5

AT the tavern, Seamus put down his fiddle and stick upon the table at his side. He had momentarily lost his passion for making music. Three men had, seconds earlier, walked through the door, their leader shouting at the tavern keeper to bring them ale. The innkeeper appeared in no rush to respond. The ambience of the bar had been completely altered by the entrance of the newcomers, the music had stopped, conversation had quietened. A few drinkers had swallowed the remains from their tankards and left.

The largest of the new entrants was warmly welcomed as he grinned amiably, nodding towards the other customers, a lad of perhaps twenty with two pale blue eyes smiling from a round face, centred by a squashed, misshapen nose. His tongue appeared to be swollen and too large to be contained within his mouth; it rested upon his bottom lip. To his left, a younger lad, maybe eighteen years since birth, mimicked the nodding grin of his partner, pushing his tongue out and gurgling "ell-lo ell- lo." As he parodied his simple friend, he looked to the man on his left for signs of approbation. On seeing none, he gently nudged him in the ribs with his elbow, repeating his mimicry. His reward was not as he might have hoped: the leader of the threesome glared a warning.

"Go get the tankards and keep your elbows to yourself," he snarled.

O'Sullivan was not in good humour. He'd just come from Fitzpatrick's house where the cleric had struck him with his riding crop. The blow, striking him on the shoulder, had not been hard and, in itself, caused little pain. The deeper pain, the cause of O'Sullivan's current mood, was that, after all his years of service, Fitzpatrick could treat him in such fashion, increasing the humiliation further by the presence, at the time, of other people. O'Sullivan's mind was determined to magnify the injustice he felt. It trawled the past in search of occasions of loyalty and service performed for the cleric. Hadn't he lied for the cleric ten years ago when they first met? Wasn't it the value of the lie that persuaded Fitzpatrick to employ him? O'Sullivan wondered what would have happened to the churchman if he had told what he actually saw, the traveller' girl, no more than twelve or thirteen, abused, crying, whimpering, then throttled lifeless, not by her father as he had falsely testified but by his Reverence. The accursed sights still troubled O'Sullivan at times, especially as he remembered the moments of the girl dying and her father choking to death. They were the first, the first of a number to die. He had procured many young girls since, by force or in payment of taxes. He had always waited and supped second; the cleric had first taste. He had quieted the girls, quietened their families with threats.

Hadn't he turned people off land coveted by his employer, raised their rents, increased tithes 'til they had no means left for paying save the sacrifice of a daughter's virtue or the land that fed their families? Hadn't he had a man hung by his false testimony just so that his boss could take possession of a mare that he coveted? O'Sullivan's mind triumphed. The cleric was in his debt, substantially, massively. He could bring him down whenever he chose. These thoughts salved the pain of his earlier humiliation.

Hanrahan returned with three tankards of ale to find his leader in improved humour. He passed the first pot to O'Sullivan, setting down one for himself. He deliberately spilled some of the contents of the third into the lap of the simple Sweeney. As the confused simpleton felt the liquid soak through his trousers, he apologised. The confused apology brought a smirk to the face of Hanrahan, quickly replaced by a frown and a wince as O'Sullivan cuffed the back of his head with his open hand. Sweeney was his dog: he might pet him or abuse him as his mood dictated but he protected him from all others.

When the trio had replenished their tankards for a third time, only the tavern keeper remained in their company. O'Sullivan remembered the cause of the stroke from the riding crop. Fitzpatrick needed more money. He blamed

O'Sullivan for collecting taxes at too slow a rate whilst, in reality, he had squandered his wealth at cards. To settle the matter, he was to exaggerate the tithes due, claim they had not been collected for two years and confiscate forty sheaves from the Mackens.

The tax-collector decided that he needed some reward to soothe his recent humiliation. He had always lusted after Macken's wife, had ever wanted her for himself. Maybe if Macken were transported, he could satisfy his cravings. Why work only for the cleric's cause? He would demand all of the crop in payment of past taxes. When Macken resisted, he would arrest him with the help of Hanrahan and Sweeney. When he was transported, the wife would be at his mercy. He would keep the money from the sale of the extra sheaves for himself so, in some little way, gaining revenge on the cleric. As he called for another draught of ale, O'Sullivan felt at peace. The ale always seemed to help him see his way forward more clearly.

# Chapter 6

CONNOR leapt to his feet, banging his left knee on the edge of the heavy wooden table. There was consternation in his eyes and his mouth rounded as he inhaled sharply. Kathleen reacted to the suddenness of the intrusion, all the muscles in her body tensing. She remained seated at the table. Within a moment, Connor's mood turned to rage as the drunken O'Sullivan tumbled into the room, closely followed by Hanrahan.

Kathleen regained her composure first and, sensing danger, she placed herself between the sleeping Liam on her right and her husband, the fingers of her left hand seeking out his forearm to exert a gentle, soothing pressure. The touch from his wife stilled Connor's temper. Seeing the darkness pass from Connor's face, the tax-collector was emboldened to take a pace toward him, his right arm extended both to protect himself if the mood changed and to deliver the tax demands so recently written in the tavern. Sweeney made use of the space liberated by his leader's movement to enter the room, nodding amiably to Connor and Kathleen. Connor struggled to order his thoughts. His physical being sought to release its tension by pounding the intruders. At last, the gentle hand on his forearm transmitted its message. The blood flowed again through the flesh on his knuckles. His fingers straightened and reached out to pluck the paper from the outstretched arm of O'Sullivan.

In the execution of his plan, the tax-collector had lost much of the self-confidence imbued by the ale. In the presence of his intended victim, he could feel it ebb from his thighs as if a tap had been left open. He reacted by stepping back between his two companions so that they were positioned in front of him. Then, having received no

*20*

immediate reaction to the paper, O'Sullivan sought to justify his demand.

"Man has a duty, a legal duty, on pain of imprisonment, to pay the tithes on each year's crop to help sustain the cleric (Mr. Fitzpatrick) and to pay rent to his landlord (again Mr. Fitzpatrick) for the use of the land. All sums are to be calculated by Mr. Fitzpatrick and collected by his agent, me. Tithes not paid one year are owed for the next. In your case, Macken, I've had to calculate for underpayment over a period of ten years, plus interest accrued of course, not for myself but as my duty to the cleric."

Connor's dejection as he gazed at the number on the paper was evident from his sloped shoulders, burdened by the impossibility of the demand. He tried to reason.

"I've paid my rent with free labour for the landlord. I've worked his field as well as my own for no reward. Your number's wrong; it cannot be; it amounts to all of my crop. I've a wife and child to feed. How can I?" was Connor's desperate plea.

"For pity's sake, don't take it all," implored Kathleen in support of her husband.

Sensing his power, O'Sullivan thought a short cut to his ambitions might be gained. Stepping round Hanrahan to place Kathleen between himself and Connor, he attempted to seem deep in thought. His eyes travelled to the roof, then to the floor. His fingernails scraped backwards, forwards, over the three days of bristles on his chin, lips sucked in, vanishing into his mouth, then reappearing.

"It may be that I could recalculate if I had good reason to." The cunning of his words was clear from the lowering of his eyebrows. His furtive, sidelong glance gave a silent invitation to conspire. The hope they had felt at the possibility of salvation was swiftly captured and rebottled lest it be falsely based, the tax-collector's shifty demeanour a warning to the couple.

O'Sullivan threw his left arm lazily around Kathleen's waist. Her body tightened, the tension raising her height an inch or two.

"If she accommodates me, I'll review the tax," he leered, tightening his grip around her waist. Connor's momentary confusion cleared as he absorbed the scene before him. With one deft movement he was upon the tax-collector. His forefinger stretched from his thumb as he forced the soft neck of the aggressor against the wall behind. The pressure on his vocal chords, his windpipe unable to inhale, O'Sullivan was able only to expel a rasp. The loss of his ability to give instructions to his two helpers left them standing mesmerised. Liam awoke. Connor, hearing his son cry, released his grip on O'Sullivan's throat.

"Take the corn and be damned. You and Fitzpatrick be damned. Taxes and tithes be damned. To keep my freedom, I must let you steal my corn." Kathleen laid her arm over her husband's shoulder to comfort him, her other arm shepherding Liam between their legs. Connor silently responded by embracing his family in the same manner. Locked together with Liam in the middle and their backs to the world, Kathleen and Connor protected each other.

O'Sullivan left the cottage, his two attendants having stripped it bare of all the corn sheaves. The embarrassment of their actions writ large as they kept their heads bowed, avoiding eye contact with the Macken family throughout. As the last of the sheaves were gathered up, Hanrahan mumbled, "Sorry." Sweeney following, looked at the Mackens. His stupid, doleful face crumpled as his cheeks were marked with the tracks of tears running down and under his chin. "Solly, solly, solly," he implored.

"It's alright Sweeney. There's no blame to you," Connor counselled. Sweeney left, closing the door gently behind himself.

The sight of the tear-stained face of Sweeney at last broke Kathleen's resolve. The tears spilled from the corner of her eyes. As they rolled down her cheeks, Liam, kneeling on her lap, kissed them so they might disappear, the salty taste upon his lips. Connor's right arm moved around her shoulder, caressing the hairs on the nape of her neck. His left hand held hers, stroking the back with the palm of his thumb.

"Hush now, all is not lost. We have twenty bundles hidden in the ditch by the field. We'll get by somehow."

The dual ministrations of son and husband, the release of emotion from the tears, the news of the twenty sheaves, all combined to dispel her anguish. "Yes, we'll get by somehow. We always do," she rejoined. "I was frightened you might resist and then we would have lost you to prison."

"Ssh now, I'm here and I'll always be here to protect you and Liam. I'll never leave you," Connor whispered softly into her hair as he pulled her gently, reassuringly, closer to him.

# *Chapter 7*

O'SULLIVAN had recovered his voice, though noticeably fractured, by the time his two labourers had loaded the cart with the corn confiscated from the Mackens. His fingertips moved gently across his damaged throat, intent on erasing the reddened imprints. The lightness of his touch was testimony to the injury he had suffered.

"I'll do for him. He's dead, just you see. Nobody treats me that way. Nobody ever has and lived to tell and nobody ever will. I'll fix him, the trollop too . . . You see if I don't . . . He'll regret this day . . . He'll wish he never laid a hand on me. . . . It was the surprise. . . . He sneaked up on me, caught me unawares. . . . If I'd seen him coming, he would've got it . . . The trollop distracted me . . . They planned it, planned it together . . ."

The two helpers kept their heads down, pulling the cart, one either side of the handle as O'Sullivan's diatribe continued.

"Why didn't you help me?" His verbal offensive switched direction. "Yes, why didn't you protect me? That's what I feed you for."

The two henchmen bent lower over the handle as they pushed it in front of them, eager to avoid catching the angry eyes of their questioner. The tactic failed. The lengthy tirade had failed to vent the anger. O'Sullivan stood in front of them, hands on hips, glaring and impeding their progress. He reached under Hanrahan's lowered chin, grasping him by the throat.

"And why didn't you stop him?" hissed the tax-collector, top incisors clamped to their counterparts below, forcing the words out of either side of his mouth.

"I, I couldn't. Was in . . . way," Hanrahan responded as best he could through his restricted windpipe. Unable to turn his head, he cast his eyes sideways in the direction of the lumbering Sweeney. O'Sullivan, unable to recollect the position of the two men during his ordeal, accepted the lie and released Hanrahan's throat. Sensing a problem, Sweeney started to back away, hunching his shoulders, raising his arms to protect his face. This submissive gesture goaded O'Sullivan further. Convinced now of his guilt, he began his revenge on Macken by beating his simple labourer to a pulp. The first blow was a fierce kick to the groin. This undid all defence. Arms dropped, face fell down, nose split, blood, teeth loosed, blood, eyes gouged, blood, arms up, attack the groin, kick, kick, fallen over, stamp on hand, grind heel, bones break, stamp on throat, stamp on face, kick ribs – some give, kick more, kick face, out of breath – stop. Sweeney was his master's dog to vent his fury on. Now abandoned, his purpose had been served. The mutilated Sweeney lay unconscious in the dirt.

Hanrahan was unable to pull the cart on his own. Despite the cuffs and curses of O'Sullivan, the wheels would not budge. So, to his great chagrin, O'Sullivan was obliged to aid in the pulling. Their progress was interrupted as the uneven push on the bar in front caused the left wheel to ride up upon the earth hillock in the centre of the track. Over many years, the wheels of countless carts had caused this ridge to form and its increased resistance proved beyond the power of the cart pullers. The remedy was to pull the handle of the cart sideways, to the left, to set the wheels straight in the ruts of the track. Hanrahan endured further cuffs and curses as they manipulated the handle, the subordinate pushing from the right, O'Sullivan pulling from the left.

The sharp sound of rooks *caww... cawwing...* invaded the evening air, mingling with the rhythmic melody from the distant seashore as waves washed over sand. The clump of straight, tall pines, absent of branches until the crown, was the chosen home of the large, black birds. From this lofty perch they circled the sky above, some spiralling down towards the ground, others rising, carrying stalks of corn pinched in their grey beaks like circus tightrope walkers with their balancing poles. The rooks' noise did not interrupt Hanrahan's thoughts as he trudged along the track feeling pangs of guilt for Sweeney's fate. He had meant no harm to the simple fellow and now missed his company immensely. A grunt from O'Sullivan stopped Hanrahan's concern for the big lad, replacing it with fear for his own safety. However, as the grunt was absorbed by the cool, dew-laden air and was not accompanied by a blow, he fell again to thinking of how he missed Sweeney. To his own surprise, he found himself looking skyward, silently pleading that his companion had not died.

O'Sullivan had also thought that he missed Sweeney but only for the moment when he realised the cart pulling would now fall to himself. His mind bore down on vengeance against Connor Macken. It had already presented its case as to why the absence of Sweeney and thus his current exertions, might be the fault of the corn farmer. Each step, the ache in legs, the tightening of his back and the hunching of shoulders acted as jury. Yes, his mind concluded and his body agreed, Macken must still be guilty somehow. He had relinquished his corn far too readily; he still had to feed his family during the coming year. Somehow...! He must be guilty, somehow! As he heaved the cart, his mind established guilt giving rise to the question of punishment. He'd plan to have him transported. He had lied, falsified the tax demand way beyond the avarice of the cleric so that Kathleen, Kathleen, could be his. Why had she calmed her husband? Was it in case Macken defied the false tithe claim? Did she suspect his intentions? He felt the increased effort on the handle beside him as he realised he had spoken her name aloud. Was taking all of the crop sufficient? Surely it must be. How would Macken be able to feed his family? No, no, his senses enjoined, how will that enable me to feel the warmth of Kathleen?

The arguments within his head tumbled over each other, first one on top losing its balance to be replaced by the other. The left wheel hit the ridge in the centre of the track, stopping the cart with an abruptness which thumped the handle into the tax-collector's chest. Cursing the rooks circling and cawing above, by implication laughing, he cuffed Hanrahan about the head causing him to crouch. The hedgerow beyond the stooping labourer caught the attention of the attacker. A number of rooks were on the ground, some strutting, others, bodies and beaks tipped forward above spindly legs, were pulling stalks of corn from the ditch.

O'Sullivan strode the thirty paces from the track to the section of ditch which interested the rooks. Whirling his arms, he yelled to scare off the birds. They stood their ground until he was some ten paces from the closest. One took to the air, flapping its great black wings, a signal to the rest who rose, flapping, cawing. O'Sullivan stripped the light covering of bracken to expose the twenty sheaves of corn. A sneer of triumph contorted his face. He instinctively knew the corn belonged to Connor Macken. It was hidden next to his recently cropped field. O'Sullivan needed to turn this to his advantage but instincts were not proof. How? What should he do? As he pondered the problem, brow furrowed, he dropped his hands into his coat pockets. His right hand settled on a crumpled paper which he absently rolled between thumb and forefinger as he deliberated. Recognition removed the paper from his pocket. The Mackens had not kept the tax demand; they had no official record. Now fate became O'Sullivan's friend and Connor's enemy.

Walking back to the cart and the waiting Hanrahan, the tax-collector determined his strategy. He would unload all but thirty sheaves from the cart at his cottage. The fifty sheaves he would sell for his own benefit. He would take the cart, laden with thirty sheaves, to the cleric's storehouse. The storekeeper would give him a receipt which he could take to the churchman as proof of tithes collected, ten sheaves short of the amount demanded. His Reverence could then accompany him to the ditch with the hidden corn. In hiding the corn, he would claim Macken was depriving the cleric of his rightful dues and therefore liable to arrest for theft.

His troubled mind at ease, he looked to the sky and nodded in acknowledgement to the rooks for their part in Connor's downfall. Five paces from Hanrahan, a fresh trouble clouded his face, furrowed his brow. In nearing his labourer, he realised that Hanrahan's testimony to events could be important. Kathleen and Connor would swear the tax demand was for eighty sheaves and that they had paid in full but they did not have the evidence of the tax demand.

O'Sullivan would show his copy which would indicate forty. The number collected would be his word and that of Hanrahan against that of the husband and wife. Hanrahan must lie for him. Fear would make him lie. He was afraid, a bonus from the beating of Sweeney. More was needed though. O'Sullivan needed to make Hanrahan a partner to his crime. Testifying for the Mackens' version must implicate Hanrahan in the crime. O'Sullivan would have to share the benefit of the fifty sheaves they were to steal with his accomplice – not equal shares, five sheaves would do. The smile returned to his face. He arrived at the cart placing a friendly arm across the nervous shoulders of his new partner. The gesture caused Hanrahan to flinch as he was unaware of his new and privileged status.

# Chapter 8

KATHLEEN and Connor sat at their table in the cottage, buttocks, thighs, calves compressed against each other. The warmth flowed between them, supporting their spirits.

"I'll build another cart and sell it. There's plenty of folk commented as to how they'd like one similar to mine. I have my tools left me by my father. There are plenty of trees. I can fashion the planks, the handle, the axle and frame. The blacksmith will most likely give me credit and the wheel-wright too 'til I finish the cart and sell it. If not, I could sell the one we have and use part of the money to pay for the new wheels and ironwork. Yes, I could. That's what I'll do," Connor concluded, kneading Kathleen's left hand with his right, bathing her whole body with his enthusiasm, love radiating from his eyes.

Kathleen responded, "I can take on more sewing, washing too if need be. The men returning from the wars always need someone to mend for them. They've coin too, from their pay abroad," she said as she immersed herself in her husband's optimism.

Connor's right hand stopped its ministrations on the table top, patting the back of Kathleen's left hand to signal the end of the kneading. His fingertips travelled up her back, feather-dancing on her blouse 'til they reached the nape of her slender neck. The middle fingertips fluffed up the small hairs below the hairline. Kathleen's eyes closed in response to this attention, her most favourite form of relaxation. Her head, which had lolled forward until her chin rested on her chest, rose suddenly. Connor heard the sound a moment later.

A scratching paw, on what? Paw on wood? The sound came from the closed door, from outside. Connor took the two paces to the door and, lifting the wooden latch, opened it inwards. Kathleen, now at his side, gasped in horror as the door opened revealing the battered Sweeney lying in the doorway at their feet. He had dragged himself the three hundred yards from the place of his attack, his passage marked by grooves in the dusty track where his knees, feet, elbows and forearms, supported his weight on its pain-ridden crawl. Blood-darkened dust marked his trail and a large round stain seeped beneath him where he rested. Connor and Kathleen bent down, placing their hands either side under his armpits, gently hauling him into their cottage, his feet dragging dust and bloody mud. Once inside, Connor eased him gently onto his back. The scale of the damage was so immense, Kathleen was almost overwhelmed. Where should she start? It was certain from his obvious pain when being moved that his chest was, in some way, crushed. She determined to clear the dirt and blood to uncover the injuries. Connor, with as much tenderness as he could manage, removed the man's shirt, the distress caused by the movement evident throughout. The crushed hand and the purple bruising around Sweeney's ribcage were clearly visible in the candlelight. Having bathed his upper body, the damage to the eyes and throat was exposed. Kathleen asked Connor to fetch Yomi. The scale of the problem was such that, whilst she could nurse Sweeney, she needed all the help she could muster to heal him.

Connor returned within ten minutes, Yomi at his side. After a few minutes, she had completed her assessment of the patient's upper body. Kathleen had lit a fresh candle to increase the light in the room and tucked a blanket around the sleeping Liam. Yomi loosened Sweeney's trousers, raising his buttocks with her arm beneath the small of his back. Connor pulled on the ends of the trouser legs, drawing the garment off. In the flickering candlelight, the carnage caused by the kicks to his testicles was exposed, showing them to be grotesquely swollen and discoloured.

"I saw a man tangled with a rhino once, from my old village. He had these kind of knocks but we don't have rhinos here," Yomi continued, "And you don't know what caused it or why?"

Kathleen told of the visit by O'Sullivan and Sweeney's part in it.

"He's one bad man. You want nothing to do with Mr. O'Sullivan. I think it's best he doesn't find Sweeney for a long, long time. We must move him to O'Rourke's cottage," Yomi stated, still refusing to call the cottage she lived in anything other than O'Rourke's even though he had been gone eight years, fighting for coin in the European wars.

Connor's thoughts returned from Yomi's reluctance to call her cottage her home.

"He's too badly hurt to move. Just the few yards to here caused him pain," Connor replied.

"His chest is badly broken," agreed Kathleen in support.

"If O'Sullivan did this and he finds him alive, what might happen?" said Yomi with finality and firmness. "I will try to mend him but it's best we get him away from here."

Connor and Kathleen deferred to her judgement for they knew Yomi was the simple man's best hope of survival.

Connor readied the cart, laying what bedding they had on its floor to ease the jarring from the track. Connor pushed the cart right up to the door to create the least distance to carry the big man. He eased himself between the cart and the door in order to help in the transfer of the patient. To avoid compressing his injured chest, Connor and Yomi lifted Sweeney's shoulders with their hands under his armpits and dragged him carefully, his heels on the floor. At the doorway, Kathleen took Connor's place as he climbed into the back of the cart. Bending down, he placed one hand under each armpit. When he had taken the weight, the women pulled their hands free, enabling him to drag the wincing Sweeney 'til he was laid on his back in the cart. His clothes were placed over his body. Connor embraced Kathleen.

"I'll not be too long. Take care."

He picked up the handle. Yomi at his side, he moved off at a very slow pace, wincing himself from the thought of Sweeney's suffering at each rut or stone the wheels rolled over.

"I'll go ahead and prepare," Yomi said when she realised that the half-mile journey would be painfully slow in every sense.

As he progressed, Connor's pace increased with the realisation that the slower he went, the more jarring the

ruts seemed to be. After fifteen minutes, he arrived at
O'Rourke's door. Yomi was waiting, ready to help in moving
the patient. Connor dragged Sweeney by the heels, the
bedding aiding his slide across the base of the cart. Yomi
supported his arm across her shoulders. Connor took up
position under the other arm. Between them they dragged
Sweeney upright, his toes rubbing the floor, to a cot
prepared by Yomi. They placed the whimpering man, as
gently as they were able, in it, on his back. Connor hugged
Yomi, bade her goodnight and returned with the cart and
bedding to his own cottage and family. The chill of the night
air penetrated his shirt, encouraging his body to quicken the
pace.

# Chapter 9

FITZPATRICK first saw the light of day in the summer of 1758. His mother had no particular problems in squeezing him from her womb. He was her second child, the first also a boy.

By the spring of 1760, it was apparent that the growth of his misshapen left foot would not correct itself unaided. The family had considerable wealth from their landed estate. Physicians were called to remedy the problem. Devices were fitted, left in place, squashing his foot, clamping his ankle more to the shape of his good, right foot. The pain endured by the young child was thought to be right and proper, a good sign of the efficacy of the treatment by the medics his parents employed. His mother had the devices removed after six months with no obvious improvement. Rather, his condition seemed to have worsened. Further physicians arrived with creams and potions applied to the affected foot. When one failed, he was paid and another came. At length, those who sought manipulation as a remedy for the boy's deformity, received a declaration from his mother who was adamant no further devices or potions should be applied to her son's foot.

By his fourth year, Fitzpatrick was now lame, supported on his left side by a crutch. In desperation, Fitzpatrick's mother called on an old woman from the next county who, if legend is to be believed, possessed mystic powers. On examining the child, however, the worried parent was told the news the physicians had failed to impart. The ailment was congenital; she could do nothing to help. The news caused Fitzpatrick's mother to seat herself quickly, lest she faint. The outlook for her second son was not as she had intended, dreamed, a dashing soldier resplendent in his gold braid and now, as she clutched her swollen belly, a third child was due. Would it too, suffer from the disability?

Fitzpatrick's younger brother was born four weeks after the incident with the old woman. To the huge relief of his parents, both feet appeared to be normal. The growing process of the next twelve months confirmed it: the infant was able to walk unaided sooner even than his eldest brother.

The three Fitzpatrick boys passed their childhood, as was the fashion of the day for sons of the gentry, with a comprehensive library, private tutoring, riding and swordplay. The second son shone above his brothers in academic learning and was almost their equal on horseback, a special stirrup having been cast for his left foot. He needed assistance to mount but was able to dismount unaided. Swordplay was the major activity his brothers enjoyed whilst Fitzpatrick would return to his books or ride alone. The stirrings of resentment seeped into his mind whilst engaged in these lonesome pursuits but he quickly banished them in favour of delight in the ride. The power of the animal beneath his seat, it's response to the pressure from his legs... no man, no matter how sound, how strong, could run with him when upon his horse. He found equal enjoyment in the words of others as his senses were balmed by the ambience of the library, its strong leather aroma and the light spilling through the windows casting huge, book-shaped shadows on the floor. The twitter of a bird, the chirp of another, the song of a third, all these sounds, discordant and random, surrounded Fitzpatrick as he immersed himself in literature. The words in the books imparted knowledge, making sense of what he saw around him. They painted pictures in his mind of far off places, of emotions he recognised and others he was yet to experience but forewarned to expect.

His brothers missed his participation in the swordplay. He was the link between the elder and the younger, able to relate to either in a way that they found difficult in his absence. The solution, when it surfaced, was so clear it was a puzzle as to how it was so long in coming. The swordplay tutor decided that the eldest son should advance his skills to fighting on horseback. This was a lesson in which the second son could participate. His lack of the basic skills, learnt by his siblings on the ground, was rapidly remedied. His enthusiasm, the thrill of no longer being a cripple, drove him to excel in this new discipline. Within a year he could better his elder brother, his tutor and parents delighting in his prowess with sword on horseback. Images of King Arthur's knights filled his imagination. He rode amongst them. He was one of them, righting wrongs, the foremost amongst a band of heroes. He dreamed too, of going to war as an officer, soon to become a general as his superiors appreciated and acknowledged his bravery.

The three boys enjoyed a privileged existence. Wants and needs were synonymous. If they desired food, clothing, houses, warmth, it was provided. They were not unkind to those who laboured on their behalf, in the same manner that they treated the sheep kindly which provided meat for their table. As long as the beasts and the people fulfilled their destined parts in the play of life, keeping to the script written by their father, his friends, their fathers and grandfathers before them, each generation interpreting the play slightly differently but recognisable as the same work performed two centuries earlier, all would be well.

Pre-ordained roles were scripted for the sons of the landed gentry, the part to be played dependant on the chronology of their birth. The eldest son would inherit the lands and title of his father. The land should not be divided amongst the offspring as, over time, this would destroy the estate and thereby the social position of the family. The second son was awarded a commission in the local regiment with the guarantee of rising to colonel after a few years' experience. The spoils of war tended to accumulate to the greatest degree at the top of the hierarchical pyramid. Rank was important: the higher the rank, the more booty allotted. The third son gained the benefit of a living from the church. The family controlled the stewardship of a parish able to generate an income large enough to fund a comfortable existence for a careful gentleman.

Laughter and cheering radiated from below the house as the oldest boy was knocked from his horse following a blow to the chest from the flat sword of the second son. Padding around his body ensured that only his ego was bruised though, in truth, he delighted in his younger brother's prowess on horseback. Nearing his eighteenth birthday, the successful swordsman eagerly anticipated this anniversary. It would mark his entry into military service. Despite his disability, he had triumphed. He had become a formidable force on horseback.

The day before his eighteenth birthday, the second son was called to his father's study. This was an unusual occurrence, in his experience unique, for he had never upset his parents to such a degree as to warrant such a summons. Perhaps his left foot had kept him from the more serious errors of youth. It was with some trepidation that he entered the room. He felt no guilt but had he done wrong? He was almost sure that the purpose of the visit related to his impending commission in the military service but was not entirely certain. His father's right hand arced lazily from his body. Fingertips pointing backwards indicated a leather chair with high back and rounded arms. The gesture communicated its message as the young man hobbled, one good foot, one crutch supporting him, seating himself in the appointed chair. He sat, crutch resting between his left side and the arm of the chair. His eyes rose to meet those of his father who had remained standing. The look, the moist eyes in the usually stern man caused disquiet, confusion in the mind of the seated youth. As he struggled to interpret, his father stepped forward placing a firm but comforting hand on his left shoulder, yet no comfort came; it only added to the turmoil in his mind. The father feeling, seeing the distress, proceeded quickly.

"The general has refused your commission. I am sorry, really sorry. He is aware of your skill on horseback but..." The father's pride would not allow him to tell his son how he had pleaded, entreated with the senior soldier, a good and old friend but to no avail. He understood the soundness of his lifetime friend's judgement.

"He believes it would be bad for morale amongst his troops to be led by a man with only one good leg. Any of his officers so disabled are forced to relinquish their command," the old man pressed on. He knew the wounds he was inflicting on a son he cared for deeply.

"Your younger brother will be given the commission when he is of the right age. You will take over the benefit of a living from the church but we will speak of this later." The father's strength had drained. With a final pat to his son's shoulder, he left his own study to the sole occupation of the sombre young man.

The general has refused your commission... The general has refused your commission... The general has refused your commission... The general has refused your commission... The general has refused your commission... over and over these words swirled, tumbled, cavorted within his head. They refused to leave. He did not want them. They were not welcome. They had drowned out all else his father said. He sensed more had been said but all he had heard, all he could now hear was, "The general has refused your commission." Fitzpatrick sat for hours absorbing the impact of these six words – he had counted them. He wanted to know how few words were necessary to turn his life from its ordained, hoped for, dreamed for, career. Lunchtime came and passed, teatime too. An hour before dinner, his father came and led the quiescent youth, arm around shoulder, from the room to his own quarters. No words passed. On the father's part, none he could find seemed appropriate. The son was not aware that he was not speaking and not being spoken to. Neither did he recognise the silence. It was as if he was not awake. He did not present himself at dinner. Food taken to his room remained uneaten. His elder brother tried to console him, talk to him, ease the pain, lessen the anguish. His words of comfort bounced off the shield of abjection set in place by the numbed youth. No attempt at comfort could soothe or elicit a response from the destroyed Fitzpatrick.

The youngest brother felt some unease; he was unsure how to react. He knew of his elder brother's loss, had empathy for his plight, yet as the beneficiary of the general's ruling, he would be the soldier and not the churchman. He had excitement, joy in his breast. The conflict of feelings produced guilt. The guilt kept him from his grieving brother's company.

The morning of the second son's birthday arrived through the window of his room. The daylight found him seated by the window, red-eyed, awake. It searched the room and discovered the bed, not slept in. A gentle knock on the door went unnoticed. The door opened and his mother walked in. She slid her arms over his shoulders, down his chest, kissed his cheek. The spell was broken, the shield crumbled. He sobbed, shaking from the contractions.

After ten minutes, the spasms subsided. The mother led her son to his bed, helped him in fully clothed and tucked the blankets around him. Thus cocooned, he slept for twenty-four hours.

At breakfast, the day following his birthday, the second son asked for an interview with his father. No trace of his recent anguish was discernible though the rest of the family were sensitive to any signals. None came.

"I should appreciate a better understanding of what my future prospects may be, Father, when you have the time to spare."

"Of course, my boy. Would three o'clock this afternoon be agreeable?"

"Yes. Thank you, Father."

On the stroke of three, the youth presented himself at his father's study door which stood ajar. He wrapped his knuckles on the oak-panelled door, entering when summoned from within. His father was seated, the semaphore of his hand indicating a chair beside his own. The son sat beside him, the two chairs set at ninety degrees apart.

His father began, "The tithes you are able to levy on the people should produce an income of some eight thousand pounds per annum. We must first move the incumbent but the power to do so rests with me."

"What training will I require as a churchman?" enquired the youth.

"It will require some years of study but that will be arranged."

"How are the tithes assessed?" asked the son.

"The law states that about ten per cent of the crops are to

*38*

be passed over to you. In practice, you must arrange to collect them and have good intelligence as to their size. The peasants have an interest in under-declaring."

"So, I may decide the size of the ten per cent?" queried the young man.

"Well, yes, within reason," replied his father.

"But whose reason, other than my own?" responded the son, his voice showing no enthusiasm but his questions indicating a detailed interest in the subject. Choosing to ignore the latest question and move the discussion onto different ground, the older man continued.

"The estate will also grant you an income of two thousand pounds per annum to supplement your tithes. I have spoken to your older brother who has agreed to make the payments when I am gone."

"Thank you, Father. That is most generous. I shall seek out and thank my brother too at the end of this interview."

"It may take a while to resettle the incumbent but no more than twelve months. Do you have any further questions?"

"I decide the size of the ten per cent," responded the younger man, more a statement of a fact settled in his own mind than a new question.

"Yes," answered the father, hesitation in his voice, foreboding in his heart at the cool, analytical manner displayed by his son; it followed, so closely in time, the crushing news of the end to his son's military career, shortly before it was begun. The two men stood, the younger grasping the right hand proffered by the elder.

# Chapter 10

FITZPATRICK sat in his study, surrounded by books. He did not have room for a separate library. His enquiring mind had not deserted him, neither had the need of his crutch. The knowledge to be gained from his books, the emotions to be explained, the experiences to be looked for, were not at all similar to those from his childhood library. Matters black, illicit, forbidden by law, filled the volumes he now immersed himself within. He had eschewed the theology he had been taught. God worked for him now. Five years of study, twelve years now a cleric, seventeen years not a soldier, he knew now of the plots which had stolen his future. In the hours, the days, the months, the years, sat in silent contemplation, his mind had reconstructed events leaving him with two histories, both of which he now believed to be true though there was not an exact fit between them.

In both he could recall an early childhood, running across the fields, outpacing his elder brother, no need of a crutch, his left leg and foot the equal of the right. The first history claimed that in a fit of temper, after losing a race, his elder brother had waited 'til he slept, then maimed his left foot with an axe. The parents, wanting no harm to come to the first born, had kept the incident secret. The second history proposed that the youngest son was the favourite of his parents. They determined that he should have the military career, the rightful dues of Fitzpatrick as the second son. They had therefore maimed him with an axe whilst he slept so that he might be disqualified in favour of the youngest. Between the two events, all members of his family were implicated, guilty of taking his glory.

Further proof was provided by the two thousand pounds per annum from the estate, still paid by his elder brother despite his father's death the year before. Reverend

40

Fitzpatrick had not attended the funeral. How could he now that he knew the manner in which his family had treated him? No man would pay such a sum to another, whether brother or son, unless there was a crime to hide. It was guilt that sent the money to his account each year.

He knew of neither man nor woman that was to be trusted with his emotions. What he wanted he now took. His sexual appetite was distorted, perverted by the lack of his attraction to women. He preyed on those too weak to resist, with no sharpness to their tongue. His first victim, whom he had throttled at the height of his passion, had fought for her life, increasing his satisfaction tenfold. To shift the blame, he'd had her father hung. The one witness to reality was now in his employ. His mind absolved himself of all blame; the girl should not have excited him. She had to take responsibility for her own prettiness. Her father brought her into the world: he must share the penalty. At least, his mind reasoned in its distorted way, his actions had reunited them.

His history was now reconciled; he had had two healthy legs for the first ten years of his life. He could outrun his elder brother and the younger sibling. Because his parents favoured the youngest son for the military commission, they had sought to kill him with an axe whilst he slept. He awoke as the axe fell towards his head. His protecting arms diverted the blow so that it landed on his left foot. His elder brother had witnessed the attack. His father had used the injury to his foot to disqualify him from the military in favour of the youngest. The general had not been consulted because he would have commissioned Fitzpatrick for his swordsmanship on horseback. The two thousand each year from the estate was a bribe to keep him from exposing the family.

O'Sullivan stood in the entrance hall of the cleric's house, the storekeeper's receipt for delivery of the thirty sheaves of Macken's corn, clutched in his hand. He told the servant that he had urgent business with the cleric; a crime had been committed, the cleric's corn stolen. The butler shook his head.

"The master is asleep. Drinking since lunch," he added in a softer, more conspiratorial voice. "I suggest you return with your crime in the morning," he concluded, opening the door for the tax-collector to leave.

O'Sullivan was back in the entrance hall at seven o'clock the next morning, the docket for Macken's corn in his right hand. The butler ushered him into Fitzpatrick's study at ten o'clock. The cleric listened to the charge against Macken.

"Take some militia in case of trouble and impound the twenty sheaves. Bring them to my storehouse," he intoned. This instruction agitated O'Sullivan.

"When shall we arrest Macken?" he shrieked.

"Arrest Macken? Arrest Macken? Whatever for?" The cleric saw no profit to his own cause. Macken laboured well on the churchman's crops for no pay and then bent his back in his own fields, much of his output resting in the storehouse in payment of tithes. Macken was of most value fixed in the yoke of rent and tithes, fashioned by O'Sullivan himself. O'Sullivan opened his mouth to protest.

"I . . . " he stopped, realising a different presentation of his case was needed. He left the house to carry out the instructions of his employer.

By noon he had returned, the receipt for a further twenty sheaves in his hand, the corn safely stacked in the store-house. He had used the intervening two hours to mull over the reluctance of the cleric to view Macken in the same light as he did himself. He queried his own motives. Why did he want Macken transported? Well, because he had attacked him, humiliated him. Mostly, however, to leave Kathleen vulnerable to his attentions. Why wouldn't the cleric arrest Macken for the theft of corn which the tax-collector had proven? Because he now has more corn than he expected, he replied to his own question. The answer, the reason for the disparity of view was that the cleric had no interest in Macken's arrest. Crime or no crime, it didn't matter. In the solution, he must somehow create a benefit to his employer, one large enough to alter his previous judgement. Would Kathleen be the bait? No. He had always wanted Kathleen for himself. Even if he shared her, his employer's real craving was for younger girls.

The butler led O'Sullivan into the cleric's study for the second time. The tax-collector reported to his master on the

SEAGULLS DANCE

successful completion of his earlier instructions, handing
over the receipt from the storehouse as confirmation.
Fitzpatrick took the docket, pushing it into a drawer full of
similar chits. A wave of his hand, his back facing O'Sullivan,
gestured dismissal. The servant stood his ground, ignoring
the signal. His master's head rose, his eyes fixed, his
eyebrows drawn down together above the nose, his irritation
obvious.

"I have a new girl for you," the employee rushed each
word into the next in his anxiety to start the conversation,
damp the irritation.

"Who might she be?" drawled his master, feigning
indifference, the rush of blood colouring his face as it rose
to his cheeks. The loss of the frown and the sudden keenness
in his eyes conspired to undo the secrets hidden in his voice.

O'Sullivan was aware of the transition in Fitzpatrick's
attitude. He relaxed himself. The bait was working but
would his victim accept the hook? He had to be shown it.

"A pretty gypsy girl," he avoided the usual description of a
traveller. "Long, brown hair, slender, coming into womanhood but with a way to go."

"When can you bring her to me?" croaked the cleric, his
voice husked. The bait swallowed, now he must be shown
the hook, deduced the cunning mind of the tax-collector.

"Therein lies my problem. A small group of vigilantes are
out wanting to catch the abductor of girls. There's a good
few gone missing since you came." Now came the hook.
"It's their leader drives them on."

"Do you know who he is?" squeaked the Reverend, the
pitch of his voice rising. He'd tasted the hook, hadn't drawn
back. Fear had been added to the bait. Strike now.

"Connor Macken." The two words came from O'Sullivan's mouth. His eyes bore into his employer, seeking a
favourable reaction. The churchman was startled. The taste
of the hook was not to his liking. He wanted the girl. The
description of her excited him. He didn't want his supply
interrupted by the vigilantes. It was the first he had heard of
their existence. Even worse, if they did exist and he got
caught by them? Yet he sensed the trap. He decided to take
the bait with the hook.

"You need him out of the way then?" the cleric's words confirmed the thoughts in the tax-collector's nodding head. Macken wouldn't be the first they had imprisoned, tried and transported for personal gain.

"When will I get the girl?" croaked the cleric.

"As soon as Macken's sent away," replied O'Sullivan, thinking he'd now have to find a girl to match the description he had given.

# Chapter 11

CONNOR recollected Kathleen's face as he was taken by the three militia men sent by Fitzpatrick to arrest him, the despair showing in her eyes as her fingers were gently straightened by the soldiers, to release her grip on him. For as long as he could remember, Connor had felt he had the power to protect himself. Later, when he married, he felt the same power to protect Kathleen, Liam too when he was born. When challenged by the three armed men, his power against arms was as his speed against a horse, an unequal struggle with but one certain victor. He had not struggled. He determined to stay alive, the only outcome that could help his family.

Connor clasped his hands behind his head, his back pressed against the stone wall. He was seated on the earth floor, his left foot flat on the ground, knee bent. His right leg stretched out, supported by the undersides of his thigh, calf and heel. In one hour he was to be brought to the courthouse to answer for the theft of his own corn. Kathleen would be there, Liam left at home to be cared for by Yomi. Counsel had been hired to plead his case though Connor did not know from whence came the funds to pay his wordsmith. Kathleen had not told him the cart had been sold. She did not want to burden him further.

In the courthouse, Connor smiled at Kathleen. He tried his cheeky wink; she laughed – his reward. He recognised Fitzpatrick, O'Sullivan, Hanrahan and Seamus the Joymaker (his old legs had carried him the miles to support his friend).

The trial went well. Connor's counsel ignored the charge of theft, turning the discussion. The issue became whether the Mackens owned the twenty sheaves confiscated as he contended, having paid the tithe demanded of eighty sheaves. If O'Sullivan was not lying, his testimony being the demand was for forty sheaves, he had only collected thirty, then ten sheaves remained the property of the Mackens; the other ten were forfeit in payment of the balance of the tithe. The jury, most of whom regularly took money at cards from Fitzpatrick, came down in the gambler's favour. The judge ordered that ten sheaves belonged to Fitzpatrick and ten sheaves to Macken. He cautioned him not to try to avoid his tithes in future, released him from custody and called the next case.

Fitzpatrick rose and addressed the judge.

"What of the theft of my ten sheaves? If it were not for the vigilance of my tax-collector, they would have been lost to me. I demand justice for this larceny."

Counsels for the defence and prosecution were called to confer with the judge. A heated discussion was evident from the wagging of fingers, shaking of heads. Fitzpatrick was called forward to add his voice. The jury sat in puzzled silence.

The discussion over, Fitzpatrick and the counsels returned to their seats. The shaking head of the defence attorney boded ill for Connor's cause. Fitzpatrick was also shaking his head in a way that boded well. The judge cleared his throat.

"Ahem, ahem. I find the defendant guilty as charged for the theft of ten sheaves of corn, the rightful property of the Reverend Fitzpatrick. In consequence, Connor Macken is sentenced to transportation for eighteen years."

Kathleen fainted. Seamus caught her as she fell.

"The Reverend Fitzpatrick will return the other ten sheaves, the property of the Macken family, currently held in his storehouse," concluded his Honour.

# Chapter 12

KATHLEEN'S eyes travelled over the water, searching towards the horizon ... then she saw the sails. She bade the wind die down. The ache in her jaw and the film of water sliding over her eyes showed outwardly the hurt in her breast. She stood, Liam at her side, the palm of her hand capping the top of his head, gently pressing the hair beneath. Liam's arms circled her right leg. The material of her dress stopped his hands from meeting as he clung to her limb. The wind paid no heed to her pleas as it drove the sails onward, drove the sails away, Connor in the hull below. In time, the sails were gone.

She sat down on the grass, Liam between her legs, both staring out to sea. She imagined that the waves rolling on the sand carried his voice, those same waves that washed against his moving prison. She heard them as she heard his voice. It asked her to be strong. He promised to return.

"Kathleen you must look after Liam 'til I return."

The voice eased the hurting. Her sorrow must not harm Liam. She must manage the family's affairs until Connor returned. She would do it and she would do it in a fashion that would be a source of pride to her husband.

# Chapter 13

THE cards would not fall in the cleric's favour for the spirit of luck never sat in his chair. It avoided him but rotated with the others: fortune for one, three aces, two kings; two knaves to benefit another; a royal flush the booty for a third. His opponents were three landed gentlemen of the county. They sought his company, not to be humoured by his wit, rather to be amused by his inebriated bemoaning. The more he lost, the greater his drinking. The brandy addled his mind. Fitzpatrick bet large sums on bad hands. The glee in his face when dealt the occasional good hand ensured his companions bet lightly.

His florid complexion, testimony to the quantity imbibed from his goblet, was heightened by his agitation at his lack of luck with the cards. The subject of his discourse was his tax-collector, O'Sullivan.

"His duplicity, cunning enough to outfox a fox... he tricked me! Me, his dutiful employer of many years. Why do we treat them so well? There's no appreciation, no loyalty. I've lost one of my best workers and why? Why, because he tricked me, said Macken was a rabble rouser, said he stole my corn. He lied. It wasn't true, never true. Why did I believe him you may well ask? Well, I will tell you. He promised me, guaranteed to bring me ..."

His Reverence knitted his eyebrows together. Why had his mouth stopped? Why didn't his voice continue the story? Then the warning signals from his brain seeped into his consciousness. They had stopped his tongue because he wasn't to talk of it. His friends were not privy and were not to be made privy to his darkest deeds.

His three friends waited to hear – guaranteed to bring him what? What had been promised? He answered their silent curiosity with a dismissive wave of the right hand. He would not tell them. Despite his fuddled brain, he would keep his dark secrets lest their disclosure should harm him. He would not tell that O'Sullivan had promised to bring him a beautiful, long-haired, brown-eyed, gypsy girl in the first blush of womanhood. He was sure the girl brought to him had none of these attributes, save that she might have been a gypsy. He suspected that he had first met her some years earlier. He had been cheated in his expectations. He had sacrificed a good worker. O'Sullivan would pay for his double deception.

To change the subject, he rose from the card table, excusing himself to the others to respond to the call of nature. When he returned, one of his friends asked if he might have O'Sullivan to place in a corps of local men he was sending to fight in France. Fitzpatrick sensed the man was trying to acquire his tax-collector as a paid soldier. If so, he should recompense him for his loss of a servant.

"How much will the French pay?" he asked.

"The contract is for the whole corps, not for each individual," the man replied. "I'd be more than happy to give you credit at cards for him though," he continued.

His Reverence harboured a deep grudge against his employee that evening. Within four hands of cards O'Sullivan's fate was sealed; he would be going to war. He might lose his life, probably would, in the service of France. If he had been more particular in serving his master's interests ahead of his own . . . but he hadn't, so no more thought to the matter.

# Chapter 14

HIS head struck the beam. As he stood upright his legs wobbled beneath him in sympathy with the heaving floor. Reality arrived the merest moment ahead of panic. O'Sullivan was on a ship, in the hold of a boat. He looked about him to see other slumbering, semi-conscious travellers. His head hurt on top where it had banged the beam. It also hurt behind. He felt the back of his head, finding the welt. Then he knew he was the victim of a press-gang.

How? When? His memory tried to respond to his urgent enquiries. He could recall drinking with Fitzpatrick, the first time he had ever been offered to drink in his master's company, in his master's study. He had drunk his fill, not used to brandy; ale was his drink. His employer had insisted so he felt he could not refuse another tankard half full of the golden spirit. Then, then nothing, his memory could recall no more.

O'Sullivan sat in the hull of the ship, his forehead resting in his cupped hands. His mind meandered back to his time of innocence. He had grown up with Connor in the village. Their mothers had both died in childbirth, his with his own, Connor's eight years later. Although two years the senior, he had taken to Connor. Their fathers had gone to war together, neither to return.

The year after he'd witnessed Fitzpatrick's foul deeds and gained employment, he'd tried to get work for Connor too. Then Kathleen McDonagh had come to womanhood. He ached for her, to touch her, to be loved back. The forced kiss had been his undoing. She had slapped his face. His fingertips stroked his cheek at the memory. Shortly afterwards, she started walking out with Macken and they married. He'd put it from his mind, sought comfort elsewhere but, as the years passed, Kathleen's beauty increased until he knew he must possess her.

He had plotted the downfall of Connor Macken. His wife would have been unprotected, vulnerable, his to take at his whim 'til cruel fate had spared her his attentions. Now his chances of holding her were as lost as Macken's.

# Chapter 15

CONNOR lay shackled in the bowels of the ship. The putrid smell of rotting detritus invaded his body, his eyes watering in the darkness, his nostrils lying open to the invasion whilst his mouth stayed clamped. The ragout of gases still found a route to scrape at the inside of his throat before corroding the lining of his lungs. This poisonous air, laden with the decay of once living matter was, nonetheless, life supporting, his body being able to extract sufficient oxygen to keep his heart beating... or was his heart beating?

As he straightened his right leg to relieve the pressure from his weight on the buttock of that limb, the leg iron sought once more to continue its passage through his skin and flesh towards his anklebone. The blood that seeped from the rub now lubricated the inside of the shackle. Connor felt no empathy from his heart: this centre to his being appeared to want no part of his imprisonment. Instead, it sought to expand and push away the bars that enclosed it. He could feel the pressure mounting on his ribs and sternum at each breath. With closed eyes, Connor entreated, "Please, please heart, do not abandon me now for I must live and cannot do so without you."

The prisoner to his left, a lad destined to see his fourteenth summer in a foreign land, began to sob. The lad was being transported for vagrancy. His mother had died and his father was soldiering in foreign wars so there was none to speak for him at his trial. Connor's heart ceased its struggle as he moved his shoulder so that the lad's cheek might rest against it. The comfort of an arm was not possible as wrists were shackled in the same manner as ankles. The hold in which the prisoners were being transported housed two hundred and twenty men and boys. There was room for five prisoners between each rib of the ship. Either side of the raised centre were channels for waste matter which were sluiced with sea water six times each twenty four hours, at the beginning of the watch. These channels did not always constrain the waste material, particularly during the sluicing or in rough weather. The raised platform had planking attached to the sides. Meals were served by filling this channel, each prisoner having a metal cup to scoop up any nutrients or, at least, fluids. Though this channel was sluiced daily, there was little left in it to dispose of.

Some six weeks into the voyage, as the ship sailed along the coast of Africa, the death rate amongst the prisoners started to increase. Throughout the voyage, a few died each day. Reilly, the prison warder on board, made a daily visit to the prisoners hold. He walked along the central channel used for feeding, the raised planking providing security against any attempt to grab at his ankles. With the aid of a four-foot long blackthorn and a lantern, he would prod the prisoners for signs of life. Any not responding were smote on the head with the blackthorn to ensure either unconsciousness or death. Then followed release from their irons. A rope was placed around the neck of the dead prisoner and then the body was dragged by the rope, hauling it on to the deck, squeezing any remaining breath with the brutal action. The rope was taken off for re-use and the body thrown into the sea from the ship's rails.

Reilly was a man easily described; he was evil. He was evil in almost all the manifestations that can be attributed to the word. He found gratification in the suffering of others: the more they suffered, the better his own position suited him. He developed this element of his character into a lust for gratification. He took employment in the prison service so that he could witness suffering and then enhance it by his own actions on people that were at his mercy – a quality of which he possessed no measurable trace. The only restraint to his evilness was the fear that a superior might witness the torment he imposed and remove him from his post. He was proud of the system he used to clear the hold each day of the dead or dying.

Reilly never allowed the six crew who accompanied him on his daily forays to carry arms for fear of them falling into the hands of the prisoners. The strike with the blackthorn on the head and subsequent hauling out with the rope around the neck was to ensure that no living prisoner would gain exit from the hold.

The daily body count of prisoners being thrown into the sea had risen to four and then six. Members of the crew were also becoming sick and a few had died. The steady disposal of bodies had created an escort for the ship; sharks now swam off the port and starboard rails. The onset of disease on board ship marked the end of Reilly's daily forays into the prisoners' hold. He feared the contagion of the sickness. The dead were left to decay in the hold.

On his final foray, Reilly had only been allowed four crewmen as his escort. Coyle, the captain of the ship, could not spare more as his crew was depleted by illness. On coming to the lad beside Connor, Reilly raised his lantern and saw frothy blood being coughed up. Reilly called for a rope and moved to lasso the boy's neck. Connor pushed forward his shackled hands to deflect the rope from the boy's face. The intensity of the contact between their eyes in the lamplight started as anger in both. Reilly's eyes changed to triumph as he called the crew to rope Connor, then fear when he realised that they had backed off and would not obey him. Reilly left the hold for the last time with a curse on his lips for Connor.

As the week passed, many more of the crew were stricken with disease. The deaths increased as did the size of the shark pack. Bread and water were lowered through the hatch each day. The remaining living prisoners had more rations than ever before as the numbers eating rapidly dwindled. The boy next to Connor was released from his suffering two days after the incident with Reilly. He was not destined, after all, to see his fourteenth summer in a foreign land.

The prisoners began a roll call each morning and evening by the middle of the second week. Since the onset of the disease, only thirty-three voices remained. The rations lowered each day were too abundant for those able to eat. It would be only a matter of days until there would be no voices, only souls.

Reilly himself was taken ill and remained in his bunk.

Coyle, the ship's captain, was now responsible for the prisoners. He determined to release sufficient prisoners to replenish his depleted crew. Coyle entered the hold and immediately forfeited the lunch he had recently consumed. The thirty-three men were released from their shackles. The first duty given to them was to clear the hold of the dead. This task was completed just before dusk. The ship sailed away leaving its escort of sharks behind, feeding on the bodies trailing in the wake.

Connor stood on the main deck amid ships, his hands resting on the rail. The callouses on his palms were red and swollen. They had softened from ten weeks of inactivity and now been raised by lifting and carrying the bodies together with pulling ropes as a replacement crewman. He could feel the cushioning as his hands pressed down.

The bows rose up and crushed the water beneath them, the resultant spray dampening the lower part of the sails and Connor, standing beneath them. The mist of seawater trickled down his face, washing tramlines through the mire collected during his time in the hold. He rolled his tongue, starting at the left corner of his mouth and circling over his upper lip, past the right corner before re-entering half way along his lower lip. As the salivered tip slipped across his lips, it captured the taste of the sea's salt and brine, overwhelming the weaker taste of his own salt-laden sweat.

Three days after the prisoners' release, the illness and death abated. The wind grew stronger, thrusting at the sails with increasing force so that they, in turn, pulled the vessel through the water at quickening speed. Only nineteen prisoners avoided the disease and all those infected had succumbed to its deadly effects. The regime under which they lived had rendered them less able than the crew to resist the virulent sickness. Almost half the crew had also perished. Reilly lay in his hammock, not expected to keep the grim reaper at bay for much longer. A welcome addition to Hades, he had already outlived most smitten at the same time.

As the ship sailed further southward, there was a noticeable keenness to the air. Connor was well attired in the clothing of the lost sailors. As the wind sharpened, all hands were despatched to the rigging to haul in the topsails and then, as it blew ever stronger, the main sails were lashed down. This endeavour was not without human cost. Climbing the mast was a treacherous task, the sway of the ship being magnified with each foothold of Connor's ascension above the deck. It was as he clambered from the mast to the top yardarm that he realised he had no head for heights. By resolute control of his faculties, he forced himself to concentrate on the task in hand and forbade his eyes to wander downward further than the drawstrings with which the sail was to be pulled in. The relative comfort of the mast against his chest and thighs was now replaced by freezing, brine-laden wind, tearing at his clothing as he stood fully erect, canvas-shod feet upon the ice covered yard. His hands, at shoulder level, gripped the safety line which ran from the end of the yardarm to the mast.

The pitching of the ship determined to end his life. This thought caused Connor to inhale deeply as he slid his feet inch by inch, moving his hands along the rope above. His regained strength of purpose came from repeating his mantra, "I will not perish. I will see Kathleen again."

The further out along the yardarm he slid, the lower the safety line lay in his hands. With the line at his waist, Connor sank into a crouch, allowing his hands holding the rope to pass above his head. His left hand let go of the line above and grasped a rope holding the sail at his feet. He timed the roll of the ship as it passed through the vertical. His right hand let go above, grabbing for the rope below whilst his feet slid either side of the yard. Sitting astride, he pulled on the drawstrings with the other five crew working that sail. They tried to haul in unison despite the ferocious efforts of the wind and managed well enough to pull with the rhythm of the pitching of the ship. Each man knew that the fate of the vessel was dependant on hauling in and securing the sails as quickly as possible; better to perish in this endeavour than drown with the ship.

With all the sails secured, excepting the mizzen and a foresail, all hands were now returned from the rigging to the deck. Three men had lost their lives, two plunging into the sea, one to the deck.

The next three days, Connor spent below decks with most

of the crew as the storm raged. Twice a day, he and other members of his watch were required on deck to clear the ice forming on every available surface. Volunteers were sought to climb the rigging and hammer free the ice on the yards; the weight of this ice, so high above the deck, threatened to lever the ship onto its side. The reluctance of men to undertake the task, conjoined with his determination that the boat should not founder, drove Connor to accept the challenge along with a few of the sturdier fellows in his watch.

Connor climbed the mast with his ice hammer and a fifteen-foot length of rope. As he reached the main yardarm he was to clear, he secured one end of the line around his waist, the other to the mast. He hacked at the ice by his feet where the yard touched the mast. The sharpened end of the hammer smashed into the clear ice, mashing the frozen water into powder. He cast a further blow into the snowy pulp, then another and another, swinging the hammer with one arm, holding the rope on the yard with the other. A slab of ice creaked as it fractured and fell, bouncing and splitting upon the deck below. Having cleared a section, Connor was able to swing his legs astride the beam, pulling himself forward with his hands, freeing the ice with the hammer. The cold on his exposed hands was intense. He could feel it piercing through the flesh, plucking at the bones beneath and levering them from their purchase on the smooth wood.

A noise sounded above, a crack as the wind twisted a spar, freeing it from the embrace of frozen brine. As the ice plunged towards the deck, it struck Connor on his left shoulder. The pain shot down his arm, straightening his fingers. As he reclasped them around the rope, it was not there. He was moving, rotating slowly around the beam. His right hand released the hammer and clawed at the frozen, lashed sail but despite the instinctive transfer of all the power in his body to those fingers, they were unable to lock onto solid matter. Connor felt himself slowly slipping through space. He was a spectator, his body travelling without him. The two were reunited as the rope around his waist crushed against his internal organs. He was swinging ten feet below the main yard, a pendulum as the ship was tossed upon the ocean. On the first two swings past the mast, he brushed against it with his thigh. He had managed to haul himself upright so that he held the rope above his head. The boat pitched as the bows dug into a wave, the change of angle smashing Connor's head against the mast on the third swing. He felt the blood flowing into his eye and realised he had little time left for action. With the strength that only manifests itself on rare occasions of dire need, he hauled himself up the rope to the mast and thence down to the deck.

The sailor with the most able medical skills took Connor, under instruction from Coyle, to the captain's cabin where he tended to the crushed forehead and bruised, left shoulder.

Their survival from the storm created a deep sense of comradeship between members of the crew. They had shared the greatest challenge then known to sailors. They had sailed through the most treacherous seas in the world, where two oceans meet, at a time when the heavens were also in uproar. Few sailors could have witnessed the conditions they had met and been able to recount the experience. This feat of survival was somehow more personal than surviving the pestilence as, in the latter case, it was less their efforts than perceived good fortune. It was not that they eschewed the role of luck in surviving the storm but that their endeavour and fortitude could be readily identified as having made a major contribution to the resulting survival of the ship.

Early one morning, as he worked upon the deck sewing a torn sail, Connor looked to the south and spotted a large white bird. As he paused to look, a voice from behind said,

"That's an albatross, some say an unlucky thing for a sailor to see." Upon looking around for the source of the voice, he saw the kindly features of Coyle, the captain.

"Why is that sir?" enquired Connor.

"Because it is an omen of bad weather," replied the captain.

"I am indebted for your courage during the storm," he said, clapping his hand on Connor's shoulder blade.

"The actions of all the former prisoners were equal to those of my regular crew and they have been so since you were released," he continued.

"Whatever your reasons for incarceration below decks, in my judgement, you are all good men. I have it in mind that any of you who wish to, may sail with me when I return to Ireland," he stated before adding, "The authorities in Botany Bay will be told that all the prisoners have perished during the voyage."

As the tears welled up in his eyes and his chest rose and expanded, Connor croaked through a restricting throat, "Thank you sir. I will always remember..." His voice trailed off as he realised the captain had left.

The great white bird, wheeling overhead, drew Connor's thoughts back to the much smaller white sea birds that circled him as he worked his fields at Corryann. An unjust man had jailed him; a just man was now to set him free.

Fifteen weeks after surviving the storms and mountainous seas, the ship arrived at Botany Bay.

Dispatches published before they sailed indicated that Port Jackson, a few miles past Botany Bay, provided a more sheltered anchorage with fresh water. Consequently, the ship docked there. A wharf had been built and a thriving community established. Coyle was transporting tools, seed corn and molasses as well as convicts to provision the fledgling town.

The warden of the prison compound, a man who introduced himself as Gavin, met Coyle on the wharf expecting to receive Coyle's human cargo into his care. Coyle explained that his boat had been struck by disease during the voyage, off the coast of Africa, accounting unfortunately, for the deaths of all the prisoners and a number of his crew. Reilly, the prison service official, had survived however, after a severe and lengthy illness although he still remained very weak. He was brought on a stretcher and passed into the care of Gavin. Reilly propped himself up upon his right elbow.

"There are prisoners in the crew," he croaked.

"We'll take you to the infirmary and soon build you up man," said Gavin, signalling two wardens to take the stretcher to his carriage.

"NO WAIT!" insisted Reilly. "I tell you sir. There are prisoners in the crew. I have overheard it said."

"Nonsense man. The captain has affirmed to me that all prisoners perished," stated Gavin in a stern tone.

Reilly pushed himself up from the stretcher he was lain on.

"It is my duty sir, to deliver the prisoners. There are still prisoners on this ship."

"How many? What are their names?" asked Gavin with increasing irritation.

"I don't know how many. There were too many for me to remember their names. Even if I could remember their faces, it was very dark in the hold but I know there are prisoners on board this ship."

After some minutes' consideration, viewing the distraught features of Reilly, Gavin consulted with Coyle. The captain agreed to call all hands on deck to see if any could be identified as a prisoner. The crew walked down the deck past Reilly. He gazed at each one, racked by his effort to remember a face. As Connor walked by, the fifth seamen from the end of the line, Reilly told him to stop. As he looked into Connor's eyes, a look of triumph spread across his face. There was an easing of the muscles around his eyes and mouth as the furrow in his brow disappeared. The ends of his mouth extended into a wide smile exposing his brown, cracked teeth.

"This one is a prisoner."

Coyle interceded to say he must be mistaken but Reilly grabbed at Connor's trousers and exposed his ankle. The marks of an ankle iron were still clearly visible. Insufficient time had passed to dispel the scars. Gavin addressed Coyle.

"Captain, is it necessary to examine the ankles and wrists of your whole crew or may this man be released to the prison service?"

Coyle's eyes met those of Connor. He saw the fear, the loss of liberty, the hopelessness. He was to be sacrificed so that the surviving fifteen ex-prisoners may remain free.

"Take your prisoner and leave my ship."

# Chapter 16

KATHLEEN'S feet were reluctant on the road. Her toes curled under to shorten the step, gripping the dirt beneath. The knuckle of her toes, white with the effort, slowed her progress. She had lain on her bed for many nights, mulling over the role of Fitzpatrick at Connor's trial. He was the man responsible for her current predicament; he had caused the charges; he had spoken up at the assizes; he, his Reverence, had sent Connor away. She could have nothing to do with him contended the prosecutor in her mind ignoring her need for food.

She was grateful to Sweeney for planting the field. He had promised to crop the potatoes when ready but it would be many months before food came from this source. Meantime, she must feed Liam and herself. She entwined her fingers to support the underside of her swollen belly, the new child, the baby she carried. She needed more food, needed money to buy it, needed work to gain the money. Her current income from mending and washing clothes needed to be increased. Fitzpatrick was bound to have work for a seamstress. Perhaps his role in Connor's prosecution was not as strong as it appeared. Maybe he was the dupe of O'Sullivan; thank God, he was gone to the wars. In her mind, she felt she had pulled the argument back in favour of the churchman, excusing an appeal to him for work. The fear of disloyalty to her husband stopped her from reaching a verdict. The turmoil in her head would not abate.

Resolution of the myriad tortuous thoughts revolving around Fitzpatrick's role at Connor's trial came, not at night as she lay on her bed, but one morning outside her cottage. The warmth of the spring sun on her shoulders, the change in the smell, the taste of the air, the scent of new growth, new life announced its presence. A white gull landed on a post.

Its head turned, black eye towards her. Her own eyes travelled over the white feathers 'til they met the gull's eye. No sound came. The landscape, the form of the gull, all disappeared; Kathleen's eyes locked on the black eye of the bird. She sensed the wisdom; it was her oracle, the question unspoken, the reply unheard. Kathleen blinked. The gull took flight. She was to be strong. That was the message that passed between them. If she was to be strong, she must banish fear, banish the fear of disloyalty. If she could do that, the argument fell in favour of seeking out Fitzpatrick.

As she made her way along the dirt road to Fitzpatrick's house, Kathleen did not feel the strength that had started her on the journey. Fear was now regaining lost-ground. It was the unease created by the struggle which took all the enthusiasm from her feet as they tried to interpret the instructions from her head. Kathleen determined to end the nonsense. She was going to see Fitzpatrick. It was what she must do, feed herself, feed her children to survive. Her feet, responding to the clarification, set upon the road with greater purpose, lengthening her strides to the house of his Reverence.

At the door, Kathleen's hand grasped the solid ring which hung from the mouth of a brass lion's head on the thick oak timbers. She raised the ring, then let it fall, pounding into the groove on the wooden door caused by previous usage. The sound of contact echoed into the room beyond. With no response evident, she raised the ring and let it fall again, then immediately repeated the exercise, a double echo thus resounding in the room within. Almost as the sound abated, the great door was swung open inwards, the movement a welcome gesture, perhaps an invitation to enter. The way was blocked by the presence of the butler who inferred no welcome nor entreaty to step in. His demeanour was belligerent, eyebrows forced together, eyes almost crossing as they peered along the length of his nose. Body erect, chest puffed out, hands on hips, he filled the doorway. His eyes travelled down Kathleen's person, intent on analysing, the task complete when they arrived at the bare, dust covered feet. His eyes swept back to Kathleen's face, irritated at having been summoned. The summons had been repeated, duplicated as he reached the portal, by a barefooted peasant, pregnant too, banging on his master's front door.

"The likes of you should be knocking on the pantry door. You have no business at the front of the house," he intoned. "Be off, before I have you imprisoned for vagrancy," he concluded, stepping back and pulling the door to close it with his left hand, his right hand flicking out in dismissal to re-enforce his words.

Kathleen was not put off by his haughty demeanour and threats as she did not doubt that she was the equal of any other that breathed the free air. Her right hand left her side; the palm, placed firmly on the oak timbers, stopped the passage of the door.

"I need to speak to your master," she stated, emphasising the last word. The butler, taken aback by this challenge to his authority, was concerned lest he had somehow misjudged the situation in a way that would earn the displeasure of his Reverence. To be sure, there had, on previous occasions, been women of low position entertained or were themselves the source of entertainment, he subconsciously corrected himself. Usually, he was either forewarned by the master or they came in the company of O'Sullivan who vouched for them.

"What business do you have with his Reverence?" he asked, keen for assistance in interpreting whether or not to inform his master of the visitor. He knew either course could bestow a curse.

"I've come to offer my services as a seamstress," Kathleen replied, infected by the haughtiness of the butler and not wishing to admit she'd come to beg for work.

The butler was now confident he could shut the door on this distraction to his routine but, as he reached this conclusion, his master, tap tapping as he hobbled across the hallway, recognised Kathleen Macken at the door. The butler stepped aside in deference to his employer as Fitzpatrick approached the open portal.

"In what manner may I be of assistance to you?" enquired the clergyman, affecting an air of civility to conceal the curiosity which he deemed unseemly for one of his rank.

"I came to plead for work," the words burst from

Kathleen's mouth. "I am a good seamstress," more words tumbled out, the speed and directness with which the words were uttered a consequence of her doubt as she feared she might fatigue Fitzpatrick's patience.

Fitzpatrick smiled; women who placed themselves dependent on his whim were of great benefit to his ego. He extended his open hand, not to be grasped but an invitation to enter. The butler retreated, relieved not to have raised the ire of his master though irked that the woman had gained entry through the front door.

The alien experience of having a rug between her toes caused Kathleen to look down at her dusty feet as she felt the warmth in her face climbing up her cheeks. She was embarrassed lest she marked the carpet, embarrassed too that he might notice the redness of her face.

His Reverence crooked the index finger of his left hand, beckoning her to follow him into his study. He sat on a sofa, patting the cushion as a signal for her to sit beside him.

"Tell me, how may I ease the burdens of life for you?" he addressed her, concern apparent in his voice. His tone, its friendliness, slowed Kathleen's beating heart, the *thump . . . thump . . . thump* against her chest diminishing. Composure returned to her body giving the confidence to absorb his question, to select the words in response.

"I am with child," she cupped her hands against her pregnant stomach. "My young son, Liam, needs to be fed." She hoped the appeal for her children would soften the heart. "The potato crop will not be ready for some months." She didn't seek charity; she was taking action to help herself and her family; the problem was short-term. "My husband has been sent away and is, therefore, not in a position to help." She had, she hoped, avoided any implied criticism of the cleric in her last words.

"Connor Macken. Yes, I remember. Deported for eighteen years for stealing my corn." Fitzpatrick's words struck jabs to her abdomen, forcing the air from her lungs. She had erred in mentioning her husband.

"I am sorry, truly, truly sorry that your husband was wrongly convicted by the false testimony of O'Sullivan," he apologised, then placated.

"He has paid the price as I have sent him to fight in France," he stated smugly.

"I will write to the judge and plead for clemency for your husband," he offered. "Meantime, I'll provide you with work to help you through," the churchman concluded. Kathleen struggled to interpret, make sense of what she was hearing. He would give her work. The mention of her husband had not been a mistake. She was right. He had been duped by O'Sullivan. Fitzpatrick was to plead for Connor – her husband could be home soon.

The confusion in her mind had dulled Kathleen's senses so she did not realise Fitzpatrick had moved beside her. For his part, her apparent acquiescence was his reward for exposing O'Sullivan's role in her husband's misfortune. He had no intention of writing to the judge but he did intend to give her work. Kathleen arranged the tumult in her brain, bringing order to the notions colliding in her head. It was then she realised that her thigh and buttock were squashed against the man beside her. The hope he held in his power for her future contentment and the happiness of her family cautioned her. She would need some wit to extricate herself without upsetting the cleric. By the faintest tickle from her womb, her unborn baby came to the rescue. She clutched her swollen belly feigning labour pains, the ploy completely perplexing his Reverence. Kathleen was able to rise, giving no sleight to her host, able to thank him. She arranged to collect the mending of his servants' uniforms from the housekeeper and was able to leave the house on good terms with the owner, if not the butler who scowled as he let her out the front door.

# Chapter 17

CONNOR was housed in a prison compound with sixty other unfortunates. Within the confines of the camp, fifteen huts had been constructed, each with the capacity to sleep twenty prisoners. The carpentry was of a high order, the positioning and size of the windows delivering fresh air as a constant breeze ventilated the sleeping quarters. The wind blew in from the nearby ocean, the salty tang forming a link with his cottage, Kathleen, Liam and his home, Corryann. The rhythmic pulse of the surf, waves breaking upon the headland, came in on the wind, whispering, losing its power; the distance of greater than a mile dissipated the sound.

The hut closest to the guards' living quarters was used for new prisoners. It was easier to break them in there, to make them gain acceptance of the yoke, back straining, muscle fatiguing labour. Connor was billeted with five men. There was ample space for each to choose a bed beside a window. Every day of the week, at six each morning, the prisoners left their beds to sample the first meal of the day, a form of boiled oats. By seven, they were walking towards a plot of land on the seashore where the ground was covered in boulders, the largest being the size of a man's head. The ground was to be prepared for cultivation as the colony must grow its own food. Each stone must be picked up, prised from the earth and carried to the seashore to take its place in a breakwater being formed there. Over time, the length of journey increased, the rocks closest to the shore having been moved first. The hand irons, chains clanking, swung against the stones being carried. The sun beat down hotter than any Connor had experienced working his own land, too hot to remove his shirt for any length of time lest he burn.

Over the next few months, his resilience to the burning rays improved. The sand on the beach by the land they

66

sought to cultivate was too hot to walk upon barefooted. So, in common with the other labourers, Connor wore sandals. The stones became so hot in the sun, the prisoners fashioned canvas gloves to enable them to be picked up and carried to their final resting place. The gloves were soaked in the sea on each visit to the breakwater. Connor had been told that before his arrival, the rock carriers had waded into the sea, placing their loads at the end of the breakwater as it grew out into the ocean. The swirl of a black fin, the scream, blue water with scarlet stain, had stopped this practice. The men now walked out along the breakwater, dropping their load at the end, dipping gloved hands into the sea.

The motivation to toil in the heat was provided by six armed guards spaced around the perimeter of the area being worked. Two unarmed enforcers also wandered amongst the men. The reach of their right arms was extended by the whips grasped in their hands. They could lay a bite upon the back from twenty feet. No man, however, was expected to suffer thirst and a water barrel was brought out each day. Eleven o'clock marked the end of the morning's work, the heat of the sun fit to broil their brains as it beat upon the labourers' heads. Lunch was taken at the camp, soup with bread being the usual diet. The men were able to rest on their beds until three-thirty in the afternoon. By four, they were once again clearing the land, this task stopping at eight in the evening when a meal of oats, similar to breakfast, was supplemented by meat of unknown origin. The daily routine had altered little in the eight weeks of Connor's confinement. Those with more experience told him that the hot, rainy season would abate soon, to be followed by milder warmth. The long midday break was a feature only of the summer.

Time not used for sleeping or clearing the land was mostly passed in conversation. Some conversations were personal, conducted silently within the mind, privacy respected by the other inmates. Open discussions were generally of times gone by, each man telling tales from his own history or times to come, of what to do when freedom came, what to do to accelerate its coming. Talk of early freedom held little interest for Connor. He had propositioned himself with the notion that, if reunited with Kathleen and Liam, they could start a new life in a new land, beyond the reach of the law which had convicted him. His view of the future was on his own land, with his people, living in his cottage, Kathleen and Liam at his side. Therefore, he couldn't be an escapee, wanted by the law. He needed to go home a free man in the eyes of the law.

Farrelly was the closest friend Connor had in the compound. They slept in the same hut, their beds opposite, each under a window. Connor's tales of Kathleen, his delight in the ordinary accomplishments of Liam, his small son, were a source of wonder to Farrelly. He himself was unmarried and was aware of no children of his paternity. A philanderer with women, it was this trait in his character that had caused his downfall. The general's wife and he were mutually attracted, she, some thirty years the junior of the military man sought, in her words, the smooth skin of a plum, not the corrugated caress of a prune. The stables were their rendezvous of choice. Unfortunately, the general returned early from hunting. His mount had cast a shoe causing him to ride her home prematurely, his ostlers jogging in his wake. Arriving at the stables before his stablehands, he led his horse to her stall. Hearing the approaching sound of hooves on the cobblestones, Farrelly and his amour sought rapidly to restore their clothing. The proximity of the *clip, clop, clip, clop* told them they had not the time. They determined instead to secrete themselves. The general dismounted his horse within the stables and put her in her stall knowing that the ostlers would see to the tack shortly, on their arrival.

Misfortune struck Farrelly. The stall in which they had secreted themselves was shared with a horse and the animal proceeded to relieve itself in both manners. Dung cascaded over Farrelly's bare legs, his feet awash with urine. The beast stepped back, shod hoof on Farrelly's left foot. He strangled the cry in his throat. The odd sound that emanated was enough to catch the interest of the general. Looking into the stall, he saw his naked wife. Whilst the perplexed man tried to make sense of the scene before him, Farrelly, having freed his foot, made a dash for freedom. His appearance as a third party cleared the horse of all impropriety. The general, still clutching his riding crop, was able to land a few hefty strokes on the bare buttocks of the fleeing Farrelly, spurring him to greater speed. Unluckily, as he outdistanced the old soldier, the stablehands arrived. His progress was stopped.

Women had played no part in Farrelly's life for some little while. He had arrived at Port Jackson the month before Connor. He was intrigued that Connor was able to gain such contentment from the love of just one woman. He did not doubt the sincerity of Connor's claims of happiness. It was evident from the fervour in his voice, in his eyes, in his hands, when he spoke of Kathleen. Connor responded well to Farrelly's easy-going, happy-go-lucky outlook on life. A man who was able to laugh at his own misfortunes and capable of creating the most outrageous fantasies as to what lay waiting in his future, was agreeable company.

Gavin, the warden of the prison compound had, on first impression at the dockside, given every indication of being a fair-minded and kindly gentleman. Connor's experiences of him since had confirmed this initial appraisal. His regime, whilst hard, was not harsh. Most of the prison guards responded to his lead and did nothing to unnecessarily disturb the prisoners' lives. The food was as good as that which the guards ate, rations being scarce in the colony. The long break from the worst of the sun in the hot season and attention to providing ample drinking water were examples of consideration. Hand irons had been removed for a time a year earlier, to ease the task of carrying the rocks. Four prisoners used this extra freedom to attack a guard, killing him in their bid to escape. Hand irons had thereafter been restored. The four prisoners were recaptured and hanged.

The enforcers, able to sting the backs of slackers, were a necessity to ensure productive effort. The ground had to be cleared and cultivated so that more food could be produced. Rations shipped in were both uncertain and dwindling. Connor had felt the rasping kiss of the leather tongue on his back when he had dallied too long at the ocean's edge. It was there that he felt communion with his homeland, with Kathleen, the white gulls above, the seagulls' dance.

# Chapter 18

THE sun was in the ascendant, close to its yearly high. Yomi had been sent for. She made her way along the track, no urgency apparent from her stride. On her arm hung a basket, a cloth on top hiding the contents. As she walked she smiled, noticing things familiar. The swallows returned, swooping, climbing and swirling with never a fear of collision. On the ground, older rabbits stretched, sunning themselves whilst youngsters chased each other in perpetual motion. A squirrel scrambled up a tree, curling its fine, feather tail over its head.

At her destination, Yomi pushed open the door, strolling inside without invitation. She placed her basket on the table, went to the bed and caressed the hair on Kathleen's left temple with her fingertips. Soothing sounds came from her mouth, not words but noises able to convey tenderness and instil confidence, signalling the arrival of her help and companionship. Yomi uncovered the bulging stomach, exposing the white stripes where the skin seemed close to splitting from the pressure beneath. The distended navel, exposing the knot tied at birth, now threatened to come undone. She laid her hands on the drum-tight abdomen, moving them over the surface, her fingertips feeling, probing gently.

Liam sat by his mother's side, his small face earnest, disquiet in his eyes.

"Tis only time for your new brother or sister to meet us, to say hello," Yomi confided.

Liam's anxiety was not quelled. He understood, knew they were to have a new baby. His unease came from his mother's apparent illness; she was in bed, crying. Her sickness coming as the new baby was due, his father not here to help, increased the young boy's feelings of vulnerability. He did not want to lose his mummy too.

A knock on the door interrupted Yomi's attempts to allay Liam's fears. Yomi called out for the visitor to enter. The door pushed open as Sweeney ambled in.

"Can I help?" he enquired.

Liam was pleased to see the simple man; he enjoyed his company. They both delighted in the antics of insects, spending many contented hours watching the smaller animals at play. Butterflies were special to both.

"Yes," replied Yomi. "Could you help Liam? His mother is in childbirth; he's worried for her."

Turning her face from Sweeney to the young boy, "Off you go outside now and play." Liam remained reluctant to release his mother's right hand, her fingers clasped between his two small hands.

Kathleen smiled at her son, "I'm fine now Yomi's here; she knows what to do. Off with you, outside and play, before it's your bedtime." She tried to introduce a note of mock sternness into her voice. His mother's words and her improved condition persuaded Liam that he could leave her for a while with Yomi whilst he played with Sweeney.

The position of the baby within the womb was of some concern to Yomi. She had no direct experience of birthing an infant positioned so. Yomi had witnessed her grandmother delivering such an infant, much effort being required both from the mother and midwife though the pain, the dreadful pain, was endured solely by the patient. Contractions were at an early stage and so it would be some time before the serious business would begin. Yomi decided she would stay although at least one night would pass before her skills would be called upon. Perhaps, hopefully, the baby would turn upside down to exit in the preferred headfirst manner. If the feet were to exit first, she must work quickly. Kathleen would be in agonies of pain, draining her strength. That strength was needed to squeeze the infant through the birth canal. It was important now that she should rest between contractions.

"Hush now. There's a fair way to go so do your best to

sleep. I'll prepare supper. Liam's happy enough outside at play," Yomi concluded, brushing a wisp of hair from Kathleen's brow. Kathleen tried a smile, the corners of her mouth turning up only to be caught by another short sharp contraction.

Whilst Yomi busied herself preparing a meal, Kathleen dozed fitfully which pleased her midwife as it was the best possible preparation for what was to come. The smell of food drew the interest of Liam and Sweeney who appeared through the door. Yomi's index finger, pressed upright on her lips just beneath her nose, was sufficient signal that the two new entrants were required to keep silent. Liam was reassured as he saw his mother sleeping. They took their bowls, laden with food, outside to eat lest they disturb her slumber. Kathleen's meal was kept ready for her awakening.

After the meal, Sweeney left having ensured that he could be of no further help. He pledged to return in the morning to play with Liam. The lad himself was put to bed, the emotions of the day soon causing his eyelids to close.

Kathleen awoke, the contractions now less sharp but stronger, stronger and they seemed to last much longer. Yomi brought the food which her patient was able to consume in the respite between cramps. The evening, the night, the dawn, the morn, all passed slowly. Kathleen rested whilst her body allowed. Throughout the night, Yomi hummed a soothing sound from the back of her throat. Sweeney arrived, as promised, bringing milk, bread and some honey. Liam awoke, breakfasted and then left with the simple man to examine the rock pools on the shore. The retreating tide always left pools of water trapped in crevices of rocks, the smallest creatures of the sea often stranded there 'til rescued by the incoming tide some hours later. Liam was thrilled with his discoveries, a tiny fish, a small crab, a sea anemone.

With Liam gone and Kathleen awake, the breaks for rest became much shorter. Yomi made the labouring woman drink some milk she'd warmed and spiced with honey. She rolled her hands over Kathleen's swollen womb to find the baby inside was still upright and would come out feet first. The whole womb had moved lower; the infant's journey into daylight had begun.

Two women from the village arrived, great pots in their arms, menfolk toting the water from the adjacent well. Two fires were started outside the cottage, the pots overhanging on tripods of stout sticks. The fire within the cottage was stoked. Buckets of cool water, pots full of warming water, strips of clean cotton piled upon the table, the conductor gazed about her.

"Clear the table. It'll be better to lay her on it." Yomi's instructions were obeyed instantly, without question. The strips of cloth were transferred to the bench, the wooden surface of the table scrubbed and dried and a sheet placed over it. The door of the cottage was closed. Yomi and her assistants supported Kathleen, helping her to lie upon the table. Her dress was drawn up above the waist, knees up, legs apart, soles of the feet on the flat surface. A sheet was draped across Kathleen's knees, a gesture to preserve her dignity. The screams, the yells, the impediment of the sheet on her knees, soon dignity would be sent to take a walk, bade return when all was done.

Kathleen sensed the time was near as her waters broke and she tried to push. Yomi held her hand and stroked her back, "Not yet, not yet. The time will come. When I ask, look into my face, then you must push, hold, push as I dictate."

Hot water had been mixed with cold, buckets full of warm water at the ready. Yomi moved to the end of the table, positioning herself now between Kathleen's outstretched knees; she asked an assistant to bathe Kathleen's forehead. The toes appeared. Kathleen pushed the ankles out and Yomi was able to grip them, drawing them further out. Kathleen squeezed even harder now, pushing the baby's buttocks out. Kathleen pressed, squeezed, pushed, Yomi encouraged, held Kathleen's gaze. "More, more." The soles of Kathleen's feet pressed hard on the table, the veins in her neck protruding, eyes bulging in danger of escaping their sockets; the baby was stuck. Yomi managed to expose both

the tiny hands and then she did what she had suspected or
known was likely from the start. She took a short piece of
wood from the basket at her feet, placed it between
Kathleen's teeth, uncorked a bottle from her container and
spilt the contents between Kathleen's legs. She waited a
moment for the fluid to produce its numbing action, then
she cut, she cut to widen the opening. Kathleen's body
bucked. She had not believed that more pain than she
currently endured was possible but the cutting told her
otherwise.

"It's now, it's now. Push, Kathleen! Push, push, push!
Yes, keep going, push, push!"

Kathleen obeyed. The pain was endurable, she told
herself. She had no choice; she could feel herself splitting
but still she pushed. She could no longer see Yomi's face for,
in its place, was her baby, held aloft by Yomi still with the
cord attached.

"Just as fine as the last one," stated Yomi, "but with one
small difference; you have a daughter."

Kathleen clutched the tiny infant to her breast allowing
her to suckle, thus causing the expulsion of the afterbirth.
Yomi and her assistants bathed the battered perineum, the
bleeding needing to be stemmed. Potions from Yomi's
basket were applied; the magic worked. As Yomi stood, she
looked upon her friend, the joy of her newborn baby
exploding from her eyes.

The midwife wept, Kathleen wept and the two women
from the village wept. They had brought new life into the
world. Their hearts were overflowing with the joy of it so
they wept together in happy celebration.

Those waiting outside the cottage had set up a barrel of
ale. Seamus, Shaun and Eoin were ready with their music.
The cries from within had caused whoops without. Fiddle
started, ale flowed; they would celebrate. It was possibly
the strongest skill that most from the village possessed, the
rare ability to celebrate well. It was to this confusion that
Liam and Sweeney returned, knowing some distance from
the cottage that the news was good. Liam was ushered
inside to see his mother, new baby wrapped, cuddled to her
chin.

"This is your sister, Kirsty. Kirsty, meet your elder brother, Liam." Pride wrapped around each word that Kathleen uttered.

# Part Two

SEVENTEEN YEARS LATER...

# Chapter 19

LIAM stumbled. His toes buckled and turned under in the soft sand. He crashed, face down, arms out, to soften the fall into the edge of the sea. Giggles came from Kirsty close behind, her push on his back the cause of his fall. He rolled onto his back, buttocks in the water, resting on his forearms. His eyes smiled as his delirious sister, Kirsty, consumed with fits of laughter, clasped her sides in an effort to stop herself from exploding from the devilment.

As Liam's body rolled, placing him closer to her, his right arm shot forward to grasp her by the ankle, flipping her to the sand. Kirsty's reactions were too quick. Despite the tears of laughter streaming from her eyes, she skipped clear of his outstretched, left hand, taking flight with her bare feet making patterns in the sand. Liam rose and jogged after his sister, his lack of energy submission to her speed. On seeing her challenge thus deflected, Kirsty slowed her pace 'til Liam reached to take her hand. The ball of her foot dug deep, sand sprayed back against his legs and she was off again. Liam responded, his thighs raising, knees driving, feet extending. The match was even as they tore along the sand though the length of run was beginning to make harsh demands upon Liam's lungs. A final effort to close the gap, despairing dive, arm outstretched, fingers tapped her ankle. The gentle touch was enough to rob her of her balance as she tumbled to the ground.

They lay within arms' reach of each other, sucking air into their lungs with short sharp pulls. As time passed, the breaths grew deeper and longer.

On their backs they lay, gazing into the blue sky above, gulls wheeling, the gentle *ssh* sound of waves caressing the sand at their feet. Content in each other's company, they were excited that Connor was due home that year. Liam's only memory of his father was of a blue butterfly dancing in the sunbeams as he watched Connor scythe the corn. Kirsty had no memories at all but a vivid picture in her mind, created from the tales of others, adapted to encompass her heroic aspirations of her father.

Liam's eyes left the sky to glance at his sister, stretched on the sand beside him. Though five years younger, she was even now only two to three inches shorter. In stature, as in all matters, Liam never considered Kirsty to be in any way junior to him. In many ways it was she who took the lead, he who followed in her energetic footsteps.

Having arrived into the world feet first, Kirsty had managed to keep her feet firmly planted on the ground in the years since. She was not lazy in the sense that Liam was; it was unusual for her to take the time to lie in the sun. She was never at a loss to find something to do, always a task that needed action. Relaxation was the doorway through which danger might pass so she made sure the portal was always shut.

Kirsty was concerned for her mother. Since the earliest days she could remember, they had instinctively shared each other's troubled thoughts. She threw herself into activity for, although unspoken, the precarious hold the family had to sustain its existence lay behind the kindly smile her mother bestowed on her children. Liam seemed unaware of his sister's deep-rooted anxiety. Kirsty read beneath their mother's smile and did her best to work hard for their future. She knew her mother was distracted. Though she sensed the troubled thought, she could not identify the cause. Perhaps the bother lay in Fitzpatrick's interest in her these past few years. She could not bear the company of this bloated man. A prick with a pin, she imagined, might release the puss that surely filled his skin. Thus emptied, perchance, nothing would remain. She knew for sure that her mother worried on her behalf but this was an old concern, fading since Kirsty had whipped the cleric's ears with her loathing for him after he'd placed an arm about her waist.

She searched for other reasons of disquiet, O'Sullivan, the name she knew, the man she'd never met. His part in her father's deportation, dark tales of missing girls, both related to her a figure to fear, to avoid. Were the whispers in the village that he was back in Ireland the key to her mother's concern?

Her mother's mysterious refusal to come with them to the beach bothered her. She puzzled, right index finger tracing circles in the sand. O'Sullivan was the new factor. The concerns were new. They had to be connected. She would make an effort to reduce her mother's fear of O'Sullivan. The cloud that had covered the sun blew by. The warm rays struck her legs, bared by the hitching of her skirt. "Raise my spirits," her words, directed at Liam, a challenge, a plea.

Liam smiled at his sister as he sat up. "By the look on your face, the raising of your spirits requires a man with ten times the strength I own."

"Be done with your messing and do as I've asked. I'm in sore need of a lift to raise a cheer in my heart," Kirsty pleaded.

Liam rose, walked a few paces from his sister, turned to face her, the sea as his backdrop.

"*The Wonders of Birds by Liam Macken*," he intoned, pleased with the result. Kirsty's face melted into giggles again.

"Who made it so?
On the wing, gulls so high,
White specks upon light blue sky.
From on high, the downward plunge,
Beneath the waves their caws lunge.
Fish in beak, swallowed whole,
Soar again, repeat the role.
Who made it so?"
Liam continued, confident in his flow.
"Golden ears of corn to crop,
Confuse the insects as they drop.
As the aphids take to flight,
They come within the swallow's sight.
Swooping on the rising host,"
Liam struggled for a last line.
"To the cropper raise a toast.
Who made it so?"

Undeterred by his difficulties with the last line, he embarked upon a third verse.

"Tiny birds that sing each dawn,
To tell all the creatures of the morn.
The sounds you make so sublime,"
Liam's creative well had run dry. He finished.
"My best attempt to make it rhyme.
If perchance you're ever thirsty,
Well come and call my sister Kirsty."
Kirsty smiled at her introduction to the verse. "Well done," she acclaimed his effort.

"What do you remember of O'Sullivan?" she enquired of Liam as he sat on the sand beside her.

"I cannot recall him at all but Sweeney cowers at his name. I've tried to find the reason why. The questioning upsets him so I no longer ask him. I've heard in the village that he's returned from the wars. If he has, we will know of him soon enough... Why do you ask?" Liam looked into his sister's face, tears gathering in her eyes.

"Life is so hard, so much to go wrong. My father sent away, never seen his face, never clasped in his embrace. The world is supposedly so dangerous that I must wear disguise, morning, noon and night. My hair is kept dirty, my face too; clothes so oversized, they hamper my movements; colours so drab, they lower my spirits." By now Kirsty was sobbing. The tears spilled from the corners of her eyes, tracked through the grime, dripped grey onto the sand. "In your verse you asked 'who made it so?' Surely no God exists that can allow the existence of people like Fitzpatrick and O'Sullivan and all the suffering they've caused."

Liam moved closer to his sister, his arm across her back, his left hand clasping the corner of her left shoulder firmly. "When I look around, all I see is beauty, in you, in our mother, in the fields, in the sky, in the creatures of the earth. Only something good could have created these. Fitzpatrick claims to represent God but we have only his word – what value is in that? The God he claims to represent is not the one I know. There is no good in him, only greed, lust, self-serving."

Kirsty nodded her agreement, kissed Liam's cheek. "Let's go home," she said.

# Chapter 20

KATHLEEN left the well. She pushed open the door of the cottage, a cloth wrapped around her head, damp hair beneath. Her face was flushed, freshly scrubbed with no grime left upon her. She arranged her drying hair in the fashion best liked by Connor, soft brown curls drooping either side of her face.

She fetched the dress she had been married in. It had been Connor's favourite dress. The fit was as good as the first time she had worn it over twenty years before. The royal blue background had possibly lost some colour. She set the rich green shawl, an anniversary present from Connor, on her shoulders, draping it through her arms.

Kathleen closed the cottage door behind her and walked along the path to the headland where they had courted, where Kirsty had been conceived. She walked towards the headland where she had watched, almost eighteen years ago, the white sails fill with wind taking Connor away. When she arrived at their special place, she sat upon the ground watching the waves roll in. She had a history to recount to Connor. The pain in her stomach was a signal that her end was close by. This was likely the last earthly conversation she would have with him on this spot.

"Connor, we have a daughter. I gave her the name Kirsty. I hope you approve. Yomi helped me with the birth. I had forgotten how much pain there is in childbirth. Perhaps it is female nature to forget the pain so as not to discourage the want of another child. Kirsty was a strong, healthy child, seldom struck by illness. By her first birthday, the fifth of June – she was born seven months after your ship sailed – she was able to walk unaided. Within two years she could talk. I taught her your name. She could say 'da-da' before she could say 'ma-ma'.

"You'd be so proud of Kirsty. On her fifth birthday, we spent the day on the beach. The weather was grand. The children played in the surf – 'twas a good means of cooling the effects of the warm sun. Liam plunged into the ocean. He'd been swimming a few years by then. Kirsty plunged after him. I ran to rescue her but there was no need of it. She could keep herself afloat, splashing with hands and feet. At the end of the day she was able to pull herself forward in the water in the manner Liam had taught her. The sparkle in her eyes that night from sheer delight – well, it put the twinkle in the stars to shame. That sparkle has never left Kirsty. When she smiles or laughs, the green flecked with brown makes her eyes look like two golden diamonds; her gaze enough to swell my breast in pride. My body has been bathed by the kindness within her, spilling from her eyes. She's the daughter any person would wish to have and she's ours, yours and mine.

"Connor, she has rare beauty though you must make your own judgements when you see her. Perhaps I favour her too much over other girls- what else would one expect of a mother? Did I tell you that she reads words, can understand them? Whole books she has read to me. She reads so well. Liam taught her and writing as well. Both our children can read and write. Liam's taught me too, after a fashion. I thought of writing their histories for you, the parts of their lives you've not been able to share. I'm better able to tell you though. I feel more at ease, closer to you, talking rather than writing.

"You often complimented me on the speed of my feet. You said Seamus' elbow was never able to keep up, the dance outran the tune. I thank you for the praise. It certainly lifted my spirits at the time, encouraged me to dance quicker still. Well, Seamus' elbow may have slowed as my feet have done for sure. However, whatever skill I had has been passed on to Kirsty magnified. She has feet so quick, they are faster than an ant's blink! She has grace and flair too. When you're home, you'll see for yourself that I'm not exaggerating her talent at dance.

"Do you remember the tune, 'As the river flows?' I'm sure you must ... it was one of your favourites. Kirsty sings the lament, no fiddle, or pipes, just pure notes from within her.

The hairs on the back of my neck stand. I do not sob though the tears always wash my cheeks. Although the villagers in the tavern often ask her to sing the tune, she is loathe to do so. I think that she has sung it only three times. I've asked her why, what is the cause of her reluctance? Connor, it's because I have told her it was a song you favour. Although she has yet to meet you, the tune reminds her of you. The sadness of the lament comes from within her and is truly felt.

"A few months ago, I was struck by stomach cramps which carried on for some weeks. Yomi has given me some potion which eases the discomfort. Whilst I was lain abed, Kirsty cooked for the family. Liam was very appreciative, as was Sweeney. He comes to eat with us frequently as he helps with the land. Myself, I was only able to sup soup. Though Yomi's potion works – I am able to be up and about- I cannot eat more than soup still. Kirsty's cooking, though mostly learned from me, has also been influenced by Yomi's instructions on the art. The combination of the two with Kirsty's fertile imagination, produces dishes that, for sure, delight the appetites of the men folk; a good attribute I think when she has the desire to find a man to marry.

"During my illness, Kirsty has taken over all my needle-work. For many years past, she has helped with a willing pair of hands. I'm not able to sit with any degree of comfort because the position seems to worsen the stomach cramps. She sews well. When we went to the market last spring, we bought a few yards of blue cotton. Kirsty has fashioned it into a matching blouse and skirt. She looks very becoming when wearing them, the cut showing her figure to great advantage. Unfortunately, I have had to limit the occasion upon which she is able to wear them. Fitzpatrick, although much weaker, still has an unhealthy interest in the young girls of the village. For the most part, I've tried to keep Kirsty well clear of him, always dressing her in ill-fitting clothes. I've tried to keep her beauty disguised, dirty her face, tangle her hair for, when scrubbed clean, wearing her blue blouse and skirt, she's fit to break the heart of any man that sees her dance, smile, laugh, or hears her sing. There is a young fellow who appears to be particularly taken by her. I don't think she is aware or has noticed the time he spends looking at her from the side of his face. The lad seems unable to gaze on her lest he be caught doing so. He's a nice enough fellow; lives on his own I believe. His father died a few years back and his mother passed on giving birth to him. He's a great friend to Liam so he's at the cottage a fair while. Good looking in a dark sort of way and about the same age as Liam; you may have seen him when he was a tot but anyway, he's changed a lot since then. Jim Cassidy is his name.

"Kirsty has her own friends. She gets along fine with all the other girls in the village. There is a group of five who spend a lot of time together when the work is done. Mary is probably her best friend but she's three years older and looking to wed soon. Kirsty will be her bridesmaid. If the wedding's next year, you may be back by then Connor. She's going to wear her blue skirt so you'll see what a fine daughter you have.

"When you're back, measure yourself against Kirsty. She's a fair bit taller than me, only a few inches shorter than Liam. I've marked their heights on the wall alongside our own. Do you remember the day we measured our heights? You said you were at least a foot taller than me. You argued, wouldn't listen to reason as you teased me. We settled to mark the wall, then measure the difference. You tried to stand on your toes 'til I trod on them, making your heels fall to the ground. The measure was only half a foot difference, six inches. You still didn't accept you were wrong. You claimed that it was the length of my foot you had intended as being the foot difference. Well, Kirsty's mark on the wall is just below yours. The floor has taken some wear through the years so it will be interesting for you to see which of you is the taller. Without a doubt, Liam is the tallest in the family whilst I am surely the shortest.

"We have fresh eggs now Kirsty keeps chickens. She earned the money with needlework. The return on a few grains of corn is brown-speckled eggs each day. They sell well, better for some reason than plain white or brown! Each week we keep three for our own enjoyment. The one bird she began with has earned enough money to buy a further two fowl. Kirsty will go to the market in the spring. She's unsure as to whether to buy two chickens or perhaps a chicken and a duck. A pregnant duck would give her a chance to grow the ducklings. She's worried that she would not be able to sell them as food. Somehow, an egg is more difficult to become emotionally attached to than a fluffy duckling. I think she will end up buying two more chickens.

"Though Kirsty worries for the well being of living creatures, there's flint to her character too. She takes no nonsense from anyone. She knows her own mind and is stubborn too; she's not to be deflected. There's no boy around who would dare to take her on. I doubt even there'd be few grown men that would risk her anger. Perhaps it's her height that gives her the confidence or maybe it's the part of you in her Connor. Yes, now that I consider it, I'm sure she takes after you in the way she's able to stand up for herself. When she has need of it, her tongue is sharp enough to slice a stone. I wouldn't want you to think she's hard though she can be when the need is there. For the most part, Kirsty is kindness itself. She has a gentle way, a softness for those about her. These past few months, I've come to value her, lean on her. In truth, I am unsure as to how I may have coped without Kirsty's tender, caring love for me. I hope she knows how much this has meant, how it has helped ease the pain. I wonder if she realises. Maybe I should tell her of the admiration, pride, I feel in her. Maybe I'll tell her this evening. I'd hate to go with her not knowing how deeply, how completely, how well, how much I love her.

"Am I being too sentimental? I've no wish to make you sad, Connor. The legs on the girl, she runs as fast as Liam, he five years older, a young man. It's not because he's slow for he's a match for any youth his age in the village. You'd think her skirt would slow her down. Not a bit of it, it just billows out behind, a full sail, driving in the wrong direction.

"You're not to think that because I'm singing Kirsty's praises, she's a complete angel. She's had her fair share of scrapes over the years. Nothing really bad you understand but enough to warrant a slap on the leg when she was younger. I'm trying to recall the worst of them. Oh yes, I remember. One day in June, just before her eleventh birthday I think it was, she was nowhere to be found at dinnertime. Liam and I ate and she still didn't return. Liam searched the village whilst I searched the beach. Liam came back with Mary's parents, Kirsty's best friend. They were looking for Mary. Seamus had seen them together earlier in the afternoon. He wasn't able to say in which direction they had gone, only that he had seen them together, near the tavern, a while after lunch. Connor, we were distraught; you remember the young girls who've gone missing in the past when O'Sullivan was here, never to be seen again. By the time darkness fell, most of the village was out looking. Their names echoed over the countryside, "Kirsty! Kirsty! Mary! Mary!" as we spread out and searched.

"When we were at our wits' end with despair, they boldly walked into the village arm in arm as though it was two in the afternoon rather than almost midnight. I cried, I hugged her, then I scolded her. Where had they been? Did they not know the whole village had been looking for them? Did they not realise the worry they had caused? Well, they'd come across a donkey on their way home. The donkey was carrying a baby, not on its back, inside it; the donkey was pregnant. As the birthing started, they'd stopped to watch. It was this event that had caused them to lose track of the time and their hunger. Kirsty slept that night with the heat of my hand on her leg to remind her of the concern she'd caused. Mary suffered the same fate, so her mother told me the next day. That was easily the worst of the scrapes that she's been in; for the most part, she has been a source of almost constant joy to me. Now she's a young woman, she's become a good friend to me as I hope I am to her.

"Yomi has taken to Kirsty. She is teaching her the secrets of her plant medicines, instructing her in the skills she was taught by her grandmother and mother in Africa. They get on very well though Yomi does not always understand Kirsty's quick wit with word play. I suppose it's because she was not brought up here. She has had to learn our language so she's not aware of all the tricks that can be played with it. Yomi does understand when Kirsty mimics Fitzpatrick, the voice, the manner in which he talks, the way he holds his hands.

"Connor, I hope I have painted a true picture for you of our daughter, her beauty, her skills, her tenderness, her toughness. For sure, when you meet her for the first time, your chest is like to burst with pride at the fine young woman she is.

"Liam still talks of the day you harvested the corn together, of the blue butterfly. He's changed a fair bit since then, grown to be a young man. He's a good bit taller than you Connor, maybe as much as three inches. He worries because he knows I'm not well and is desperate to help where he can. We don't plant corn anymore; the memories of it are too bad. Perhaps, when you return, perhaps then the land will bear the golden ears once more. The potatoes we do grow don't have the same value though they do provide enough food when added to the eggs. We are able to buy extra due to the sewing work.

"Liam turns the sod, buries the seed potatoes and pulls them from the ground when ready. The storing of them is a problem, to keep them in fair condition. We have the cart back to carry them. I didn't tell you before but I'd sold the cart to pay for your lawyer. He did a good job. At one point, I thought you would go free but it wasn't to be; no blame to the lawyer though. Well, we bought the cart back some years ago. I remember how you fashioned it with your own hands, the pride you had when you'd finished. Liam pulls it now; the potatoes weigh heavier so it is not possible to fill it in the manner you did with the corn. I don't think there'd be enough potatoes to fill it anyway. Sorry if I'm blathering on. I was telling you of Liam. I'll try to fill in the time since you were taken away, the things he's done, the nature of him, the person he has become.

"You'll remember from your time with him, how he would spend his days with the small creatures, watching the insects go about their business, never doing any harm to them, careful not to tread where they might be, the wonder he had at the tasks they undertook when compared to their size. The questions he asked, the depth of them was such that, more often than not, the answers were outside our knowledge to bestow. He has many of the replies now, gained from his own observations. He delights in the birds, the small animals. He once found a squirrel that had injured its leg. I think his attempt at kindness for the poor creature was misunderstood; the bites and scratches to his hands testimony to that. Undaunted, he removed his shirt and enclosed the animal within, only its head visible. This procedure had an unfortunate effect on the nerves of the squirrel. I spent some while trying to remove the result from the shirt but that's by the by.

"Liam took the lamed animal to Sweeney. Sweeney has a great deal of skill in such matters. Within three weeks, the creature was able to scramble up the trees as if no harm had ever come to it. Liam has such a love of nature, most of his waking hours are spent outdoors. Even if it's raining, he'll stand under a tree to watch the raindrops' journey. He has a kindred spirit in Sweeney: they both gain great joy from the natural things that surround them. Things that you and I notice only occasionally, if at all, they seek out and spend many hours absorbed in. When you next go for a stroll with Liam, test him on the calls and songs of the birds. He can discern each, even when their sounds overlap one another. The robin, the lark, the swallow, sparrow, thrush, blackbird, crow, rook, raven, pigeon – he knows them all. He can tell the calls of the different seabirds. I didn't know there were so many. He knows from their sound whether it's a mating call, warning of danger or just sheer happiness that makes them sing so. Some songs he can mimic well enough that the birds respond to his sound.

"Liam's excitement at the wonders he encounters each day is infectious. He has dragged us, Kirsty and myself, from the cottage to see a leaf unfurl, to watch newly hatched chicks in a thrush's nest, ants burdened with loads larger than themselves. What troubled him was that he was unable to describe to us what he saw with words that would paint the picture he wished us to have. I took him to see old Mrs McGarr, you know, she that writes the letters for a fee, reads them too if need be. She's well past sixty now. Well, she took Liam on as a student. She's no family of her own and was happy enough to teach someone her trade for the future. Connor, you'd not believe the progress he made. For the want of words to describe what he saw, he gave up much of his time outdoors and took to the books. I'm not sure

Sweeney understood at first but he was soon reconciled to wandering again on his own.

"Within a year, Liam had mastered reading and writing. His skill with words was like that of an acrobat; he could make them turn, twist, somersault. He's since taught Kirsty and me the skill of reading, writing too after a fashion. Kirsty writes well but Liam has the mastery, the vocabulary. He is able to describe an event in a way that you feel you are present as it happens. Mrs McGarr's no longer able to write letters because her eyesight's failing; the reading of them is also beginning to trouble her. Liam's taken over the writing, some of the reading too. The fee he gets, I believe he shares with Mrs McGarr but I'm not sure for certain. He's never talked of it. The money he earns is a useful contribution to our income. You couldn't begrudge anything he gives to Mrs McGarr. She's taught him well, given her trade over to him. In truth, it is part of Liam's nature to show kindness to all whether they be on two legs, four or six. His gentleness and reverence for others is a virtue I've not seen much of elsewhere.

"Before you start to believe that he's a quiet, nature-loving scholar, there is an active side to him too. He can dance though I wouldn't say he has the skill that Kirsty shows for it; neither would he have the energy that you put into your feet when the fiddle's warm. Liam's height is against him but, nonetheless, he has a fair skill at dancing. His preference, when the tune is right, is to sing. Speaking as his mother, he has a wonderful voice capable of raising goosebumps on my arms. To be fair to the lad, it isn't only me who's affected by his singing; the rest of the tavern ask him to sing at least as often as I.

"The first time he was allowed ale, on his fourteenth birthday I think it was, he was too intent on pleasing the audience. Having downed one tankard in the manner of a seasoned drinker with a thirst neglected for a week, his friends pushed forward a second. Encouraged by the banter of the youths and intoxicated with the attention the whole tavern seemed to bestow on his initiation, he tipped the second down his throat. The reaction as the bitter fluid landed on his first effort had him rising in a rush from the table, tumbling out the door to lose both pints in the dirt at the side of the inn. A good meal exited with the ale to the merriment of the assembly. His pale face as he re-entered the tavern, eyes downcast, was soon enough restored to its usual style with the light of his smile. Hands crashed on his back; he'd done all that was expected of him, hoped for, by those assembled. The evening passed in song, talk and dance. Liam even managed to drink a tankard of ale with more deliberation so that it remained with him, inside of him. He's not a heavy drinker now; two or three tankards are all that he sups of an evening at the inn, modest quantities in comparison with some of your efforts, Connor! You've not always managed to stop the ale exiting in the same manner it entered but I love you for it and have no intention to scold.

"Eoin, that plays the pipes with Seamus, has spent some time this past year with Liam. Seamus fashioned a pipe which he gave to Liam on his eighteenth birthday. He's making good progress. The simpler tunes are easily recognisable. Some of the more doleful pieces, he plays with such tenderness. I slip into the trance that sometimes overcomes you when you watch the flames in a fire; you know, when your eyes start blinking to an unconscious rhythm without any apparent effort or thought. The evenings of fun you've to look forward to when you return Connor, the lost time to make up, song, dance, music, Kirsty, Liam.

"Although I've recommended Kirsty's cooking to you, especially the dishes influenced by Yomi's African culture, Liam's efforts at the stove are not to be overlooked. He is very inventive; he places ingredients together that I'd never think to mix. The results are sometimes surprisingly good. Other times, it's all I can do to swallow but he's mostly finished his experimenting now so you can look forward to some subtle mixing of flavours to delight your appetite.

"Did I tell you of his swimming? He's developed the art to such an extent that I wouldn't wonder he could outpace a fish. He stays beneath the waves for longer than I ever thought possible, unless of course you were to drown. One day, when Liam was fourteen, or maybe it was when he was fifteen, we were on the beach. Kirsty and Liam were swimming in the surf. They swam out clear of the breaking waves, then both dived under the water, bottoms in the air, then feet, until they disappeared from view beneath the surface. I watched for a minute or so and Kirsty's head popped out of the water, gasping for breath. It was a competition between them to see who could stay down the longest. I waited, expecting Liam to follow but there was no sign of him. After what seemed like an age, Kirsty out in the water was obviously agitated. I ran to the water, soaking my dress as I ploughed in. Liam's grinning face broke the surface; he hardly seemed out of breath! No harm done. My dress dried in the sunshine; the sand brushed off once it was dry.

"Liam wasn't always so fortunate. A few years earlier, he climbed the big oak tree close by the mill. His friends ran calling for me as he'd fallen from the tree. When I arrived, the poor lad lay on the ground, the set of his face showing the pain he was in. I was near to certain that his left arm was broken. Yomi confirmed it, then set the arm straight in splints for nigh on three months. It mended well though the inactivity it caused for Liam sore tried his patience. Why is it that boys feel the need to climb trees? What drives them to do it? His friends are a good bunch of lads. They're almost the same crowd now that he was with six or seven years ago, climbing the tree. Jim Cassidy is probably the closest of his friends. Do you remember? I told you of him before; the fellow who seems to have some regard for Kirsty, so abashed he can only look at her sideways!

"Liam's friends warm to his kind-hearted personality. He's never a cross word for anyone whatever their fault may be. Liam's so popular, I could imagine that he could win a seat in Parliament one day!.... though the business wouldn't suit him. He's best outside in the fields, in the woods, on the beach, absorbing nature and recounting what his eyes see, that which his heart feels. He puts his words into verse, to be spoken or sung so that others may understand the contentment nature can yield.

"So Connor, we have two fine children to be proud of, now grown to adulthood. They've been blessed with many talents though they've suffered the loss of their father for most of their childhood. I hope, when you return, you gain the pleasure, the satisfaction from their company that I've enjoyed these past years.

"The reason I've come to talk with you, to tell you the histories of Kirsty and Liam . . . Do you remember the dress and the shawl you gave me? I hope you do; I'm wearing them now, in memory of you. Well, to get back to why I'm here, the pain in my stomach has been worsening. I take more of Yomi's herbs to try to ease it but it grows in intensity each day that passes. I can feel something inside of me; I can feel it growing, squashing my vitals. Yomi's felt it too as it's developed, grown larger over the weeks. She tells me that she has no means of mending me, only the herbs to ease my time, ease my time 'til I must leave you, leave you, Kirsty and Liam. Perhaps as an angel I'll be able to look after all of you, care for you, keep you all from harm. As the devil in my stomach tries to deny me the night, my heart fights against his venom. I fear I am close to losing the battle; I sense I've not much more time. Look out for our children Connor. Let them know all they mean to me. I love you Connor with every nerve in my body. In your absence, the love has intensified. I don't understand how, for each day I feel I love you absolutely, then tomorrow comes and I love you more. I'll be your angel Connor. Listen out for my voice in the wind."

Kathleen rose from the grass, her eyes fixed on the horizon, the place where the sky met the sea. She trusted the ocean to transmit her message. If not the ocean, then the wind should be her messenger. Her eyes gazed skyward. The seagulls had listened. They would ensure Connor heard her words.

She brushed away the few pieces of dried grass that clung to her skirt and they floated back to the ground. With a deep breath of the ocean air, she swung on her heel to walk home to Liam and Kirsty. The thought of leaving them encouraged tears to spill from her eyes, slide down her cheeks, drip to the ground.

Her way was blocked. O'Sullivan stood in front of her, a canvas bag at his feet. The tears impairing her vision, it took a moment to recognise him. She had heard he was coming back. He'd changed, become older and skinnier – were his teeth always that cracked and brown?

"Do you remember me, Kathleen?" the words formed at the back of his throat.

"You look as pretty as a picture," he advanced a step towards her.

"You're not a day older since I last set eyes on you. Isn't it a good omen that you're the first person I meet on my return?"

Kathleen backed away. There was menace in his demeanour for all his attempts at civility, flattery.

"Kathleen, I've dreamt of you these past seventeen years, dreamt of what we'd do together. Others say dreams don't come true, well this is one dream that will."

He pounced, right arm outstretched, fingers closing on the dress above her left breast. As the talons sank into the fabric, pinching the skin beneath, Kathleen turned to flee. The material ripped setting her free. The sight of her exposed left breast stopped O'Sullivan's on-rush. Short, sharp breaths hissed between his rotten teeth. Another lunge and Kathleen was away towards the ocean, towards the cliff. Triumph glittered in the evil eyes of O'Sullivan for there was no escape as Kathleen turned to face her attacker. She crossed her arms over her breasts to cover the tear, no fear now in her eyes, just a hatred for the evil lifeform in front of her, the man who had lied, cheated, taken her Connor away from her, the monster who had caused such devastation to Sweeney's body and left him in the dirt to die.

Calmness descended upon her. She would entice him closer then pull him with her to the rocks below. At least, in her own departure, she would rid the world of the evil which O'Sullivan personified. Having fixed on the plan, her heart immediately vetoed the notion. She had not much life left in her but she'd not sacrifice a second of it. She'd words to say to Kirsty and Liam.

O'Sullivan's feet shuffled forwards; no step was taken. He closed the gap between them a few inches with each slide of his foot, first the left, then the right. Now he was within arm's length, he could grab her at will. He raised his right arm, no speed required now, nowhere to run as his fingers reached to take hold of her. Kathleen dropped her arms from across her chest, the exposed left breast ensnaring his greedy eyes. He did not see her right hand, fingers curled in the shape of a claw, slashing through the distance between them, nails scouring the side of his face. He felt the heat in his cheek, the trickle of blood. Kathleen darted forward on his left side, passing his mutilated cheek but his foot tripped her. He pulled her upright from the ground, fury in his eyes. As his left hand held her by the throat, his right hand swung in an arc towards her face. Fingers clenched, his fist landed on her jaw, splitting her lower lip, jerking her head backwards. Free from the grip on her throat, she was falling, falling, falling to the ground, on the ground still falling – no ground there, nothing. Kathleen's body lay part on rock, part on sand. O'Sullivan stared over the edge of the cliff, his dream gone, a fragment of dress at his feet. He kicked it over the edge watching its feathered flight as it landed on the sand close to Kathleen's left hand.

Terror took hold of O'Sullivan. He mouthed his fear.

"I could hang for this...but...but not if people believe she took her own life...That's it. She killed herself," he decided, regaining his arrogance.

"I'd best go and re-acquaint meself with Fitzpatrick for I've unfinished business with him," O'Sullivan schemed; he had his own plans for their future relationship. Lessons learned in France, he would apply in Corryann.

At Fitzpatrick's house there was no butler to answer the door. O'Sullivan pushed it open. The hallway had the same aura of dereliction he had noted in the garden. He knocked on the study door and Fitzpatrick himself opened the door to him. The worried frown ebbed from the cleric's face as recognition of his old tax-collector suffused his features.

"Come in...come in," Fitzpatrick waved O'Sullivan into his study. The air of neglect permeated this room also. Most of the books were gone. Horsehair bulged from splits in the leather armchairs.

"When did you return? What have you been up to?" the cleric asked, sweeping his right arm towards one of the two armchairs.

"I've come straight here," O'Sullivan replied, irritated by the questions but taking the proffered seat.

"A glass of wine?" Fitzpatrick offered, picking up an empty bottle from his desk. "Sorry, my cellar's empty," he apologised. "These past years have been hard on me."

O'Sullivan's temper unleashed. "Hard, hard you say. I've spent seventeen years of hard...in Bonaparte's army. Do you know how cold Russia is?...Do you know the taste of dead men's flesh?... Hard's not a word you've ever had to befriend."

"Yes, yes, well that's as maybe but I am thankful to the Lord for your safe return," he replied. O'Sullivan was not placated.

"Was it you set those press gangers on me? If it was, you'll be able to thank the Lord in person..."

"No...no. I had no part in it."

"If it was, I'll soon be finding out, mark my word."

"Calm yourself. Why should I have you press ganged? You're the best collector of rent a man could wish to have. It's been har...difficult to find one half as good. So, would you like to resume your old position?"

"No, citizen Fitzpatrick. The world, your world" (gesturing to the dilapidated study) "has moved on. I will collect your rent and tithes but the greater share will be for my pocket. Oh and if you've a need of sewing, though by the looks of you I doubt it, just forget it for all the sewing girls will be attending to me...So, as you've no further business with me, go and arrange my rooms as I'll be living here," O'Sullivan finished, placing his booted feet on Fitzpatrick's desk.

"Oh and I heard in the village on the way that the Macken woman jumped from the cliff. So be sure that she's not buried in the churchyard," he said to Fitzpatrick as he left to prepare O'Sullivan's new quarters.

# Chapter 21

THE breeze blew in from the ocean. Connor stopped, rock in hand, sensing a change in the sound of the breeze. The death throes, *sssh, sssh . . .* of the waves was also different.

He was close to serving his time. By his reckoning, at the end of winter, he would be a free man, free to return to his land. He would hold Kathleen in his arms, inhale the perfume of her hair, the sweet, special smell of her body. What would Liam be? How would he look? The plans he'd made for the future . . . so many ideas, thoughts colliding. Over the years he'd ordered them, put them in sequence 'til he was confident all could be achieved. The next eighteen years, he would live at twice the pace of a normal man in which manner he could recover the time he had lost.

He chided himself for disowning all that had happened in his time at the prison camp. There were many good experiences, good people he had met, learned from, laughed with, had fun with. In particular, he had gained much from his association with the prison warden and his family. The Gavins had filled part of the void in his life created by his absence from Kathleen and Liam.

Mrs Gavin was plump, not much over five-foot tall. The combination of shape and stature ensured a sense of energy to her every movement. The bustle of activity that always seemed to surround her was added to by the presence of three children about her legs. She loved her children, husband too – that much was evident from her demeanour when surrounded by them. Her attention was not solely focused on her family though. She had enough love in her to adopt all the community of the prison compound. Guards, cooks and prisoners alike were treated to her ready smile and kindness.

In his second year at the compound, Connor had

collapsed in the field of rocks. The enforcer, whip in hand, moved in, first calling to the armed guards to pay attention to the incident. He did not use his lash but rolled it into coils instead, bending over the collapsed prisoner. Cold sweat on the prisoner's brow convinced him that this was no malingerer. Two prisoners were called to support Connor, to place him in the shade of the tree beside the water barrel. At the end of the working day, his condition had deteriorated. He was no longer able to walk even though supported either side. A space was made to carry him on the cart that was used to transport the water barrel.

Once back within the compound, he was carried to his bed. Too ill to eat, he missed the evening meal. He sought the release of sleep but no relief to the malaise he felt came from that source. Nightfall came and stayed, unwelcome visitor that it was. Other guests came unbidden by Connor; friends of the night, they entered his fevered brain. They told him of his demise, showed visions of the hell he was to enter, teased him with fleeting glimpses of Kathleen, Liam, his land, tormented him with the news that he would never return to them. Through the never-ending night, there were times when Connor doubted he had the strength to repel them. The struggle sapped his energy; sleep to replenish him was denied. Just as he felt he must fall to those dark forces, daylight came; night left taking all unwanted guests in tow. As the sun rose, it brought Mrs Gavin to his side, damp towel in hand. He saw no wings; he expected her to have wings. His chains were removed, his body bathed. Was he dead? Were they burying him?

He was being lifted, floating, no longer on his bed, no longer in his hut. The breeze cooled his face. Now it was gone. He was no longer floating. He lay upon a bed and sleep came taking all responsibility from him.

Mrs Gavin mopped the brow of her fevered prisoner. It was two days since she had asked for him to be unchained and moved to a spare bedroom in her own house. Warden Gavin had not demurred at his wife's request: the only sign of argument was the raising of his right eyebrow which quickly dropped upon seeing the determination writ large upon her face. For two days, Connor had not opened his eyes. Now, as he felt the coolness against his temple, his eyelids slid back across the blue surface. Mrs Gavin's crinkled, smiling face filled his vision.

He was kept in the warden's home for a further seven days as Mrs Gavin sought to rebuild the strength he had lost in his struggle with the fever. The Gavin children came to see him, the eldest two both boys, the youngest a girl. They brought his food, soup for the first few days, bread and stew thereafter. Connor's affection for the family was bonded by his treatment that week. All were kind to him, the wife and daughter became particularly special to him.

As the years went by, Connor spent much of his spare time during the summer cultivating a vegetable plot beside the warden's house. Mrs Gavin was grateful for the produce, Connor for the chance to share in some small way the family life he was missing. He had watched the children grow and develop. He wondered if Liam was progressing through life in the same manner. He hoped he was as the Gavin boys were, growing into honest, hardworking, young men with an obvious respect for their father. The daughter, Anne was her given name, was already quite a few inches taller than her mother. Her tenderness, care for those around her, impressed Connor. He noticed the particular rapport she had with her father, gentler, closer than her two brothers' more formal behaviour in his presence. Connor determined that, on his return, Kathleen and himself should have more children. If a daughter came, he'd be delighted. If Anne Gavin was a reliable guide, Kathleen would be as happy as Mrs Gavin so obviously was with her daughter.

Connor considered that he would miss the company of the warden's family when he departed for his homeland, miss too the association with many of the other prisoners, particularly his friendship with Farrelly. Poor Farrelly, eighteen years for dallying with the general's wife. They were due to be released about the same time.

A lot had changed in the seventeen and a half years of Connor's enforced presence in Port Jackson but some difficulties remained. When he arrived, provisions were in short supply. Now there were still difficulties in feeding the colony. The work he did each day was not entirely the same.

Instead of moving rocks all day, summer afternoons were now spent cultivating the land from which the rocks had been cleared. The breakwater they had been constructing had been completed a few years back. Rocks were now taken to the beach and piled, creating small hillocks. There was a marked difference between work times and the hardships during the wet summer compared to the dry winter. Connor had a strong preference for the cooler time of year. In the wet season, the prisoners toiled for eight hours a day beneath a broiling sun. Their bodies lost copious amounts of fluids as they sweated throughout the day. Water was always plentiful but sweat ran into the eyes, the drops magnifying the heat of the sun. Dirt and dust from the hands transferred to the brow and carried to the corners of the eyes as perspiration ran down. Connor felt drained by the extra energy needed as his body sought to cool itself, the muscles still demanding the effort to raise and tote the rocks.

The warden had split the working day into two with a rest period from eleven in the morning 'til four in the afternoon to avoid the hottest part of the day. This free, hot time was of little use other than to lie abed. Connor much preferred the regime of work in the dry season when work started at eight in the morning and finished at five in the afternoon. Lunch was taken in the fields, the temperature much, much cooler. Free time after work had more value as Connor was not confined to bed by the excessive heat of the hot summer. He enjoyed cultivating the land cleared of rocks. For most afternoons, in the wet season, this was the task allotted to him. Fertile wasn't the best description for the cleared land, only a third as productive as his own land at Corryann. However, the satisfaction of working the land again, planting and seeing a crop grow, then harvesting it, fulfilled a deep need within Connor.

Longer evenings, the working day finishing at five o'clock, enabled greater intercourse between the prisoners. Music, singing, dancing and other pastimes all played a larger role in the social life of the camp when the hot season had passed. Connor had noted that arguments, frayed tempers, were most times prevalent at the height of the hot season. The seasons in Port Jackson seemed upside down, hot at

Christmas, cool in June, wet in summer, dry in winter. He looked forward with relish to the return of the four seasons that were common to him; the snugness of winter, tucked in his cottage, peat fire to warm him, early morning frosts, the air so clean, crisp, you could bite it as the smoke of your breath billowed from your mouth; youthful promises of spring, new shoots and leaves, new life, time to turn the sod, time to plant; summer, all the land green, the ocean and sky blue, playing on the beach and dancing in the village; autumn, time to harvest, time to fish, golden, russet, sunset, yellow, brown, the multi-hued colours of leaves in the trees soon to carpet the ground beneath.

Connor carried another rock to the beach and tossed it onto the pile with the others. It stuck fast in a cleft between two other stones. As he turned away, his reverie was once more disturbed by the tone of the breeze, the death tune of the waves. The seagulls stopped their dance in the air. Turning towards him, they called to him, his ears straining to interpret their song. A sting on his back interrupted Connor's concentration, the lash summoning him away, back to the land, another rock waiting.

# Chapter 22

NEWS of the call to a tavern meeting spread throughout the village as Seamus waited. The night breeze ruffled the wisps of grey hair atop his crown. Around his head, a denser growth of grey-white was interrupted by his high, smooth, brow. Two ears, well out of proportion to the rest of his head, looked as if they had been clumsily stuck to each side of his face, their lobes pulled downwards by the loose flesh that sagged from his cheeks and under his chin. His eyebrows were forced together, only held apart by ridges of skin. His eyes were deep-set. Seamus' feet were shod in brown leather boots. He clenched a clay pipe between his gums, empty but a comfort. Seamus' seriousness was evident to all who stood before him.

Yomi arrived to join the throng assembled outside the tavern. Seamus took his pipe from between his gums and held it by the bowl. Using the stem as a pointer, he first indicated Liam to his left and then Kirsty to his right.

"Kathleen is missing. When Liam and Kirsty returned home this evening, there was no sign of her. They're fearful for their mother's safety. As you'll all have noticed, she's not been in the best of health these past few months," Seamus paused. "When's the last time any of you have seen her?"

The question was directed at the faces before him. Kirsty spoke first, "We left shortly after lunch. Mother was in the cottage then. She had no particular plans for the afternoon. I asked her to come with us but she said we were to go off and enjoy ourselves."

"Has anyone seen her since midday?" Silence; no one responded to Seamus's question. "We'll split into four search parties. Divide yerselves into four groups."

The four teams assembled as Seamus continued his instructions. "Yomi, take your people to search the fields

*103*

and meet back here when you've finished. Send a messenger if you come across anything."

Yomi departed in the company of six or seven people. "Liam, you go with this group; best you search the woods. Kirsty, take these people with you. Walk the beach. There's a good moon to help us."

The final group waited for their instructions. "We'll search the village. Ask any you meet if they've seen Kathleen since midday. We'll meet back here when we've finished. We'll wait for the other groups to return and if there's no sign of her, we'll have to widen the area we're searching 'til we find her."

O'Sullivan walked past to enter the tavern. "Yer back then, have you seen anything of Kathleen Macken today, since midday?" asked Seamus.

"No, I've not. Why do you ask me?" was the sharp response from O'Sullivan as he turned to face Seamus.

"She's missing. We've sent search parties to find her. Jes, what have you done to yer face man?" queried Seamus as the tax-collector's face came into view.

"Toothache," he hissed from between gritted teeth clamped by the white bandage which covered the left side of his face, ran under his chin and was tied, the knot behind his head.

The moonlight did not discern the pinkness seeping through the white cloth as O'Sullivan entered the tavern. Seamus led his team to the far end of the village to begin their search.

Liam's group was on the edge of the woods, a mile or so from the village which lay between the cottage and the trees. His mother would have normally passed through the village if she were bound for the woods. Surely somebody would have met her. Though not a large village, it made no sense to him that you could pass through it on a Sunday afternoon without being greeted by a host of people. This thought increased the sense of foreboding he felt, tightening the muscles across his chest, the murmured encouragement from his friends unable to penetrate. They walked in amongst the dark trees, the moonlight only able to break through the canopy above in rare places where an old tree had fallen. The gloom of the woods settled on Liam. At other times, he'd sat and watched for hours the shafts of sunlight spearing through the trees, dust suspended in the rays. Tonight, his heart had no place for wonder, no room for delight. He felt the weight of it, felt its pulse pounding on his ribs, pulling tight upon the muscles within his throat.

Yomi spaced her group one hundred paces apart, the moonlight lighting the open countryside. They moved in a ragged line half a mile wide, sweeping across the fields. Two sweeps, each of about two miles would cover the terrain they were to search. Yomi forced herself to concentrate, forced her eyes to pry, seeking some sign of her friend Kathleen. A thought forced its way to the front of her consciousness but it was rebuffed, scolded for interrupting the concentration needed by her eyes. Again the thought came and she fought it; she had no time to think. She must look. The second sweep complete, there was no evidence of Kathleen as Yomi's team followed her back towards the village. The silence of their progress was disturbed only by hushed conversation as if the folk were in church where conversing was frowned upon and by the distant echo of Kathleen's name, called through the darkness by members of one of the other teams. The thought she'd fought came again to Yomi as she walked. She knew of Kathleen's condition, knew the pain she suffered. She knew too that it was only a matter of a short time before the growth within her would end Kathleen's life. Had she left to die? The elephants did, she knew from her memories of Africa. Had her good friend, Kathleen gone away to die alone, to spare her friends and her children the witness of her torment? A tear leaked from Yomi's right eye, tickling her nose as it passed. She had planned to be with Kathleen, to comfort her at the end, to tell her of the spirit world she would enter, meet again her mother and father, prepare the way for the rest of her family. Yomi's sadness that Kathleen might die alone consumed her on the walk back to the village.

Kirsty walked along the sand, the only time in her life that the softness beneath her feet had failed to exhilarate her. Why had she not been more forceful? She felt sure her mother would have come with her that afternoon, if only, if only she had pressed her to. Where could she be? Where would she have gone? She'd not talked of going anywhere. Why wasn't she at home in the cottage? She was always there. It was her presence that made it their home. Kirsty pulled question after question into her mind. If she could just keep asking questions, she could put off the fear, her fear that something was wrong. Mindful of the stomach cramps her mother had tried to conceal, Kirsty's intuition told her it was more serious than Kathleen pretended. Why had she thought of her mother as Kathleen? She only ever though of her as her mother. The questions again tried to block out the fear. Kirsty walked on.

Ahead of her, the rocks tumbled from the cliff to rest on the sand, touching the ocean. As she closed on them, she could discern a dark shape close to the cliff face. During their search of the beach that night, they had, a few times, thought that clumps of seaweed washed upon the shore might be other than what they were. This shape was too far from the water's edge. As this calculation emerged in Kirsty's mind, she recognised the material lying upon the ground and the ball of her foot pressed down on the sand. Her stride lengthened as she ran towards the dress. As she neared, she saw her mother's face washed by the moon's light. She quickened her stride, anxious to aid. Kirsty's fingers stroked her mother's face, brushed a lock of hair from her forehead, the coldness of the skin, the message she had never wanted to hear. The muscles of her face contracted; her mouth, her throat, her chest, they ached; she could not breathe. She stroked the hair, kissed the eyelids, caressed the cheeks but nothing changed. Her mother lay dead. The only parent she had ever known, her best friend, lay dead. As the sobs shook her upper body, her tears washed over the blood on her mother's lower lip. The diluted blood ran down Kathleen's chin, the only sign of life. Kirsty saw the tear to the dress, pinchmarks on the upper breast. She picked up the torn material from beside her mother's left hand. Nothing registered in her brain; it was a subconscious action to tidy for her mother. Her whole consciousness was consumed with the knowledge that the smiles, the warmth, the counsel, the presence, had all gone. Without her mother to take pride in her, she could never again dance or sing, never again do anything. She'd heard people sing of broken hearts; hers was not broken, it was torn. Every nerve-ending within it screamed, implored that she should join her mother in death.

Yomi's team returned to the village where Seamus' group was already waiting in front of the tavern. Neither had met anyone who had seen Kathleen since noon. As they waited, the hushed reverent conversation continued until silenced by the sound of sobbing drifting towards the tavern on the breeze as Kirsty's people were heard returning along the track from the beach. Sweeney walked ahead carrying Kathleen in his arms. Her head rested against his breast as though she was sleeping. Kirsty held her dead mother's hand as they walked, pressed, caressed, stroked the back of it, hopeful still of bringing back life to the fingers that had fashioned her life. Seamus' old eyes took in the scene, from the way she was carried to the grief of the approaching party. His eyes watered; his lady was no more. He signalled for Sweeney to follow him into the tavern. Sweeney laid Kathleen gently on the table with the care he used on a newborn chick. The big man's face was awash but no sound came from him. The teardrops flowed freely from his swollen eyes. As the bar filled with the searchers, O'Sullivan slipped out of the door, his fresh pint hardly supped. Kirsty placed the scrap of material to cover the breast exposed by its loss. Seamus asked Sweeney to find Liam and his group in the woods and bring them back to the tavern. The big man shook his head, tears dripping from the surface of his cheeks. He would not leave Kathleen's side. A volunteer offered to do Seamus' bidding, setting forth immediately with news for Liam which no man would wish to impart.

Yomi began to chant, the sound captured deep in her throat, her eyes closed tightly. Kirsty still held her dead mother's hand, still tried to stroke life back into it. Sweeney stood at the end of the table close to Kathleen's head, embarrassed to be present, shuffling from foot to foot, not wishing to leave the woman he would have died for, still would sacrifice his life for if he could bring her back to smile again.

SEAGULLS DANCE

The searchers drifted away once there was no more to be done. Seamus stayed, waiting for Liam to arrive. He was not long in coming, the effort expended apparent from his heaving chest and rasping breaths as he sucked air into his lungs. Kirsty placed her mother's hand gently on the table. She clasped Liam to her, looking into his eyes in shared despair.

"Who . . . how . . . why . . . ?"

Liam searched for an explanation to the tragedy.

"I found her on the beach. Her body was cold. I don't know how she died but I think her neck may be broken. She was below the cliff where the rocks have broken away. You know how special that place was to her. If we had found her sooner, if we hadn't been away . . . I don't know the answers."

The flow of tears increased down Kirsty's face.

"Why was she wearing her wedding dress? Why the precious shawl? A link with our father? I don't know, I just don't know. I only know she's dead and I can't see how I can live without her."

As her body heaved and sobbed, Liam tried to calm his sister.

Seamus at last persuaded Sweeney to leave Kathleen. He was to fetch the handcart from beside the Macken's cottage, place a blanket from the cottage on the floor of the cart and then bring the cart to the tavern. Able to do this last service for Kathleen, Sweeney ambled off.

Kathleen's body was carried on a blanket from the cart into the cottage and lain upon her bed. Sweeney and Seamus departed. Yomi offered to stay but Liam assured her they'd be alright 'til the morning. At last, Kirsty and Liam were alone with their mother as it had always been but tonight was no longer the same. Now their mother could not hear them, she could not speak to them, nor hug, nor smile. She lay lifeless, cold, the warmth gone from her. Liam cried; he cried and cried, the numbing ache of his grief descending as the loss of her took hold. All that he held precious, took for granted like the air he breathed, was no more. Kirsty sobbed, her shoulders shaking with each stuttered breath. Their

*108*

nightlong vigil had not sapped their grieving when Yomi returned in the morning.

Yomi bathed the body of the tranquil Kathleen, taking such care as she had ever done on any living being. She talked to her friend as she ministered her last service.

"So many seasons, so much of our lives, we have spent together. When first I came to your land, your body was no different than a boy; the blush of womanhood had yet to transform you. In those days you honoured me with much kindness, friendship and love, and I, a stranger to your land. When O'Rourke departed, I thanked all gods, all spirits too for the friendship of you, my little sister. I've known you longer than any other person, longer even than my time with my own mother and father, sisters and brothers. We've giggled our girlish stories. I watched you fall in love with Connor. What an illness that was! You were so giddy with the excitement of your newfound passion, no thought of artfulness ever crossed your mind. I remember the pride I felt at your wedding and the coaching I gave you beforehand. When Liam came, we were so close; I felt of him as my son too. Kirsty, I have always considered as my daughter. Don't tax your soul, my good friend Kathleen, I will look out for your children, keep them from the spirits that harm. My spirit sister, I will always keep my love for you. Come and sit with me any time you feel the need."

Liam and Kirsty sat at the table listening to the manner of Yomi's conversation with their mother and the notion that she was still there. They learnt that Kathleen could still be talked to, could still go and visit Yomi in some way, was still somehow with them all and this added balm to their grief. Their feelings of absolute loss dissolved. Kirsty had washed the wedding dress whilst Yomi bathed her mother's body. Patching of the tear proceeded very deliberately; the very best of her skills with a needle was required to please her mother. The realisation that she still sought her praise meant that she believed her mother was, in some way, still able to judge her efforts.

The patching and bathing complete, Kathleen was re-dressed, hair brushed, face serene, lain on her bed, ready to receive the final visits of those wishing to say goodbye.

Sweeney was the first to call. He had been waiting outside since early that morning for the opportunity to see Kathleen. The big man shuffled in and nodded three times to Liam, Kirsty and Yomi before his eyes shifted to the body lain on the bed. He knelt beside it and picked up Kathleen's left hand, pressing its palm to his cheek. The same he did with her right hand. Then, bending forward, he pressed his cheek against hers, the tears that flowed running from his face to hers. Sweeney rose, wiped his eyes with the back of his left hand, nodded again three times and walked out of the door. Yomi went over to the bed. A small knife was placed in Kathleen's right hand.

"He has given her his knife," she said, looking towards Liam and Kirsty. Her brow furrowed with the effort of understanding the significance of the gift.

"It belonged to his father. It's the only link he has with his own family. He treasured it above all else." Liam's voice was husky as he interpreted the meaning of the present. Kirsty wept at the generosity of the big man. Tears rolled out of Yomi's eyes as she comprehended the sacrifice, the quiet manner of giving. Liam sobbed, uncontrolled with a rapid heave and fall of his chest. His friendship with Sweeney, the time they'd spent together . . . he knew more than any other person what the possession of the knife had meant to the big man; now he had given it up.

Throughout the afternoon, the villagers came to say goodbye to Kathleen Macken nee McDonagh, raised in the hamlet since birth, a friend to all, the enemy of none. The flow of kind words continued well into the evening. Seamus was the last to call, bringing his fiddle with him. He kissed Kathleen upon her brow.

"I first met you, my lass, when you were but a young girl. Your pa bade me come from my village. Your ma ill, he tended her whilst I took care of you. She never recovered. The fever took her and your poor pa was distraught. Then he took with the fever too, joined your ma. Before he died, he made me promise to look out for you. Well, I promised and up 'til now you've done just fine. My own wife died before I came here, three children too, a fire in the cottage whilst I was off at work. Perhaps it was the loss of a family of my own that spurred your pa to make me promise to look out for you. Well, now you're gone too. Maybe it's my lot in life to bury those I love. There's an air I'd like you to hear before you're gone. I'll play it for you now."

Seamus took up his fiddle and stick. The sound, as he caressed the strings, melted the bones in your body, exuding a plaintive air of such serenity that the angels from heaven came down to listen.

Seamus clamped his right hand in the middle of Liam's back, bade him stay strong. He kissed Kirsty on the cheek, squeezed her left hand and looked deep into her eyes. "You're a strong one. You'll do just fine," he said, increasing the pressure on her hand. He kissed Yomi's cheek, squeezed her left shoulder with his bony right hand, nodded to her. With no more words, he picked up his fiddle and stick, kissed Kathleen's brow between her eyes and was gone through the door.

The next day, Yomi prepared Kathleen for burial. Kirsty helped but was limited by her lack of experience. They folded her hands so that they rested in the centre of her abdomen. Sweeney's knife was placed between them. A lock of Connor's hair that Kathleen had kept since before they married was pressed between the thumb and forefinger of her right hand. Seamus had given Kathleen a silver locket worn by her mother on her wedding day. This was taken from her box of precious things, hung around her neck, the locket resting between her breasts. Liam penned a poem which was held to her body by her left hand. Kirsty tucked the rag doll which had looked after her each night for the whole of her life under Kathleen's arm, its head resting between her right shoulder and chin. Yomi placed a small wooden carving under the little finger of her left hand. She explained to Kirsty that it would ward off any bad spirits that came to call. Thus adorned, they wound white cotton strips around Kathleen's body until it was totally encased, save for her face upon which a small square of white linen was placed, the edges tucked into the surrounding cotton strips. Kirsty kissed her mother's lips. Liam followed her lead, then Yomi and then one last kiss from Kirsty before the linen square was tucked in place.

*111*

Crunching pebbles, the iron-clad wheels rolled along the track. Ahead was the clippety-clop of the hooves of the horse that pulled the cart. A tall, unshaven man led the horse, his long, black coat hanging on his lean frame, almost to his ankles. In the bed of the cart, a rough wooden coffin was tied down with broad, brown, leather straps. The ends of each strap were tied to an iron ring set in the base of the cart. The lid of the coffin was fastened on one side by a small iron hook that clipped into a leather ring set below the hook in the side of the coffin. The far edge of the lid was fastened to the side by three iron hinges spaced along its length.

The cart driver, who owned and rented his coffin for burials, pulled on the harness gripped in his left hand. The horse stopped outside the cottage. Liam, having heard its approach, was waiting. The undertaker released the straps from the rings on the left-hand side and, standing in the bed of the cart, he pushed the coffin with first his feet and then, as more space became available, crouched down and pushed with the heel of his hands. Liam balanced the other end as it overhung the edge of the cart bed until the coffin owner was able to jump down, lifting his end clear. The two men carried the empty coffin into the cottage, placing it alongside Kathleen's bed. Yomi, dressed in her finest, brightest dress, took hold of her friend's feet. Kirsty, wearing the blue cotton blouse and skirt Kathleen favoured her in, lifted her mother's shoulders. The two women tenderly placed the body of Kathleen Macken in the coffin as the undertaker held the lid open. The closing and fastening of the lid brought a sob from Kirsty's chest. As her tears rolled, Yomi and Liam let their emotions run down their cheeks in solidarity. Seamus entered, followed by Sweeney. As their eyes were drawn to the coffin, empty bed beside it, they too were overcome. Sorrow, tears filled the room – no word was spoken. Soon the whole village was assembled either inside or outside the Macken's home. Kirsty, Liam at her side, bore the front of the coffin. Seamus and Sweeney supported the rear on their shoulders. They placed the end on the edge of the cart bed, sliding the coffin forward 'til it was completely supported. The undertaker strapped it down.

Nostrils flared with each great breath, red, pink of the

interior visible each step as the horse exhaled. His master's knuckles tickled the side of his face as he walked beside him, gripping his harness in his left hand. The long, black coat flicked his right foreleg each time he led with it. In his experience, all humans were doleful and sad for, in his work, he so seldom met any that were not. He trudged slowly onward, leading the procession to the church.

Kirsty looked up at the dark grey clouds, in sombre mourning too as they drifted slowly by. Patches of white, emblazoned by the sun, appeared and the sun itself broke through, casting off its dark grey blanket, blue sky displacing retreating grey. It was a morning such as to delight her mother. Did she watch them from on high? The choir rejoiced, singing their alleluias full throat as the birds bade their farewell to one who had cared for them. The squirrel scampered forward, bowed, turned, skittered up a tree. Liam's feet kicked up the dust as they led the village behind their mother's coffin.

# Chapter 23

HIS Reverence mopped his brow, kerchief in hand, a sudden burst of sunshine beating down upon his heavy coat. Armed militia surrounded him, six on either side. O'Sullivan, face still bandaged, stood behind the phalanx with Hanrahan (now relieved of his duties as tax-collector) for company. The fifteen men waited.

The cortege arrived at the churchyard, their passage blocked. Fitzpatrick raised his right arm, flat palm, a signal to stop. Kirsty, Liam and Seamus strode past the coffin to confront his Reverence whilst villagers spilled either side of them. Sorrow slept whilst anger awoke the fury of the village that stood before the cleric. Unnerved, Fitzpatrick turned to O'Sullivan, himself stepping back half a pace. O'Sullivan stepped forward and addressed the villagers.

"Kathleen Macken took her own life. In the eyes of God, she has no right of a place to be buried on holy ground. If you threaten us, the troopers will fire their weapons. You must leave for you have no business here." He vomited his words, eager to finish.

"For pity's sake, let us bury our mother for she was always a Christian," Kirsty's eyes fixed on the troopers. "You all have mothers of your own. You know what it means to us, would mean to you," their eyes, unable to return her gaze, were downcast in shame that they should be the cause of these new tears for the grieving girl before them. Doubt seeped into their minds, loosened the stern resolve of their duty. Shuffling feet, they lowered their weapons, sideways glances questioning each other's eyes. "Stand fast!" cannon roar exploded from the mouth of their captain, shattered doubt blown to smithereens.

Kirsty turned in search of an answer. The faces of the villagers, they could force the passage. She would not ask that sacrifice. Yomi stepped forward, standing sideways in the path with militia to her left, the crowd on her right.

"I do not come from your land. I do not have your religion. I know of no religion that refuses to accept the body of the mother, the mother that brings life to us, nurtures us through childhood, worries in our absence, dies a little each time that we are sick, gives us love regardless of ourselves, creates a home, a place of warmth for body and spirit, hides her own infirmity lest it concerns us. Such a mother was my true friend Kathleen whose passing took a part of me that never can return. She had not long to live; the growth in her stomach advanced each day. These past few months, the pain was past enduring. She hid this from you to save you from worrying. There's no one saw her fall, no one saw her slip."

The murmur of assent rose in the crowd as they began to move forward. The captain looked to the cleric for instruction. He looked to O'Sullivan and then mimicked the shake of his head in response.

"Stop! Any further and my men will shoot!" boomed the captain lest his words would not reach the ears of all.

"We can't allow injury to others, Liam," Kirsty sought her brother's accord.

"No, we must go," Liam replied. The undertaker coughed to gain their attention.

"I'm sorry to press but I need the coffin for another funeral. The family would be sore put out if I don't turn up," he half whispered, not wishing to inflame the situation.

"Turn the horse. Take us back to the cottage." The words dropped dully from Liam's mouth.

"Please, all of you, return to the village. We'll be at the tavern this evening to celebrate the life of our mother." Kirsty's words released the villagers from their passion to rush the troopers, saving them from harm.

Kathleen lay again upon her bed, the clatter of the undertaker's cart fading. Kirsty was relieved to have her mother once again at home. The sense of relief yielded to one of guilt. It was her duty to bury her mother's body, not to keep it as a comfort to assuage her own loss. The sun, high in the sky, flooded through the open door, warming the still cold body of Kathleen.

"Vikings set their dead upon a burning boat and floated them out upon the ocean. We could entrust Kathleen to the care of the sea. She would be closer to father; the sea may take her to his shore," Liam surmised, romantic notions filling his mind.

"I don't think so," Kirsty replied, "Her body would sink and we would never know its whereabouts. I need to be able to go to her, to visit her grave so it must be on land. Liam, do you believe that when we are dead we will be able to see our Mother again? If we can, will we be the age we are now or might we be older than her if we live longer?"

"I believe that we will all meet again when we die but we will not have bodies; we will have left them behind. We shall live on as spirits, able to commune in thought, to feel in thought, to love each other in thought," Liam concluded.

"I'm not sure I really understand yet," Kirsty responded. "Where shall we place the grave?"

"Overlooking the ocean and our land with a view of the birds in the sky... that is what I should like. I think it would suit mother too," was Liam's reply.

"At the headland, close to where she fell, you can see the ocean and our land too. There are forever birds overhead. That'd be a fine place. She'll be the first to see father's ship when it brings him home. He will come home, won't he Liam? He is still alive, isn't he?" Sadness and foreboding quivered in her voice.

"That'd be the right spot, on the headland as you suggest. Of course he'll be back, a year or so at the most," confirmed Liam, his voice giving the reassurance his mind lacked.

Kathleen's body was carried for the last time from her home. Her children laid her carefully on the base of the handcart Connor had constructed with such pride in his workmanship so many years earlier.

Kathleen's children shared in pulling the cart as they passed their land and the ditch where the corn had been hidden, to the headland, Kathleen's most favoured place. Liam cut the shape of the grave with his spade, stripping the grassy sods with care, intending to re-cover the grave at the end.

Kirsty took her share of the digging, rocks and stones blunting their progress 'til, at last, a hole some four feet deep, was complete. Kathleen's body was carried with great tenderness from the cart and placed on its back alongside the open grave. Kirsty removed the linen cloth that covered her mother's face. Her peaceful sleep continued now, caressed by the soft light of the moon. Kirsty stroked Kathleen's stiff cheeks with the back of her fingers.

"I'm sorry that I thought you had abandoned us. I knew you were not well but had no notion that you were close to death. I thank you for sparing me the pain of knowing. I thank you too for my life, what you have made of me. If I ever have a daughter of my own, I'd fill with pride if she has half the love for me that I, your daughter Kirsty, have for you. I hope you like your resting-place. I'll come often to talk with you. God bless and goodbye Mother." Kirsty touched her lips to her mother's and as she rose from the ground, a single tear dripped from her cheek to land beside Kathleen's lips.

Liam knelt at his mother's side, "I thought it best to express my feelings for you in verse. You have it written in your hand. No matter, I would as soon you heard the words from me."

"I've loved a love so peaceful, so serene
No pain it caused, heartbreak none
Its balm it salves my soul
In never-ending stream.
My love for you eternal
Rests in the wind that blows
Sung by the birds above us
And all small beings down below."

Liam kissed Kathleen's right cheek, the salty taste of his sister's tear still upon it. As he rose, Kirsty replaced the linen square over her mother's face and tucked the edges into the cotton bindings. The two children gently lowered Kathleen Macken's body into its last resting-place. Kneeling at the edge of her grave, they placed stones upon her body 'til it disappeared from view. Liam lay a wooden cross that he had

*117*

fashioned upon the stones. They tipped in the earth, covering all with the grassy sod. Little disturbance to the ground was to be seen when they had finished; in fact, one good wash of rain would disperse all trace.

The seagulls danced above the grave, calling to each other the news of Kathleen's burial below.

# Chapter 24

CONNOR paused as he walked back up the beach, his last rock just dropped upon the pile. The gulls above were calling, the breeze carrying their message to him. For all he could not understand, he turned to face the ocean, dropped to his knees upon the sand and cried aloud for the first time since he was a boy. The tears swept down, striping his face, tightness in his chest. The guard raised his whip hand, a kiss to bestow on the back of the kneeling prisoner.

Mrs Gavin entertained the sea captain with tea in her drawing room. His ship had brought much needed provisions for the colony at Port Jackson. Although some twenty years since its founding, the colony was well short of self-sufficiency. Official documents had been entrusted to the captain, a few addressed to the prison warden. Warden Gavin had taken possession of these, their contents the reason for his absence from tea with his wife and guest. His shoe-shod feet buried with each step through the sand as he strode onward, right hand clutching the open document, left hand catching the guard's wrist that held the whip, the kiss never reaching the kneeling Connor. Connor felt the kindly hand of the warden and heard the words of comfort; the document announced the end of his imprisonment.

Emotions engulfed the kneeling prisoner. He sensed the trouble in his homeland though he knew not the cause. Now he was a free man, free to return to his wife Kathleen, his son Liam, to his land, to Corryann. His shackles were, at this moment, being taken from his wrists and ankles. A blizzard of feelings swept over him, threatened to overwhelm him. Through them all, he felt the constant throb, "I am free, I am free, I am free." Connor's next meal, his lunch, he would eat unshackled, free to return to his home. The earlier feelings of foreboding dispersed amidst the euphoria of his

119

unexpected freedom, three months earlier than he had anticipated, than he had calculated.

Warden Gavin and the enforcer left Connor to his thoughts. Passing prisoners laid hefty palms upon his back as they passed by, joy in their hearts at the release of one of their own. Connor's heart and his thoughts were filled with the love he had for Kathleen, for the moment when he would see her face, feel her warmth, bathe in the aura of her gorgeous smile. These thoughts intoxicated him as he stood facing the ocean, its waters lapping at his toes, washing the dust away. Connor sought to overcome his light-headedness, blinked and rubbed his eyes. He had much to say to Kathleen and wanted to clear his wits before he began.

"Kathleen, my time is done. I've waited so long, despaired of the day ever arriving. Today, I have my papers. I am a free man again. I'll work to earn my passage home. Be sure, I'll not take a day longer than it needs," Connor drew his right foot over the water, wetting its sole.

"This ocean will carry me back to you. I'll never let go of you, your hair to caress, your head pressed against my chest, my arms about you. If O'Sullivan comes by, he'd do well to steer well clear of me for it's him that has caused our separation these past eighteen years." He lowered his eyebrows and narrowed his eyes with a scowl dark enough to put the fear of God into O'Sullivan if he were to witness it. "But I'll not dwell on the past. I've a son that's grown up now. He'll have such stories to tell. I was thinking it may not be too late to grow our family; a daughter's a fine thing for a mother to have, a father too, from what I know from here. Well Kathleen, it's time for me to make a start on my journey to you. I've work to find, coin to earn."

Connor kicked at the water's edge in exultation, joy writ large across his grinning face as he turned, walking up the beach, a free man. The sight of his fellow prisoners still in chains, still moving rocks, caused a sense of guilt which momentarily reduced the joy in his heart, in his face but he knew they'd be happy for him. Their day would come too.

# Chapter 25

AS darkness ebbed away, it's retreat brought form to the landscape before him. Arms of silent ogres ceased to palpate his heart. Branches, trunks of blackened trees and cobalt bushes took shape. Mist cleared from the grey sky; mist still settled as a cloud taking rest upon the ground. Blacks and greys changed to greens and blues as the trees and sky were illuminated from an unseen source. Clouds covering the land melted as the warmth of the light bore upon them. Grey-pink slashes of colour lay low down in the eastern sky. Mountains loomed to the south where, yesterday, the sea had been. Mottled brown bark lay as fragments clinging to the smooth fawn trunk of the eucalyptus as the light burnt off the blackness of night. Dark clouds atop the ocean rolled away, mountains no more. Sky above, lightest pale blue, below grey, then a strip of white light, more grey, slightly darker, rested upon the mist that covered the land. An orange glow warmed the eastern horizon as the crowns of trees broke through the mist. The sun rose through a veil of wispy cloud.

Connor sat, watching it rise, on his first morning of freedom. He'd imagined this morn, replayed it in his mind through the months, through the years. Not wishing to miss any part of it, he'd sat watching throughout the night. The orange orb now turned to gold, it's light too strong to gaze upon. His right hand sought out the wrist of his left, the fingers gently caressing the worn skin worked smooth by six thousand five hundred and twenty days of iron bracelets. Almost half of his life he had been chained and now he was free, fifty-five days before he had expected. Thoughts of freedom intoxicated his body, the lightness in his head the equal of at least ten tankards of ale from the tavern. As he made this calculation, visions of the tavern appeared before his eyes, Kathleen dancing, Seamus' elbow flicking back and forth as the tune spilled from his fiddle, his friends, the gaiety . . . now he was free to return. Connor's nostrils flared as he inhaled as much freedom as his lungs could accommodate, the air of freedom surging through his body. Contentment, tranquillity such as this was but a far memory, now rekindled to sit with the easy comfort of an old favourite shirt upon his shoulders.

"*Mmmph mmmph,*" the sound behind, to his left side, broke into Connor's reverie. He turned from the window, his eyes upon the bed before him, tousled ginger hair protruding from the brown blanket that encased the waking occupant. Farrelly's eyes peeked above the upper edge of his woollen shroud. Flashes of blue as he blinked, light from the sun pouring through the window spilled onto his bed. "'Twas a grand night alright," he shifted, taking the weight of his upper body upon his left elbow, his right hand shielding his eyes from the bright light flooding through the window.

"Mr. Gavin's a kind man; fair play to him for that," he continued, responding to questions asked only by his own subconscious. Connor's response was to smile kindly down on his friend, his expression concurring with all that Farrelly had said.

The previous day, Farrelly had also been given his release papers by the warden. The two friends, freed together, had been permitted to celebrate with the other inmates of their hut. Warden Gavin had made available a modest but agreeable amount of rum to enable all to toast the good news. He reasoned that the morale of those left in captivity might benefit though, in part, he felt it proper that his two longest serving prisoners should have the opportunity to say a proper goodbye.

Eighteen voices, well lubricated, had sung with a vigour fit to burst their chests. They danced until their calves and thighs screamed for mercy, their croaked throats pleaded for rest. Then it was time for the singing and dancing to end and for Connor and Farrelly to leave the hut for the last time. With slaps to the back, knuckled fists gently punched to the upper arms, rough embrace, strong, tight handshakes, the occasional tear, "God speed" and "Good luck," the warden closed the door behind them, leading the two free men across the compound to a two-bedded room in his own house where they would spend their last night in his care. It was in this room that Connor had spent much of the night gazing through the window, waiting for the morning sun.

Farrelly beat the pillow with his right hand, holding the corner of it between finger and thumb of his left hand. Having re-established it's plumpness, squashed by the weight of his head through the night, he placed it at the head of his bed above the neatly folded, brown, woollen blanket which covered most of the straw-stuffed mattress. He stepped back to examine his handiwork, to compare its neatness with Connor's bed tidied some hours earlier. Happy with the comparison, he grinned and nodded his head, his left eye winking in the direction of Connor. Connor's right arm swung, the arc taking his hand above the pillow on his bed, his fingers plucking it from the bed as his arm continued on its sweep. Fingers released, the pillow continued unaided 'til its progress was arrested by the grinning face of Farrelly. Farrelly caught the pillow in his arms as it slid from his face, retaliation momentarily an option, speedily dispelled as he tossed the pillow onto Connor's bed, his grin wider still, the sides of his mouth almost in reach of his ears.

"What time were we to meet with Mr. Gavin?" asked Connor, eager to consolidate his free strike with the pillow by a change in topic.

"We're to have breakfast first with his family. I'm sure he said he would talk to us after breakfast. He's arranged some employment to get us started though it'd be up to ourselves as to whether or not we wished to take up the offer. He said he's no wish to push us in a direction that doesn't suit. He'll not be in the least offended if we choose to find our own work." The width of the grin on Farrelly's face had now subsided as he finished his response to Connor's question.

"Do you recall the nature of the work he's to offer to us?" enquired Farrelly.

"I don't think he said what it was to be other than it would be working with the sky above, with fresh air in our faces. I think we'd best be finding the kitchen. They may be waiting on us to appear," replied Connor.

Further discussion of the subject was cut short by a gentle rap on their bedroom door. Connor was across the room in three paces, his right hand enclosing the knob, drawing the door inwards towards him. Mrs Gavin stood before him, bright, blue eyes smiling through the crinkled flesh. Connor returned her smile, gazing down upon the warden's wife.

"Time to eat, boys," she addressed the two men, both of whom had witness to over forty summers.

She spun on the heel of her right boot, then bustled down the corridor past closed doors. The two men followed, the proximity of the kitchen now apparent as a medley of aromas from cooking food drifted in the air from the half open door. As they entered, they were greeted by Mr.Gavin's hearty handshake and bade sit at the two chairs drawn up to the table opposite his own seat. Mrs Gavin placed a pot of porridge on the table betwixt the seated men, the steam rising from it's mottled surface evidence to the freshness of it's preparation. As she took her seat beside her husband, opposite Connor, she dipped the wooden ladle in her right hand into the oats, moving the contents into a wooden bowl held in her left hand. She passed the full bowl to Farrelly and bade him eat lest it should get cold. Repeating the procedure, the second bowl was passed to Connor. Her husband received the third bowl whilst she served her own portion last. A bowl of sugar was offered for each to sweeten the porridge to their own taste, salt too for any that had preference for the sharper tang. Whilst Connor's normal preference would have been the salt as he was partial to the keener flavour, the chance to taste sugar was unique in his experience. He cast the sugar across the surface of the porridge in the manner directed by Mrs Gavin who had noted his confusion.

"Let it melt awhile," interjected her husband.

Within moments, the brown crystals became fluid, covering the surface of the porridge. "Now you can eat," said Mrs Gavin, a note of authority in her voice.

Connor dipped his spoon through the liquid sugar into the porridge, scooping the contents of his spoon to his mouth. The varied flavours burst upon his tongue competing for his attention, for his comprehension. His reaction pleased the attentive cook.

"I've used milk today. Normally, it's water that I prepare the oats with," she said, by explanation. It's a special day for us as well as you two," she continued, happy to build up the intrigue as to what she was to announce. Having gained the attention of the two men and the knowing smile of her husband, she went on, "This is the last such breakfast David and I will be giving," she paused, intent on watching the reaction to her words.

Connor thought he had never heard Warden Gavin called by his given name before; he had not known, never even considered what it might be.

"There are no more men due to be released before we finish this Christmas," she concluded.

"Our children have all grown up to make their own way. The boys have gone inland to raise sheep and Anne's to be married in the spring," said the warden by way of explanation. "We've been here more than twenty years now," he concluded.

"More porridge anyone? You must clear the pot," declared Mrs Gavin. Farrelly and Connor dutifully proffered their empty bowls.

"Where will you go to when you retire?" enquired Farrelly as he waited for the sugar to melt on his second bowl of porridge.

"We . . . " Mr. and Mrs Gavin spoke together. With a nod of his head in the direction of his wife beside him, the warden deferred. "We have built a home along the water's edge at Sydney cove. It's been six years in the building and is all but finished now. It's a fine home, built to David's plan," she turned to smile at her husband, her pride evident in the roundness of her eyes which accompanied her smile. "There will be plenty of room for guests, six large bedrooms, enough for all the family, grandchildren too if we're so blessed," again the eye contact with her husband expressed an empathy of wishes. "There's a large verandah with views over the wooded hills on the other side of the cove. All the ships at anchor are in view. We can see them sail into the cove, see them set sail when they leave too."

Mrs Gavin interrupted her discourse on her new home to attend to her guests. The porridge had been eaten, bowls and pot all empty. She cleared the table of the porridge pot.

"Keep your bowls and spoons; you'll need those for the mutton stew," she confided, proud of the scope of the meal she was able to offer them.

Fresh baked bread was placed on the table, butter too. "Tuck in boys," beamed the warden's wife for she knew the feast that she set before them was way beyond their experience of the past eighteen years.

Connor tore a chunk from the loaf of bread, spreading the butter with the flat underside of his spoon. His teeth sank through the golden butter, through the soft white dough, a shake of his head separating the bread in his mouth from the chunk in his right hand, exquisite memories rekindling with the taste upon his tongue. Home, his cottage, Kathleen, Liam, appeared within his tightly shut eyes.

"I can see that you approve of the bread," remarked Mrs Gavin, mistaking the closed eyes as delight in her produce, unaware of the memories it stirred. "We shall be able to grow our own maize, sugar cane, vegetables too, beside our new home. We have some twenty or so acres of good soil about us on our plot."

Her guests now serviced for a while, the warden's wife returned to her discourse on their retirement home. "We've planted out the flower garden close by the verandah. The yellow flowers, clustered in the manner of grapes about the shrubs, are a sight to behold. There are flowers of blue, red, orange, golden, purple and shades and shapes I never did see before I came to this land. The scents in the evening air...," her muse discontinued as she attended once more to her guests.

Rising from her chair, Mrs Gavin wrapped cloths around the handle of the stew pot sitting on the stove and carried it to the table, presenting the aromatic contents to the three men. Connor sensed the pride she had in her creation. He feared his appetite would let him down and disappoint the cook. His belly was already so tight, he felt the skin might split. With a smile, he proffered his bowl at the asking, accepting a ladle of stew. All four bowls brimming, Mrs

Gavin signalled a start to the final course of their grand farewell breakfast. Her expectant eyes surveyed her two guests from above the spoonful of stew she sipped. Farrelly gulped his spoonful and returned for another, his appetite unsated, tongue flicking out, licking the dribbles from his lips to the delight of the cook. Connor made an effort to match his friend's enthusiasm on the first spoonful but, thereafter, ate at about a third the pace of his comrade.

"Do you have news of the employment you remarked upon last evening?" enquired Connor of the warden. Farrelly slowed his spoon to attend to the answer.

"There's a sawmill looking for labour. The owner was an inmate here some years back. I've spoken to him concerning both of you and he's more than willing to pay for a good day's work," Gavin paused to allow his listeners the chance to absorb his words.

"Of course, you're under no obligation to me to take the work. You must follow your minds' will now that you're free men," he added.

"How far is the sawmill from the wharf?" asked Connor.

"Less than two miles by the track, I'd say," responded Gavin.

"That'd suit me fine as I wish to stay close to the ocean to find a boat home," said Connor.

"How would that serve you?" he enquired, turning his head to the left to face Farrelly.

"I've no problem with that. Chopping trees is fine by me," spluttered Farrelly through another spoonful of stew.

"That's settled then. I'll give you directions and a letter of introduction after breakfast," beamed the warden, content that he could offer this last useful service.

"More stew boys?" asked Mrs Gavin upon seeing Farrelly's bowl empty.

"Yes please," he replied, holding his bowl forth.

"More stew for you Connor?" enquired Mrs Gavin.

"No, thank you ma'am. I'm still to finish what I have. Never in my whole life have I eaten so well. All credit to you ma'am; it's been a grand meal." The compliments from Connor were well received and truly meant, deflecting any slight disappointment Mrs Gavin may have felt at the lack of need to refill his bowl.

Farrelly, finally defeated by the food still before him, raised his hands, palms facing Mrs Gavin in amicable submission.

"I can eat no more, not today, probably not for another week," said Farrelly as he dropped his hands, clapping them about his bulging stomach. "If I'd died and gone to heaven, I couldn't have expected a finer feast."

As he finished the compliment, he rose from the table and walked around to the seated Mrs Gavin. Stooping, he grasped her by the shoulders and placed his lips against her cheek. Unused to such emotion directed at her, Mrs Gavin rose from her chair to busy herself with clearing the table. Her husband chuckled to see her in such confusion, her cheeks flushed in the manner he could remember from thirty years before, on the day that they wed.

Mr. Gavin rose from the table, mirth still shaking his body, "I'll go fetch the letter of introduction for you. I have it written in my study," explained the warden.

As he crossed the kitchen, his left hand squeezed his wife's side as he passed her, bending to bestow a kiss to the crown of her greying head. Connor, realising it was time to say goodbye, pushed back his chair. As he approached the busy, bustling Mrs Gavin, she stopped her chores. This good man she had nursed, taken from the arms of the black angel. He had tended her garden and played with her children. Now he must leave. She would miss his presence. She knew he must return to his own family but...but her mouth felt dry. Through the ache in her jawbones, she could feel the tears gathering at the bottom of her eye sockets, threatening to overflow and run down her cheeks. She must be quick whilst some composure still remained. Connor wrapped his arms about the warden's wife and placed his lips upon her wrinkled brow, "Thank you for all you've done for me. A part of my heart will always bear your image. I'll come to say goodbye before I leave for home." He gently squeezed her soft body, the action, the words enough to release the tears which flowed along the creases of her face.

Mr. Gavin returned, letter in hand which he passed to

Farrelly. He was not surprised to see his wife's tears for he too would feel the loss of Connor's presence. Right hand grasped right hand, fingers out straight, the V's between thumb and index finger met, fingers curled, exerted pressure, first with Farrelly, then with Connor. Handshakes complete, the warden opened the door. The dusty track before them, the two free friends stepped forth, the start of their journey.

As they walked from the warden's door, neither man spoke. Their eyes cast at the path in front of them, at their bare feet stirring the dust with each footfall. Minutes passed and the distance from the Gavins' lengthened. Connor's thoughts turned from the people he would miss at the prison, to the people he would see, hold once more, Kathleen, Liam, to the working of his land at Corryann, to the tavern, his friends, singing and dancing. Such thoughts raised his spirits, raised his eyes from the ground. As he walked, his fingers from his right hand kneaded the leather necklace he had worn night and day since the morn he was wed to Kathleen. A lock of his wife's hair was sewn into the tube of leather, fashioned by Yomi, her gift to him on his wedding day. His fingers could still discern the symbols carved into the leather to ward off evil from the wearer. Connor's feet carried him over the track. Huge trees overhung their path, grey-green bark with blotches of fawn, smooth to the touch, their height perhaps twice that of a ship's main mast. Plants of gigantic proportions covered the ground where the trees supported leaves the length of a grown man. Four men standing on each other's shoulders might touch the crimson flowers atop the stem. Blossoms had fallen to the ground large enough to cover the whole of a man's hand.

Sweat tickled the centre of Connor's back as it slid down beside his backbone, gently tugging at small hairs as it passed. Though early in the morning, the sun's rays scorched their shoulders as they walked westward toward the sawmill. Each man carried a change of clothes wrapped in a shirt and a pair of boots, laces tied together, were slung either side of their left shoulders, heels bumping into ribs with every stride. Connor determined to sell his boots, the money useful to help pay his way home. He had never owned a pair of boots before, apart from those borrowed for his wedding day, never had the need to wear them. In his pocket, his fingers could tumble five coins, the five shillings all prisoners were given on their release to aid them on their way.

A bend in the path lay ahead of them; the ground thus far had been rising enough that their legs were aware of the incline. At the point of the bend, Connor's leading foot planted firmly in the dust, his left foot trailed up alongside, hands rose to rest upon his hips, air whistled as it was sucked fast through his open mouth, across his teeth. Beside him, Farrelly was likewise stunned, the point of the bend marking the summit of a hill they had been climbing. Before them lay a vista fit to take their breath away. Port Jackson harbour was set amongst the wooded hills. Fingers of water insinuated into the rocky cove, bare cliffs plunging to the water line, seagulls flecking the blue sky with their gliding white forms, a ship, sails set full, exiting to the ocean, sun's rays radiating from the surface, a giant shimmering sapphire dropped from the skies. Having feasted on the scenery, his senses near overwhelmed, Connor's eyes picked out the settlement at the quayside at which he had arrived so many years before. Even from this distant view, it appeared to him very much larger than he could recall.

"Heaven, if that's not heaven, I've no wish to go there," sighed Farrelly. "I've never thought any land could hold my attention for more than a year or two, but now, but now I've walked the path to Damascus, now I see," concluded the awe-struck Farrelly.

"I'd not give up Corryann, even for all this," Connor responded with a broad sweep of his left arm, a shake of his head to emphasise his rejection.

# Chapter 26

CONNOR was keen to make contact with the owner of the sawmill in case he changed his mind on their employment. His eagerness to arrive was reinforced by the heat from the sun now burrowing into their heads. They had no water but were in need of a drink. Their path took them to the right of the settlement, towards the river, above the town. At the water's edge they drank freely, scooping water to cool their faces and the backs of their necks. From the riverside, Connor noticed the logs stockaded in the river perhaps a quarter of a mile further upstream. Having sated their thirst, the two friends continued up the track towards the lumber mill. Connor felt a slight tightening of his stomach as they approached the entrance to the mill.

"What's yer business?" The black-haired, black-bearded, giant of a man demanded as they entered the lumberyard. He walked out of the sawmill to meet the two friends stood before him. Connor and Farrelly, similar in height, were at least a head shorter than their questioner.

"We're looking for work. We've a letter of introduction from Mr. Gavin." Connor almost spewed the words, so eager was he not to raise the big man's ire. He became irritated with himself for the speed of his delivery and the lack of confidence it signalled. A huge paw grabbed the letter from Connor's outstretched hand. It took a moment for Connor to realise that a smile was spreading on the face beneath the thick, black beard.

"Pleased to meet yer," the big man had transferred the letter to his left hand. His right now gripped Connor's right hand, then Farrelly's. "I dunno why that Mr. Gavin writes me when he knows I don't read. He's spoken to me of yer an' I said I'd give yer work. If yer works well, I'll keep yer on." Connor relaxed, warming to the giant as he finished his offer to employ them. "You'd best come with me. I'll show yer where you sleep," the giant signalled to the pair to follow him as he walked inside the sawmill. The huge structure was full of the dead torsos of trees, crowns, roots chopped off, branches stripped with only the trunks remaining. There were white woods, dark brown woods and most of the shades between. In the corner of the great shed, wooden steps led up to a platform. The giant gestured for them to climb. "There's two beds over to yer left unoccupied. Best take them. There's four workers out cutting lumber what fills the rest." Connor and Farrelly climbed the ladder to the platform. "When yu's dumped your stuff, come on back down an' I'll set yus some work fore lunch," said the big man, anxious not to have idle time. Yu'sll have t' put yer boots on. There's plenty a bad snake living in the forest; yu's wouldn't want to be treading on one without a boot on yer foot". His words aimed at the empty ladder but with enough force to be heard by the two friends above.

"No chance to sell the boots now," thought Connor as the mention of snakes determined his next action. Shod in their boots, the friends descended the ladder to be met by the big man who put them to work.

Connor did not dislike his time spent at the lumberyard. He knew each day's earnings brought him closer to a berth home. He found the physical aspect of the tasks set, for the most part, less demanding than moving rocks. Amongst the shade of the trees, the sun was less of a tormentor. His nose enjoyed the experiences, perfume of different resins, aromas of varied burnt trimmings from the trees, the scent of leaves when pressed between the fingers and crushed beneath the heel, the smell of fresh, sawn wood. He lay in his bed at night, listening to the chatter of the other men, an agreeable group, talking through their dreams and the manner in which they would be achieved. Food was plentiful, good, wholesome fare to yield the energy needed for the day's work. Connor gained satisfaction at his skill in moving across the floating logs, in his use of the flow of the river to carry each trunk to the position he needed it to be in, directing all with his long pole 'til he had constructed a huge raft of logs to be steered downstream when next a ship arrived to transport them. Despite the warning from the big man, he had not yet encountered any snakes. He hoped this situation would prevail and, for safety's sake, continued to wear his boots although they rubbed the skin from his feet. In fact, as he reflected on all matters, it was the wearing of the boots which was by far the most disagreeable feature of his time at the lumber camp.

Some four weeks or so after Connor had started his employment at the sawmill, news came from town of a ship sighted half a day's sailing from Port Jackson. These tidings prompted an excited agitation in the big man as he prepared himself to go to town to meet the incoming ship, hopeful that it might be the means of transportation of his eucalyptus mahogany for sale in Europe. Connor's heart stirred too. Would the ship be returning close to his home, he wondered? Even if it was, he hadn't enough funds to pay his way. This realisation dampened the pace of his heartbeat.

On his return the next day, the big man made preparations to float the raft of mahogany trunks to the quayside. Connor was to ride on the logs with the black-bearded giant whilst the rest of the men were to make themselves handy at the quayside on the pulley and chains that would lift the trunks from the water and place them in the hold of the ship.

Connor woke early on the morning of his river journey. Breakfast raced down his throat. His stomach, unappreciative of the rush, rebelled and sent it back. He couldn't remember the last time he had vomited. Perhaps the mixture of excitement at the trip and nervousness lest he failed the big man with the use of his pole were the cause or maybe it was the promise of twenty shillings bonus to him if all went well. That would double his funds to bring him four weeks closer to seeing Kathleen. These thoughts in his mind, he waited on the riverbank for the big man to arrive to give him his instructions. On the far bank, the branches of some of the trees dipped to trail their leaves in the water causing a swirling motion on the surface of the slow-moving flow. At about one o'clock, from where he stood, Connor watched the small stream join the main river. A duckbilled platypus played in the gentle current. Kangaroos stood at the water's edge, dipping their heads to the water. Connor feared for their balance; they seemed close to tipping over their short front legs as their heads met the surface. Cockatoo's, black with crimson tails, green lories, patchwork parrots-green, red, yellow and blue, all perched in the trees opposite, taking flight from time to time, brilliant flashes of colour as they sought a different branch. Connor's study of the wildlife was interrupted by the arrival of his black-bearded employer.

Tranquillity marked their progress down-river, the gentle gurgle at the back of the raft, the progress of the current slowing as it shouldered the burden of pushing the massive trunks. '*Caw, tweet, tweet, tweet, caw.*' A shrill melody of sounds came from the birds either side as the raft drifted through a ravine that amplified their music. Rhythm came from occasional plops as a fish turned, flicking the water with it's tail as it consumed the insect foolish enough to alight on the surface. With an easy, languid movement of feet across logs, pole pushing off the bank, swirling in the water as a paddle, the two men worked. Despite the untroubled progress of the raft, Black-beard maintained his concentration at the leading edge of the logs, speaking only infrequently and then only with single words of instruction to Connor at the rear.

Left. Right. Push. Paddle. Enough."

At the mouth of the river, Black-beard, on the front left-hand corner, stretched his pole forward in great arcs, sweeping through the water right to left around the corner he stood upon. Connor, at the opposite, near corner, pushed his pole through the water, twisting his body to sweep from left to right. The great raft turned slowly to the right, nudging into the stockade at the top end of the quay. Applause broke out from the lumber men standing on the dock.

"Nice work. Well done," shouted Farrelly to Connor.

Tension ebbed from Connor's back. He grinned in reply to his friend's compliment. Black-beard crossed the angled logs towards him, his smile so large that not even the bush on his face could conceal it. The hug he bestowed on Connor as he lifted him off his feet, squeezed all the air from Connor's lungs – he could sense his ribs bending.

"Good man, time fer some ale. Our work's done. The

134

others will load the ship," said the big man, replacing Connor's feet on the logs, releasing his arms from the crushed ribs whilst nodding in the direction of Farrelly and his other men standing on the quayside.

As they walked up the hill away from the shore, Connor noticed a number of fine white buildings on the far side of the river. One stood away from the rest with a sizeable verandah on the three sides of the property that faced the ocean. If this was the Gavins' retirement home, for sure, it balanced with Mrs Gavin's description of it, "Well, good luck to them," thought Connor. They deserved all the good fortune available to them.

Black-beard stooped to enter the tavern some hundred yards or so above the quay.

"Two tankards of ale for men as 'ave earned them," roared the big man, once inside.

The mugs were at their table almost before they could seat themselves. Froth from the ale was trapped in the black curly hair that surrounded his mouth as the base of the tankard smacked the surface of the table.

"Two more!" bellowed the giant. Fresh tankards before them, the worst of the thirst satisfied, the big man asked, "What's yer story then? How d'yer come to be here?"

After two more refills, Connor reached the end of his history.

"Aye, I've 'eard similar tales afore, mebbe with less misfortune than yerself," declared Black-beard with a note of conciliation in his voice. "But there's no sense to dwell on the badness. Best be getting on with yer future. That's how I've settled myself quite nicely," his great right paw clapped on Connor's left shoulder, the vibrations shaking his teeth. "I've a hunger now. Landlord, some food!" roared the big man.

Having eaten his fill and waited whilst the giant sated his prodigious appetite, Connor rose from the table, a lightness in his head. Black-beard was ready to check on the progress of the loading of his cargo. As they exited the tavern, the big man mistimed his stoop, cracking his brow against the door lintel and landing inside on the seat of his pants. Picking himself up, he wiped the smear of blood from his forehead with the back of his right hand, shook his shaggy head, bent earlier and lower as he re-exited, great chuckles shaking the ribs in his chest.

The two men walked down the hill to the quayside, Connor mightily impressed by Black-beard's jovial reaction to the crack on his head. Men, women, children were all busy hurrying east, south, north, west, carrying, pushing, rolling barrels, horsedrawn carts, handpulled carts, people shouting, each louder to be heard over the maelstrom of activity that enveloped the quayside in front of the ship. Cargo was being stowed, barrels of whale wax, barrels of whale oil, bales of wool, more bales of wool, a mountain of them to be loaded. The mahogany tree trunks, swinging in the air over the heads of those below, secure in their chains, were released within the hold of the ship. Provisions to be stowed, sufficient to feed eighty men for two months, livestock, fowl to be slaughtered on the high seas, fresh water, all pushed for their place in the loading queue.

Black-beard strode over to his foreman who noticed the drying blood on his brow but thought it best not to enquire.

"How much longer?" asked the big man.

"Half an hour should see us finished now," replied the foreman.

"Good. Good. I'll stands yus all a drink when yer done," responded the amiable employer. "I've just to have a word with the capt'n and clear some paperwork but I'll be back here within the hour." The giant strode off up the plank leading onto the ship, no need to wait his turn, the throng in front of him parting as the sea before the prow of a boat.

Connor removed himself from the émelee and propped his back against the wall of a wharf-side rope merchant. The twenty shillings bonus awarded him by his employer created a comfortable weight laid against his thigh in his pocket. As he gazed at the scene before him, he wondered where the ship might be bound for, whether the captain might have need of additional crew. For sure, he was well short of the funds to pay for a berth but might he be able to earn one? His body tingled with the excitement of the thought that his means of return to Kathleen lay before him, likely ready to leave within a few days. Caution threw ice chilled water in his face. He had no good reason to believe the ship would be heading for his homeland. He had no evidence to think that the captain might be in need of more crew and even if he had the need of an extra pair of hands or two, wasn't it probable he'd want to employ experienced seamen? Whilst caution diffused his earlier optimism, Connor refused to let it extinguish the flame entirely.

Farrelly picked out Connor leaning on the rope merchant's wall and walked over, the loading of the mahogany completed.

"Why so glum?" he enquired as his friend's face failed to mirror his own cheerful demeanour.

"I was just thinking of home, of Kathleen. Do you have any knowledge as to where the ship is bound for?" The anxiety in Connor's voice was difficult to disguise.

"I heard she's bound for Bristol," replied Farrelly.

"That would not be too far from my home...," mused Connor as one of caution's hurdles had been past. "Do you happen to know if they are in need of extra crew?" he asked, eager to remove another barrier.

"No, I've not heard it mentioned," answered Farrelly. "Are you coming to have a drink with us? You can tell me all about the raft ride down the river. You looked a real expert the way you turned it into the pen here."

"I might find room for just one more tankard of ale though I've not much of the taste for the hard liquor," replied Connor, his mind still working on how he might find the answer to the question of a place in the returning crew.

"There's the big man now, over there with the rest of the men. We're to join them. He's to stand the first round. Come on now Connor, it's an age since I had me fill of ale."

Farrelly's words trailed after him as he began to walk towards the black-bearded giant, a flagpole amongst the crowd. Connor followed, his thoughts focused on finding the means of becoming a crewmember on the ship, the idea of ale seeming of less import.

Black-beard was conversing with a much shorter, sandy-haired man wearing the tunic and braid of a sea captain as Farrelly and Connor arrived. The captain was flexing the fingers of his right hand to restore the circulation stopped by Black-beard's farewell handshake.

Connor seized his moment, "Captain, do you have a requirement for new hands on the return journey?"

Black-beard stared intently at the captain. He too had an interest in the reply. He knew of Connor's desire to return home but he liked the man and appreciated the skill he had for the logs; he'd be sorry to lose him so soon.

"Aye, I've a need of eight men who've experience of the sea," replied the captain, "Do you have any such expertise?" enquired the ship's master.

"I spent a month as a deckhand with a Captain Coyle though, in truth, it was a long while ago. I do learn quickly though. Warden Gavin will vouch for that. My current employer," Connor nodded towards Black-beard, " may have some good words to say on my behalf."

"Aye, Connor's a good man," Black-beard interjected, having determined to help Connor in his cause despite the possible loss of a man he valued. "He has a good pair of sea legs, balanced the logs as soon as he first stepped on one. He helped me to steer the raft downstream today, a rare skill," the big man completed his eulogy.

"You say you worked under Captain Coyle and your name's Connor? Would you be Connor Macken?" asked the sea captain. Connor was baffled. Confusion covered his face, furrowed his brow and knitted his eyebrows together, the corners of his mouth drawn down. He had no fame, nor notoriety that he was aware of. How had the Captain come by his name?

"Yes, yes, my name's Connor Macken," came his delayed response. The captain's right hand left his side, the speed of it catching Connor unaware. He grasped Connor's right hand and shook it firmly.

"I'm Captain Liam Davy," said the ship's master, still grasping Connor's hand, still shaking it. "When you sailed with Captain Coyle, I was Billy, little Billy, the cabin boy. I tended the needs of Captain Coyle, know the regard he held you in, the pain it caused him when Reilly had you taken off to prison but if he hadn't let you go, it might have gone badly for the other eighteen men. I'm so glad that you've survived, so very pleased to make your acquaintance again."

A broad smile lit up the captain's face as he continued to shake the hand of the perplexed Connor. Black-beard, sharing Connor's confusion, resolved that all should go to the tavern for a drink to celebrate. Whatever it was they would celebrate, the need of it was clear (the reason less so, apart of course, from the successful embarkation of the valuable mahogany lumber). Nine thirsty souls trooped up the hill towards the inn followed by one joyful questioner, the bemused Connor. Black-beard's command of the inn-keeper still held sway when six full tankards soon arrived on the table, carried three in each hand by the hostelry's host. He hastily scurried back, shortly returning with a further four and then took the further precaution of filling two large flagons of ale in anticipation of the big man's next command.

"Captain Davy, I do recall Billy, a cabin boy on my last voyage though I have some difficulty in matching him with you," the words spilled from Connor's mouth. His anxiety affecting their composition, he pressed on. "As you were on the ship the last time I sailed, you may have your own opinion of my experience – for my part, I pray that it is favourable. I would be forever indebted to yourself if you allow me to sail with you when you leave," he finished with a plea.

"Connor, there isn't another man in the world I would rather take," responded the captain.

Connor's mind took some moments to decipher the portent of the response. Slaps on the back from those seated close to him and raised tankards of those opposite confirmed his interpretation, agreed that he was not mistaken. He had a place on the boat which was to sail in a few days. He was on his way back to Kathleen. A whoop of joy exploded from his mouth, fire flew from his eyes, infecting those about him in his utter exultation. Sounds of a pipe caught the moment as one of the lumbermen struck up an air. Connor, boots off, leapt on the table, his feet flashing in dance to the tune. Ten hands rescued the tankards in unison as his feet flicked over the wooden surface. At the end of the dance, on a signal from Black-beard, the innkeeper carried two flagons of ale to the table.

Ale flowed down their throats and they sang. William Davy related the tales of Connor's deeds at sea, his rescue of the boy from the bully Reilly, his heroism in cleaning ice from the bucking yard arm, his near death in doing it. Deep in his heart, Connor was pleased of the praise from the captain but, on the surface of his face, he could feel the blood rise. He was happy enough when the acclaim stopped. As more ale flowed, he infected others around with the delight of his return home and, in his merriment during the course of the afternoon, persuaded the captain to take Farrelly on as a crewmember. Black-beard, although disadvantaged by the loss of two good workers, accepted the new position with fair grace. Captain Davy rose from the table and shook the hands of Black-beard, Farrelly and Connor, nodding his farewell to the rest of the men.

"I'll see you two on the ship tomorrow, at noon," were his parting words to the two friends.

Connor returned to the sawmill with his employer. Farrelly and the others who had loaded the lumber onto the ship remained in town to make better use of the bonuses they had been paid.

A lump of light brown soil slid into the water, the ripples from its entry rolling lazily away from the bank. The river flowed by, licking at the newly exposed soil that contained its passage, determining it's route to the bay. Connor sat watching the ripples, his elbows resting on his thighs, his face cupped in his hands. The course of the water was somehow new, different. Then he realised the log raft was gone making the river appear wider than before. The bank beside him, protected for so long from the flow by the mahogany trunks, now crumbled into the water. His joy at his new employment aboard the ship that would take him closer to home was now settled, absorbed within his body. This allowed new feelings, feelings of sadness about the land, the people he was to leave behind. It was unlikely he would see any of what he left again. He sat, consuming all that he could of the scene before him, the river, the forest. Each exuded distinctive odours; he inhaled deeply to lock them in his memory. He captured flashes of colour in his mind as the brightly plumed birds winged by, form and hue stored for future recollection.

"Connor," his reverie disturbed, Connor turned towards the voice, rising to his feet.

"Connor," repeated Black-beard, "No doubt you'll be off early in the morn, so best I say me goodbyes now." The big man coughed to clear his throat and raised his chin, his eyes now locked on Connor's. "Yu've had yer misfortunes; there's many a man has but, when life knocks yer down, you get up again, fer if yer stay down, yu're down for good."

The big man offered his right hand which Connor grasped. "I'm grateful for the work you gave to me, for the good opinion you expressed to the captain on my behalf, thank you. I'll always be indebted to you." Connor finished with a final shake of the black-bearded giant's hand which he now grasped in both his own hands.

As they disengaged, Black-beard clapped his left hand between Connor's shoulder blades, nodded, turned and walked into the sawmill. Connor followed, climbed the steps to his dormitory and arranged his few belongings for tomorrow's departure. As he lay contemplating his journey home, Farrelly's head appeared from the top of the steps, consternation on his face. He walked over to Connor's bed, sat on the left corner and addressed his prostrate friend.

"Connor, most people smile when I tell them my plans for the future. They see me as a dreamer, aiming too high for a person of my standing. They're right. I am a dreamer but I do believe I can make my dreams happen. One day, I will live in a mansion with servants at my beck and call and horses in my stable, the equal of any others. Connor, this land is new. Anyone with the will and the wit can make a success of it. Black-beard's a fine example. I know you have strong reasons for returning home. I would too if I had a Kathleen and a Liam waiting for me but I have no such pull on my emotions. Sure, I miss the land of my birth, the land of my childhood but my dream, my dream rests here, here in this land of endless possibilities... What I am saying Connor, in my own long-winded way, is that I can't come with you tomorrow. I see my fortune in this land. There now, I've told you. I'll miss your company but it's plain we're to go our separate ways now."

Connor sat up, hugged his friend, arms about him. "We've both to follow our destiny," responded Connor.

Farrelly returned the embrace. "Connor, when I've made my fortune, I'll come visit you. I'll have my own ship by then, perhaps a fleet of five or ten even."

"If any man can do it, you'll be the one," confirmed Connor, nodding his head to reinforce his words.

"I'll work at the sawmill for a while, then, when I have saved enough, I'll be off inland, staking a claim for gold, diamonds too if what I've heard whispered is true." The certainty of success carried in Farrelly's voice might have enticed Connor to follow him in his fortune-hunting but Connor was certain that his real wealth lay at home in the company of Kathleen and Liam.

"I'll say goodbye now, wish you all the luck in this world and any available from the next for I am away early in the morn." Connor squeezed the shoulders of his friend between thumb and fingers as he bade him farewell.

"Best of luck to yourself and give Kathleen a kiss from me. It's perhaps better I'm not tempted to deliver it myself," quipped Farrelly.

# Chapter 27

CONNOR woke as the sun rose. All about him still slept. He picked up his bundle and quietly left the sawmill, passing along the river, down the track he'd taken a month before. He climbed the hill. Through the towering trees he walked, retracing his steps to the prison compound. Arriving to see no activity, he sat on a rock close by the track, staring at the hut in which he had lived for over seventeen years. Blackbeard's words, echoing in his mind from the previous day, served to rescue him from his melancholy. He turned his thoughts to the voyage home, to his arrival at his cottage, to his wife and son, to the land at Corryann. As the sun rose towards ten o'clock in the sky, he saw Mrs Gavin hanging her washing out to dry. Connor walked over to her, causing her to start.

"Sorry to startle you," apologised Connor. "I'm to set sail for Bristol tomorrow. I didn't want to go without saying goodbye to you and Mr. Gavin," he explained.

"Good to see you, good to see you," repeated Mrs Gavin, wiping the palms of her hands on her apron. "Do come in. Have a cup of tea. Would you like some breakfast? There's still some left. I cooked extra because Anne stayed overnight." The torrent of offers flowed from Mrs Gavin's mouth.

"Thank you ma'am, I'd appreciate a cup of tea and now that you mention breakfast, the fact is, I've forgotten to eat this morning," replied Connor.

He followed Mrs Gavin into the house, into the kitchen.

"Sit yourself down. I'll fetch a bowl. Porridge alright for you?" enquired Mrs Gavin.

"Yes, thank you, porridge would be just grand," responded Connor. As he spooned the porridge to his mouth, Mr. Gavin walked in.

"Bless my soul!" he exclaimed.

"Connor's off to Bristol on the ship that leaves tomorrow," explained Mrs Gavin, before the now standing Connor could greet the warden. "He's come to say goodbye. Wasn't that a kind thought?" she concluded.

"Sit yourself down and finish your porridge man," instructed Mr. Gavin. "It's a pleasure to see you – you've added a few pounds since you left us," he added cheerily.

Porridge finished, Connor rose, "I'd like to thank you both for all that you've done for me, the friends you've been to me." His thanks delivered, he shook Mr. Gavin's hand and embraced Mrs Gavin. "I'd best be off. It wouldn't do to keep the captain waiting."

The door to the kitchen opened. The Gavins' daughter, Anne, entered.

"Connor's to set sail tomorrow," again Mrs Gavin was the first to impart the news.

"I wish you all the best. We shall all miss you," said the young lady standing on tiptoes, hands holding Connor's shoulders for balance as she kissed his left cheek. Connor felt the poignancy of the moment as his eyes swelled.

"I'll miss you all too," he replied.

Standing by the open front door of their house, the Gavins waved as Connor walked away down the track until he reached the bend in the path which took him from view. A final turn, a final wave from Connor and he disappeared. His goodbyes completed, Connor strode up the path 'til he reached the crown of the hill where the whole bay was set out before him. He could see his ship alongside the quay. He turned onto the path that would take him down to her.

# Chapter 28

LEFT foot following right upon the steeply inclined planking, Connor stepped down into the waist of the ship. The tautness he felt in the muscles of his midriff was the physical consequence of the dread in his head lest Captain Davy might, on reflection, withdraw his offer of employment, perhaps having found more experienced hands. His disquiet was soon quelled. Captain Davy strode along the deck toward him, all the enthusiasm of the previous day still evident. The outstretched right hand, the wide grin upon his face, the slap to Connor's shoulder with his left mitt as the right clasped and shook Connor's right hand with great vigour, assuaged all his doubts.

"Good to have you aboard. Welcome. Where is your friend, Farrelly?"

"He's decided to stay and seek his fortune in this land," replied Connor, "but he's grateful to you for the offer and wishes you well for the future," concluded the new crew member.

"I had a feeling that might happen. Don't worry about it. Well, let's get you settled in. I'll pass you over to the first mate. He'll refresh your memory on the ropes and show you your berth," the captain explained.

The first mate, though slightly older than his captain perhaps by five years, seemed, on first encounter, to possess a jovial nature similar to his superior officer. He led Connor to the crew's quarters so that he might stow his small parcel of personal belongings. This task accomplished, they climbed the companionway to the deck above. Connor listened with deep attentiveness to his instructions on the ropes, the meaning of each order. Though eighteen years had passed since he had last stood on the deck of a ship, the mate's words and phrases rekindled memories of the actions required. By the time lunch was called, Connor felt confident that he could respond to orders.

In the afternoon, Connor bent his back with the other crew-members, finishing the loading of provisions as the boat was to set sail early the next morning. Amongst the last items to be stowed were three live sheep and two dozen chickens together with hay and corn to feed them. Fresh fruit, oranges, lemons and melons were stowed on deck in crates.

Darkness cosseted Connor, stretched in his hammock, inhaling the goulash of aromas that seeped through the ship's timbers, mahogany, whale wax, livestock, lemons, oranges, the smell of the sea, 'til the gentle roll of the boat lulled him to sleep. His slumber was curtailed by the activity about him as his shipmates stumbled in the dark, one cursing as he cracked his head on the low beams. Another banged into Connor's sleeping form causing his hammock to sway in a manner that startled the somnolent ex-prisoner. Connor tumbled from his moving hammock keeping his head bowed to avoid the low underside of the deck above him. He climbed the steps that brought him on deck into the dazzling sunshine, shielding his eyes by a combination of squinting and creating a peak with his left hand; fingers horizontal to his brow, index finger pressed against it and thumb tucked below, his hand rested across the bridge of his nose. Having acclimatised to the change in light, he made his way across the deck to the galley where breakfast was being served.

At the conclusion of the morning meal, the ship was readied for it's departure. A small group of well-wishers were gathered on the quayside to wave goodbye. Connor scanned their faces with as quick a glance as would not distract him from his duties. He recognised no person familiar to himself. As the great ropes cast off from the quayside rings, the ebbing tide drew the ship away from the shore. The bow canvasses flapped in the breeze. More sails were unfurled and the prow of the vessel cleaved the blue waters as the breeze was captured by the mainsail. The wind pushed the ship forward in its effort to escape the canvass embrace. Connor's spirits soared as the ship pointed out toward the ocean, toward his homeland. His journey back to Kathleen and Liam had begun. Black and grey fish raced the prow of the ship as it sliced through the ocean, white foam splaying the bow above the water line. As the fish leapt from the sea, keeping perfect pace with the progress of the boat, they formed graceful, quarter-moon arcs. Connor gazed at their antics, his duties complete for the day. The easy rhythm of their dance entranced him, resting his body, emptying his mind. After a while, he noticed the sun dropping into his view on the horizon, the orange glow signalling the impending nightfall. He could see the fish no longer for, lost in silent contemplation, he was uncertain when they had ceased their escort of the ship; he had missed their going. Connor left the rail in the bows and wandered back along the deck towards the waist of the ship. Above his head, the boastful mainsail puffed out it's chest whilst the lesser sails tried to match the glory of the great one. Masts and spars groaned with the labour of holding them in check; ropes and lines squeaked with the strain put upon their sinews.

Connor sat amongst his crewmates, gathered in the waist between stern and bow under the great mainsail, unaware of the struggles above. Story telling was an art with which not all the men were blessed for, as some spoke, the interest of the assembled would drift and many other simultaneous conversations would begin whilst others would so capture the attention that none other than the narrator could be heard. Each spoke of their own history, of great events they'd missed themselves but heard other men tell of. Most of all, they related their dreams, their intentions for the future. Connor felt empathy for much of the latter kind of conversation. A constant theme was to find a piece of land to call their own, build a home, find a wife as fair as any other, work the land, raise a family. For him, this was no dream. He had his land of Corryann. His wife, Kathleen, could stand comparison with all in the district. His land was fertile and he had a son, Liam. His good fortune he did not boast about but encouraged those that thought the same to reach out for their dreams. In his experience, all was possible for any man with the right determination. As night fell, the men returned below decks to unfurl their hammocks and climb into their cocoons for the night, emerging the next morning rested, in readiness for another day's labour.

The daily routine was not especially taxing to Connor as it was easier on his muscles than either the regime at the prison or the lumberyard. Having discovered his talent for carpentry, the first mate had assigned Connor to assist the ship's carpenter because this fellow also doubled as the doctor and was thus in need of as much help as could be made available.

Days passed, becoming weeks. Weeks passed and the warmth of the African coast rolled out across the seas that bordered it, enveloping Captain Davy's ship 'til all aboard, save the officers, abandoned their shirts. The heat could not be avoided as the only shade was below deck and there the air was hot and stale, the whale wax smell by now suffocating all other aromas. Fresh fruit and livestock had all been consumed. The diet was now just biscuits and salted meat. All the crew slept on deck, the gentle progress of the boat creating it's own cooling breeze. It caressed the skin of the half-dressed sailors as they slumbered beneath the gaze of a myriad of stars which pricked the dark night sky with points of light. Captain Davy announced to his men the news that they were but a few weeks' sailing distance from Bristol. By his own estimations, they should be clear of the coast of Africa within a day, two at most.

An air of celebration infected the ship's company. Men went about their duties with grins on their faces for no apparent reason, banter flicking like whip ends across the deck. That evening, a party atmosphere permeated the crew. There were no extra rations, no extra grog, but somehow all knew that tonight they would sing. They would sing, make music and with the music, they would dance. Four fingers of the left hand flashed past four fingers of the right hand backwards, forwards, forwards, backwards, the fingers beating out a tattoo on the stretched goatskin. The piper joined the drummer's efforts, fingers slipping effortlessly over the holes in his pipe, changing the sound as he blew through it. The rhythm of the two instruments had all men tapping the deck in time with their feet 'til one sprang upright, the strength in his legs sufficient to save his hands the need of pushing. His bare feet flashed across the deck, arms aloft, fingers touching above his head, balls of feet, pads of toes beating in time with the music.

*Clap . . . Clap . . . Clap . . . Clap . . . Clap . . . Clap . . .*

The crowd encouraged the musicians to increase the tempo until the dancer collapsed from exhaustion to the good-natured applause of his shipmates. To encourage another, the tempo was slowed again. Three sailors accepted the implied challenge and rose to dance. The musicians quickened the tempo once the dancers had established the rhythm, then played faster and faster 'til only one remained standing to take a bow to his comrades. With the deck now clear of dancers, the musicians reduced the tempo again. Still no dancers so the tempo was reduced to one suitable for a lament. This tactic enticed six sailors to come forward. The pace picked up as the dancers beat the rhythm with the balls of their feet, Connor amongst them. He held his arms apart, hands above his head, fingers pointing to the sky, others joining the tips of their fingers to create a circle around their heads. Others still, placed hands on hips but each kept to the rhythm set by the drum and pipe.

*Clap . . . clap . . . clap . . . clap . . . clap . . . clap . . .* two dancers dropped to their knees.

*Clap . . . clap . . .* one more dancer down, three left.

*Clap . . . clap . . . clap . . . clap . . .* one more dancer down, two left.

*Clap . . . clap . . . clap . . . clap . . .* one more dancer left.

*Clap. clap.*

Connor took his bow, the last dancer standing.

The evening continued with boisterous songs, tales of derring-do, battles won, heroic deeds. These gave way to softer songs, songs of love, of home and, as the night closed in, sad laments of unrequited love or of loved ones lost. By now, many had settled on the deck to sleep, lullabied by those who still sang. Connor was one such as he slipped contentedly into slumber, reflecting on the fun he had that evening, his old legs still able to match the pace of those many years younger. Only the night watch remained standing, awake, vigilant, to sail the ship whilst their comrades slept about them. Little breeze cooled the sleeping sailors that night as the ship gently pushed it's way through the sea; no froth rose from the prow, only a small wave either side. All sails were set to make the most of what little wind there was.

At midnight, the ship's bell clanged to mark the change in watches. Those rostered to take the next watch, including Connor, rose sleepily, only a few hours of rest since the end of the revelry. The retiring watch dispersed to their preferred sleeping places. The new watch were cautioned to stay alert by the first mate.

"Barbary pirates sail these waters. That's why that American man 'o' war we saw earlier is here," he counselled.

Connor remembered the great ship sailing past, yellow gun ports with rows of guns waiting for action. 'CONSTITUTION' was the name emblazoned across the stern.

Connor splashed cool water from the sea, drawn up by a bucket on a rope, over his head to banish the weariness from his head. As he shook his head to clear the droplets that still clung to his skin and hair, he strode towards the stern to take up his assigned position. Thoughts of home subdued his mind as he stood awaiting orders, the tavern in his hometown, the nights of song and dance, Seamus and his fiddle. There was little activity to disturb his reverie. It was unlikely that the sails would be re-set unless a stiffer wind came by for the tack they sailed on was set for many hours to come, well beyond the end of this watch. He analysed the fatigue he felt, probably partially the result of the evening's exertions but ... but also, this was the worst watch, midnight 'til four in the morning, interrupting a few hours' sleep. Few of the sailors aboard would disagree with his judgement on that. Lack of any action increased his tiredness, his head lolling forward 'til his senses alerted him and he brought it upright with an involuntary jerk. He rubbed his eyes, pressing the knuckles of his hands into the sockets and agitating them as if they might wash the drowsiness away. He estimated that it must be close to two o'clock, half-way through his watch; the call should come soon.

The trickling water sound created by the sea as it swirled around behind the stern seemed to have changed, its rhythm interrupted. Connor moved to the rail to look down. As he realised the cause, he turned. The blow struck his temple, his knees crumpled and his unconscious head ricocheted as it struck the planking of the deck. On a signal from the pirate that had struck Connor down, more swarmed almost soundlessly over the stern rails, striking down the unsuspecting watch 'til they were almost half-way along the ship. The alarm was sounded. The ship's bell clanged out... *emergency, emergency!*

As the sleeping men were startled in their slumber, they failed to comprehend what was amiss and the dark-skinned pirates slew many. Muskets from the bow watch fired into the invaders, stopping their progress. The temporary pause as pirates fell ensured that the ship was not completely overrun. Now the defenders were on their feet, muskets, swords, knives, stout wooden pins placed in their hands. The early advantage over now, for each sailor that fell, a pirate fell also. Captain Davy fired his pistols, two pirates down. Sword and dagger in hand, he took the fight to the invaders, driving them back towards the stern. His first mate fell at his side. This distraction caused the captain to turn and help him but this selfless action ended Davy's own life. He fell beneath the first, slashing blow and then became the focus of four or five pirates' scimitars as they sought to kill the commander of their foes. Resistance ebbed once the captain and first mate had fallen. The slaughter stilled as the remaining sailors surrendered.

# Chapter 29

THE thread tightened, drawn through the left sleeve of the green serge tunic by the needle, pulling the torn edges of the fabric now clamped together, bound by the cotton. Kirsty cropped the thread with her shears, laid down her needle and cotton. She stood, holding the tunic, her fingers pegging the garment on the left and right shoulders. She held it at arm's length in the stream of light that flowed through the window. Content with her handiwork, she spread the soldier's jacket on the table. Buttons faced her as she crossed the sleeves, then folded the tunic, head touching tail.

Kirsty returned to her chair, a pair of fawn breeches lying crumpled in the basket awaiting the skill of her needlework. As with the tunic, indeed with all that she mended, Kirsty had washed and aired the garments in the manner her mother, Kathleen, had taught her. She surveyed the tears in the breeches with a practised eye for though just seventeen, Kirsty had aided her mother with the sewing since the day of her tenth birthday. She could still remember the thrill that surged through her with the joy of being able to help. Kirsty decided to sew the tear in the seat and patch the tear on the right knee. As she prepared the patch, her thoughts settled on her childhood, of the times at her mother's side. She had found a speck of blood on her fingertip the day she first used a needle and thread; her mother's kiss had removed the small crimson droplet. It was seldom now that the sharpened point would prick her finger, only occasionally when her mind wandered afar. Kirsty smiled to herself at the recollection. How many times had her mother's soft lips plucked troubles from her? The patch, now prepared, was placed above the tear. The needle was pushed through both fabrics, pulling the thread which would bind them together. Kirsty's reverie continued as she sewed. She recalled a summer afternoon, her mother playing tag on the beach, Liam running into the water to escape being tagged, the laughter, the gaiety, the sun baking the sand, browning their backs and faces, salt-water stinging their eyes and cooling their bodies. At the centre, the hub from which all enjoyment flowed, was their mother. Kathleen's eyes were sparkling jewels catching the sunlight's comfort. During the winter evenings, smoke from the burning peat scented the air in the cottage whilst Liam made music with his pipe and Kathleen's voice remained so clear, so moving as she sang; it took no effort to imagine the rent heart of the maiden whose love had gone to war.

Kirsty's fingers stitched the patch to the breeches, letting her mind go free to replay her childhood. It seemed, upon reflection, that most of her life had been lived in content-ment; joy-laden events appeared to squash against each other, jostling for a vacant space in time. Throughout her recollected history, her mother's presence was at the core. Few instances of happiness and merriment could she recall that did not feature Kathleen in a central role. This observation was sacred to Kirsty's spirit. She felt strength deep within herself and now believed that she had identified its source. Whilst she missed her mother's physical presence, she refused to allow herself to dwell upon her absence, rather she drew strength from the memories of the time they had had together. Kirsty often visited her mother's unmarked grave where she felt able to commune with her, silent questions, silent answers. She always said goodbye knowing the direction she would take.

Some four weeks earlier, as she walked the path toward the headland, she saw a figure close by the spot where Kathleen was buried. Each stride closed the distance between her and the figure until she was able to discern the kneeling Sweeney. Recognition eased the disquiet from her breast. Sweeney's unhappy eyes cast upwards as she approached him. Kirsty placed her right hand gently upon his right shoulder, bending at the waist to kiss the furrows in his brow, her heart aching to see the sorrow that so crushed the big man. She took his great hands in hers, the gesture signalling him to rise. The big man's red-rimmed eyes looked down, searching for a sanctuary in Kirsty's face.

*153*

He stumbled over his words, then out of his mouth they tumbled, "If... if... when... when I... when I... when I die, when I die, will you lie me down close by, please, please Kirsty. It's all I'll ever want. Please lay me down close by her," the huge head rocked forward in supplication as he finished his plea.

"Michael, it will be a long while yet but I'll lay you down close by when the time comes," replied Kirsty, stroking his hair, all the tenderness she felt for him flowing through her fingertips.

The anguish in the big man's face was soothed by her response as he ambled off down the path to allow Kirsty her own time at Kathleen's grave. "Michael," Sweeney turned to face Kirsty, "Kathleen's still with you; she still looks out for you." The big man nodded as the sense of Kirsty's words took hold in his consciousness. He turned again to the path and was on his way.

Kirsty's fingers had stopped sewing. Her recollection of the incident with Sweeney had so absorbed her that the patch on the breeches was sewn only on one of its four sides, her hands she found lying idle in her lap. She pushed the needle through the two materials, pulled it with the thumb and forefinger of her left hand 'til the cotton tightened. Her fingers once more active, her mind returned to reverie. She recalled the time that Seamus had joined her on the headland and he had spoken of the guilt he felt. Kathleen was his brother's daughter, entrusted to his care. His promise to look out for her were the last words he had uttered to his dying brother and then, when it came to burying her, he'd let the bullying O'Sullivan drive them from the churchyard. Now she lay here, not a mark to show her grave. Kirsty sensed the old man's need for absolution. She knew of no good reason why he should torment himself. She'd told him that there was not another place in the world that better suited her mother and, if alive, it was the spot she herself would have chosen. Unsure of the calming effect of her words, she'd embraced the music maker, held him tight for perhaps a minute, kissed his cheek and asked him that, for the sake of her own peace of mind, he should no longer dwell on the matter.

Kirsty decided that any more thoughts of graveside encounters would have to wait for another occasion as she realised, once again, that her stilled fingers rested in her lap, two sides of the patch remaining unsewn. Once more she laboured, fingers darting forward, pulling back, Kathleen again in her mind. They had talked often of Connor, the father Kirsty had yet to meet; excitement sparkled in Kathleen's eyes as she detailed the fineness of the man she had married. It was the shine in Kathleen's eyes, agitation in her hands, arms, fidgeting of her feet that best transmitted to Kirsty the special man her father was. There was a drawing of his likeness, Connor with his right arm about Kathleen's waist, her head nestled on his right shoulder, her hair spilled across his chest. Seamus had drawn the portrait, presenting the parchment with its charcoal images to Kathleen on her wedding day. From the accuracy of the likeness of Kathleen, it was probable that Connor too had been well portrayed. Kirsty kept this record of the youth of her parents safe in a box under her bed. Now, as her needle darted in and out of the fabric, she wondered how Connor's appearance might be changed from the image she had. For sure, he would be a good bit older. His face would probably be lined though not to the same extent as Seamus' for Connor would not be nearly as old. Hardship may have marked him; she knew not what he had been made to endure but reasoned that his time was unlikely to have been spent in comfort. Would he still have his fine head of hair as portrayed in the picture? She knew of some men in the village possessed only of a shaggy skirt about their ears, smooth naked skin stretching from their brows across their crowns.

Kirsty pushed away thoughts that Connor's appearance might not match up to her expectations. She'd be happy enough just to have him home, crinkled skin and no hair, his presence here all that she would pray for. She prayed that he had survived his imprisonment. She believed he had; her instincts told her so but a small part, deep within her, harboured the fear that he would not come back. He might never return. She might never meet him. Banishing the disquiet deep within her breast, she wondered how Connor might react to meeting her. Did he know of her existence?

Had word somehow reached him, telling of her birth? Would he be pleased to have a daughter? How might he take the news of Kathleen's loss? When would he return? The questions flowed, the arrival of each faster than the last, leaving no time to consider an answer.

Kirsty turned the breeches on her knee so that the unsewn fourth side was parallel with her waist. As she started to sew, she closed the door on the flood of unanswered questions concerning her father which so troubled her mind. She wondered when Liam would return. Kirsty determined to settle on this question to slow her mind's race. Liam had left that morning with Jim Cassidy. Most likely he'd be back for supper. She'd prepare enough for three; Jim usually stayed when he came to their cottage. He had a wondrous appetite for a man no more in height than she was (though broader in the shoulders and legs). She'd watched him stroll away down the path towards the village that morning, chatting to her brother. She'd noted the sheen as the sunshine bounced off his thick, black hair, the broadness of his shoulders, the fluid motion of the muscles on his back as his arms gesticulated some point to Liam. Her eyes had travelled down his back to his buttocks; Kirsty felt the heat rise in her cheeks at the recollection.

She was sure she had strong feelings for Jim, as strong as those she held for Liam but different. It was the difference that confused her. Kathleen had noticed the change in her when Jim was present and mentioned as much a year ago to Kirsty but she had not wished to discuss her feelings further with her mother. She talked of everything with Kathleen. She was her confidante so her reluctance to confide or examine her thoughts on Jim added to her confusion. Whatever her feelings were, she aimed to keep them secret, even within herself, reluctant to probe what may upset the current happy balance of things. Her girlfriends' smiles, knowing glances and raised eyebrows were all deflected by Kirsty, changing the topic of conversation.

'Snip', the shear's blades crossed as the thread was cut. Kirsty turned her attention from the finished patch on the right knee to the tear in the seat of the breeches. She would finish mending the breeches, then prepare tea for the afternoon was almost past. Potato cakes were a favourite of Liam's; Jim also had a passion for them. This last thought confirmed her decision as to how to use the cooked potatoes left over from the previous evening.

# Chapter 30

O'SULLIVAN kicked at the stone on the path. Dust puffed from the ground in front where the sole of his boot struck the earth. The toe of his boot hit a stone shaped like a hen's egg cut in two'. It skipped and bounced along the path, small squirts of dust marking each contact with the earth track. O'Sullivan continued on his way until ten paces further along when his right leg swung back and the tip of his boot again sent a stone hopping along the path. He continued this until an edge of the semi-oval struck the ground and the stone was sent at right-angles into the undergrowth along-side the path. A grunt from the tax-collector signalled his irritation on losing this diversion. His ferret eyes swept the path in front, searching for some object to kick. As he trudged, he muttered curses on most of the people he knew in the belief that they were responsible for his imagined misfortunes. In a few years, he'd see his fiftieth year, no thanks to anyone but himself. In France, in Russia, as well as at home, it had been his own skill at concealing himself in the heat of battle that had saved him although, even then, there were a few times when he might have been killed. There was one occasion when his own officer had found him cowering. The officer raised his sword in anger, only to drop it as O'Sullivan's knife twisted in the hole it had made in the gentleman's ribcage. No witnesses, the enemy was blamed for the death.

He owed no man a favour but many were in debt for services rendered by him, none more so than Fitzpatrick. Now he was the master, he'd make up for the wasted years. The sight of Kathleen Macken's daughter in her blue skirt and blouse at the churchyard had aroused his interest. He would summons Kirsty to Fitzpatrick's house to collect the sewing and then . . . he smirked as he imagined his pleasure.

As he made his way along the track to the Macken cottage, O'Sullivan gently stroked his cheek. The tips of his fingers could still discern the different texture of the new skin which had repaired the damage done by Kathleen's fingernails. It would be the first occasion since that encounter that he had visited the cottage. In the weeks since Kathleen's death, no suspicion had fallen on him. What if Kirsty was alone when he arrived? Why should he wait to lure her to Fitzpatrick's house? He had been surprised to see how comely a maid Kirsty Macken had become. Her appearance at the church-yard had stirred his own fantastic lust. Why wait? If the chance arose, he would have her in her own home.

# Chapter 31

GRAINS of sand rolled over one another, suspended in the rush of the sea, driven on shore, rearranged in uniformity. Four footsteps, toes, ball, heel, indenting the soft wet sand, their presence was now obliterated. As the footsteps climbed, leaving hollows in the sand, the beach definition ceased and dry grains rolled from the crests with no clue as to the cause until the end of the trail. Liam and Jim sat gazing out across the ocean, bare feet planted flat, arms encircling their knees. Liam watched as the surf erased their footprints at the water's edge. His eyes traced the passage of their feet across the dry sand to where they sat. He studied the nearest footfall as the rivulets of sand ran into the bottom of the track, raising it, lowering the crest, until only a slight indent was left. The breeze would finish the smoothing.

"Does Kirsty ever talk of me?" Jim asked, still staring out across the ocean.

"She talks of nothing else!" replied Liam, turning his grinning face toward his friend, winking his right eye.

"Don't mess with me; you know what I mean," Jim cuffed the top of Liam's head as he spoke.

"If you mean does she like you, I'd say for sure she takes notice of you but she's far too sensible for one such as you," retorted Liam, giving hope, then dashing it.

"In what way does she notice me?" asked Jim, fixing on the most encouraging aspect of his friend's reply.

"Well . . . well, she notices that you have a hearty appetite," Liam responded, chuckling at the disappointment his reply would cause to Jim.

"You're a donkey's arse," Jim pushed Liam, causing him to topple sideways as he lay, still chortling. Jim scooped sand onto his prostrate friend.

# Chapter 32

KIRSTY pushed the needle through the fabric in the seat of the breeches, the tear now closed. O'Sullivan pushed the door open and walked into the cottage, his eyes taking almost no time to confirm that the girl was alone. Kirsty sheared the thread and took three paces to her left, away from the door, positioning the table between herself and O'Sullivan. She placed the breeches on the tabletop and held onto the needle in her right hand, unused thread dangling from the eye. In her left hand, she gripped the shears. Kirsty could feel the increased force of her heartbeat. *Thump . . . thump . . . thump . . . thump . . . thump* went her heart inside her chest. O'Sullivan stood, considering his tactics. The girl was alone, just as he had hoped. Would she do his bidding or would he have to take what he desired?

"I've been a good friend to your family over the years," he lied. "Your father and I were close. We grew up together. I pleaded on his behalf at his trial but, sadly, to no good consequence," the tax-collector continued, hopeful of gaining Kirsty's affection.

"I've always admired your mother since before she married."

Kirsty winced at the reference to the fate of her father, knowing that O'Sullivan was lying. She held her tongue so as not to provoke him.

"Course, he wasn't really a convict and I told his Reverence so," he continued. "I've arranged for you to take over your mother's sewing but you'll need to go to Fitzpatrick's house in person." As he had been speaking, he had been sidling towards Kirsty. She now sensed his closeness.

"I'm grateful for your kindness, to be sure," she responded, "but I've more than enough sewing for the

161

moment." Her politeness hid the loathing she felt for O'Sullivan. She'd no wish to see Fitzpatrick or to work for him even if it meant that she starved to death. The village was awash with rumours of O'Sullivan's new power over Fitzpatrick and his occupancy of the cleric's house. "My brother Liam and his friend are due back this instant and I've still to cook their tea, so, if you don't mind..." Her right arm outstretched with needle between her thumb and forefinger, Kirsty pointed at the door. O'Sullivan could see that his friendly tactic had failed so now he must take what he wanted by force.

He stepped closer. Kirsty stepped back, the corner wall pressing on each shoulder. Liam and Jim then walked through the open door and took in the scene before them, Kirsty backed into the corner, the needle in her right hand pointing forward, a miniature sword for her defence and O'Sullivan advancing towards her. Relief replaced the fear in Kirsty's face whilst triumph made way for fear in O'Sulli-van's.

"What's your business here?" snarled Jim, hate mixed with fury contorting his face.

He advanced towards the tax-collector, arms forward, fingers curled, ready to grab the intruder.

"I came to offer work to Kirsty," said O'Sullivan, "but now you're here, it's as well you know you're years behind with the payment of your rent and tithes. Now I'm back, I'll expect payment."

Kirsty, her balance recovered, was eager to avoid trouble. "It's true. He came to offer sewing work from Fitzpatrick. I've declined the offer and he was just about to leave when you returned," concluded the young woman.

Jim's curled fingers tightened into fists, the pressure great enough to stop the flow of blood to his knuckles. His arms dropped to his side, fists still bunched as O'Sullivan pushed past and out the open door.

"There was more happening when we came in than you cared to state?" asked Liam of his sister, eyebrows squeezed together to indicate his concern.

"There's no sense in seeking trouble with the likes of him," Kirsty replied. "We know enough of the way the law works to be sure that Fitzpatrick could twist matters in favour of his tax-collector and against ourselves. O'Sullivan has a hold over Fitzpatrick," she continued.

The substance of her words caused Jim's and Liam's shoulders to droop, a dejected slant pulled on their faces, eyes cast down, mouths dipping in the corners, chins settling on their chests.

Kirsty asked, "Would you like potato cakes?"

Chins rose, smiles formed as the two men changed their thoughts to food. "Yes please," they answered in unison.

"Well, be off and wash," she chided. "Food will be ready in fifteen minutes or so." Kirsty was talking to their backs as they dutifully made for the well behind the cottage.

On her own, patting the potato and flour mix into hand-sized tablets, Kirsty scolded herself for the way she had reacted to O'Sullivan's presence. Why had she not stood up to him as Jim had done rather than cowering in fear in the corner? She was a good bit taller, probably stronger she thought given the difference in their age. She determined that she would never give way to fear again if circumstances were ever to repeat themselves.

Liam placed the pitcher of water that he had just filled from the well in the centre of the table. He sat down next to Jim, hands clasped on the table in front of them, wet hair slicked back, inhaling the aroma of potato cakes sizzling in butter. Kirsty carried the pan to the table and turned two cakes onto each man's plate, dribbling molten butter over the crisped coating. Quiet reigned for the few minutes it took for the cakes to be consumed, clack of wooden knife striking wooden plate as it carved through the soft potato, the only sound within the cottage.

Jim, his meal finished, sat with a furrowed brow. His dark eyebrows pressed down on the bridge of his nose causing the skin to crease. Kirsty, attentive to the change in his mood asked, "What makes you frown so, Jim?"

Jim delighted in the concern of Kirsty. The mention of his name created a sensation akin to a butterfly fluttering over his heart. His frown eased but still lingered.

"Tithes are unfair, unjust. Why must our backs be burdened with the need to keep men such as O'Sullivan and Fitzpatrick in a feathered nest of comfort?" Giving neither Liam nor Kirsty the opportunity to reply or agree, Jim pressed on, "Matters will be worse now that O'Sullivan has returned. He's a much fiercer tax-collector than Hanrahan." He stopped to survey his audience, to ensure that the import of his analysis struck home. Nodding heads confirmed as much.

"Hanrahan's a good clerk. You can be sure the records will be up to date but he doesn't really have the stomach to enforce the theft of people's labours for the benefit of the clergy." Jim paused. Kirsty and Liam were still content to follow his discourse.

"O'Sullivan's been bragging in the tavern as to how he'll collect the tithes unpaid since he went to France. The villagers are all concerned because food's been plentiful since he went away. There's none that's died of hunger in these parts in all the time I've been growing. 'Tis only stories from our elders that keep us aware of the misery it may cause. Seamus says O'Sullivan's returned meaner than he left and he knows him well. I heard he was mean enough when he left so that's a warning!"

"What's to be done that will solve the problem?" enquired Liam for he knew his friend well. Jim was never a moaner. He'd always have an answer, a plan of action to rectify a wrong.

"Desperate problems require dramatic solutions," Jim searched the eyes of his audience, determined that they should note the seriousness, the sincerity in his own eyes.

"We must destroy the records. Without the records, O'Sullivan will have no past claims on us."

"How will we get into the Records Office? O'Sullivan is no fool. He has it guarded night and day," responded Liam.

"We'll not enter the office at all. We'll distract the guards long enough to fire the building", stated Jim.

"Now that'd be some adventure," romantic notions stirred Liam's soul as he concurred.

Kirsty's heart pounded with the realisation that this was not idle chatter, that two men she held dear were determined to risk their lives, in her judgement most probably lose their lives.

"You'll both get yourselves killed. There's no benefit in that to anyone. The guards carry muskets. You've not a hope of pulling it off." She searched for more reasons to deter them.

"Your own father's a victim of the tithe and O'Sullivan's likely to do worse in future," Jim spoke quietly, softness in his voice to calm Kirsty, trying to make her see the desperate need for their proposed action.

"I must be off home now," he finished, hopeful that he had quelled Kirsty's anxiety.

As Jim stood in the doorway, Kirsty placed her open hands against his cheeks, cupping his face.

"I've no wish to see you die Jim." She held his face and pleaded with her eyes.

"Your way is too dangerous. Something needs be done but not at the price of your life," she said as she released her hold.

"Kirsty, I thank you for your concern but my head is fit to burst thinking of another solution."

Kirsty, Liam at her side, stood in the doorway, right arms waving as Jim made his way down the track.

# Chapter 33

KIRSTY stood up, the seat of her skirt moist from the ground. For the first time she had confided her feelings for Jim. No words were spoken; it was enough to think her troubles through at her mother's graveside, to gain silent confirmation.

Kirsty's bare feet pressed on the damp soil of the track leaving their imprint as she wandered home. There was moisture in the air; it carried the perfume of burning wood, the smell of autumn. Fields, for the most part, lay bare, the soil of each a different hue of brown, patchworks of tan, chestnut, sienna and ochre. Soil, recently turned, lay much darker than that ploughed earlier. Kirsty marvelled that such earth sustained the lives of all she knew. Could there ever be a more perfect place to live she asked herself, sure of the answer she would give for it was not a new thought to her? In the field to her left, the first few inches of the plant that had been cropped, corn she thought, stuck out above the soil. The next field was similarly dressed. As a matter of fun, Kirsty imagined them to be the unshaven cheeks of a giant. She sought to identify his mouth, settling for a ditch that cut into both fields, his ruddy cheeks the sienna earth of the freshly ploughed fields above. The hedge became his nose but she could not fathom out his eyes because the ground fell away in the distance. The hedgerows she could discern so they need be his eyebrows. The woods beyond made up his hair in multi-coloured hue as the leaves were yet to fall. Greens of summer were now replaced by golds, russets and rusts, the finest head of hair a giant ever wore.

Kirsty passed by her giant, it's work done, a winter's rest before the spring crop was sown. She looked down at her feet and realised that she was dancing as she went. Seagulls

166

diving, gliding above, settling on the most freshly ploughed fields, their hard beaks picking through the soft soil, juice-laden worms a delicacy to be enjoyed, a change each year from their fish fare. Amongst the gulls, the occasional hawk hovered, defying gravity, his prey beneath no longer able to move with freedom under the canopy of the crops. Kirsty followed her feet as they danced along the track, now twirling, flicking right, spinning left. Her delight was interrupted by the sound of a plaintive, tortured voice carried to her on the breeze. She followed the direction from whence the dirge flowed. Kirsty left the track, her feet sinking in the soft soil of the ploughed field, earth squeezing between her toes. She passed through a gap in the hedge, through the field of stubble, taking care to follow the earth lines between the three-inch stalks sharpened by the slash of the sickle. As she neared the lamenter, Kirsty recognised the voice of an anguished friend. Sitting on a log at the edge of the wood, Yomi hugged her knees, rocking backwards, forwards. Her song of mourning ceased as Kirsty sat beside her, wrapped arms about her, cradled the shoulders and gently pulled the dark head to her shoulder. Kirsty continued the gentle rocking all the while *ssh, ssh, sshing* into her friend's ear. She felt the dampness as her blouse absorbed the tears from Yomi's face.

After many minutes had passed by, Yomi's sobbing shoulders quieted. She raised her head and Kirsty was able to see the deep, deep hurt in the dark, brown eyes.

"Whatever's brought you down so low?" Kirsty enquired, tenderly stroking her friend's tear-washed cheek with her fingertips.

"O'Rourke's... not coming back... he'll never ...be back... he's been dead... for more than ... ten years," the words jumped from Yomi's mouth between sobs.

"How is it that you know this now?" Kirsty asked quietly.

"O'Sullivan ... he met someone ... a soldier ... fought with ... O'Rourke ... saw him die," sobbed Yomi. Kirsty caressed the last of the sobs from her friend.

"It's not the loss of O'Rourke. Perhaps I've known for some time he'd not return," Yomi continued. "It's not that I

*167*

don't have a good life here, fine land of my own, free under the stars at night, birds to sing to me all day." Yomi started to sob again, "It's just... it's just ...now ... now ... I realise ... I'm never ... never ever ... to see ... my homeland ... again."

"Hush now, hush now," soothed Kirsty.

"There's my family, brothers, sisters and little brother, Choma. He must be a full grown man by now," Yomi's sobbing had stopped but the thought of her family brought fresh tears welling in the corners of her big brown eyes, overflowing, streaming down her cheeks.

"Tell me about Choma," asked Kirsty, sensing that Yomi's young brother might be the person she missed most of all her family.

"Choma is my youngest brother. He was in his sixth summer when I was taken. I am the oldest of the girls in my family; I've two younger sisters." Talking of her youngest brother was calming Yomi.

"My mother and father would say that I was Choma's second mother; this pleased me. Choma was so content. When he was a baby, I would play with him, carrying him everywhere I went on my back. His little fingers would grasp my finger and he would try to suckle on my fingertip. It was my tenth summer; a big responsibility was given to me. I remember his first footsteps unaided, the pride I felt in his achievement. As he grew, it was easier to play with him. His small legs were always leading him into some form of mischief but I took great pleasure in this – he was never bad. At the waterhole where we bathed, he would disappear beneath the surface, then pop up some distance away in the manner of a diving bird. Sometimes the delay did concern me but he was able to swim underwater for a considerable time. His chuckle could change my mood. The sound of his laughter made me feel happy. When he slept, his eyelashes would curl almost to touch his eyebrows. At peace, in sleep, it soothed my spirit just to gaze upon him.

When I was taken, I cried for my five brothers, two sisters, mother, father and all who would miss me but, most of all, my tears flowed for little Choma when he found I was gone. Each morning, when he liked to play, I would not be there for him. Now I know I shall never see my homeland nor my family again. O'Rourke was the one person who knew from which coast in Africa I came." Yomi finished her recollection with a great stuttered heave of her breast.

"There will be a way. You're never to despair," Kirsty responded. "My father is due home soon. He may have some news from his travels, from people he's met," she soothed.

"Is it likely he might know of my land?" enquired Yomi, eager to cling to any faint chance, not wishing to stay with the abandonment of hope she felt on learning of O'Rourke's demise.

"For sure, for sure, there's a chance," replied Kirsty, grateful to be able to lift a weight from her friend's shoulders.

Yomi kissed Kirsty on the cheek. "Thank you," said the African as she rose to her feet. "Will you be at the tavern this evening?" she enquired, some of the sorrow now gone from her soulful eyes.

"I'll be down as soon as Liam and Jim return. They're working in the town today," replied Kirsty.

Yomi and Kirsty walked on together 'til the way home parted. "See you at the tavern," Kirsty said, squeezing her friend's shoulders and kissing her forehead.

Kirsty followed the track back to Corryann, the gaiety of the early afternoon now replaced by thoughtful concentration as she sought to find a solution to Yomi's plight. How might she find her homeland? She scolded herself for never having considered that her land, with all its bounty and blessings, was still foreign to her friend.

It was in this reflective mood that she arrived at the cottage. She unlatched the door, pushed it open and walked in. Half way across the room she sensed movement and jumped when the door slammed shut behind her. Sneering, leering, ale-breathed O' Sullivan barred her exit.

She instinctively backed away 'til the wall halted her progress. She knew Liam and Jim would not be walking in this time. As O'Sullivan advanced, half crouched towards her, she slid along the wall 'til trapped by the corner.

"Your brother and his ugly friend won't be back to save you this time, my girl," he hissed, "For *my girl* is what you're about to be." He smirked, pleased with his own wit.

Still advancing, the buttons on his breeches slipping out of the holes with the aid of his left hand, O'Sullivan held his right hand out to catch Kirsty if she tried to pass him. Kirsty felt his beery breath upon her face as she watched in horror, O'Sullivan's breeches falling around his ankles. Panic gripped her, froze her muscles.

"Your mother, all dressed up, talking to the convict. She escaped me when she fell. The blow was just to stun her so you've that to make up to me too."

Kirsty forgot the creature in front of her and she closed her eyes replaying the scene when she had found Kathleen on the beach, the torn dress, pinchmarks on her left breast, split lip, Kirsty's tears washing the dried blood. As she opened her eyes, she saw her mother's killer breathing stale ale upon her, seeking to take pleasure in her, this pathetic old man.

O'Sullivan was slow to notice the fury that now transfused Kirsty's face. Her fingers curled, her nails ripped flesh from both his cheeks and her right knee crashed into his groin, squashing his testicles flat. Kirsty ignored the vomit that spewed from his mouth and splashed her blouse. Her left knee sent the flattened testicles across his groin, pinned them to the bones beneath. More flesh she tore from his face. Her fingernails full, she beat the bloodied head with her hands. O'Sullivan sank to the floor to escape the violence upon him.

"It wasn't me, it wasn't me. She fell. I tried to grab her," he pleaded as Kirsty picked up a knife from the table. He scuttled across the floor on hands and knees, fearful of a stab from the knife. Kicks rained upon his body until, at last, he reached the doorway. Kirsty allowed him to tumble into the dirt outside, his breeches ensnared around his scrawny ankles.

Kirsty's racing pulse calmed slowly as she sat at the table sipping water from a wooden cup. Kathleen had been murdered trying to escape from O'Sullivan. She'd gone to the headland in her wedding dress to say goodbye to

Connor. Knowing the truth caused tears to stream down her cheeks, not from sadness but from an increased pride in her mother's strength.

# Chapter 34

SOME weeks had passed since the incident with O'Sullivan at the cottage. He had not been seen in all that time, neither collecting tithes as had been feared, nor at the tavern. Word spread as to the likely cause of his absence. Many believed they knew the reason; he was ill, he had died, left for the wars again, gone away to be married. Almost all of the villagers had their own story.

Kirsty had said nothing. Not even her brother, Liam, was aware of the damage she'd wrought on O'Sullivan. By the time he had returned home on the day, all traces of vomit and blood had been cleaned from the cottage, cleansed from Kirsty's clothing, from her hands, from under her finger-nails. She'd scrubbed the whole of her body to relieve it of the stench of the aley vomit, pummelled and thrice washed her blouse to ensure no lingering smell.

Liam clasped his sister's right hand, swinging her arm forwards and backwards in time with his own. Darkness came early at this time of year; Christmas was not many weeks away. The pair skipped through the blackness of the countryside, a little light shining from the early moon. In front of them, less than five minutes away, the lights flickered in the villagers' cottages. Brightest amongst them were the candles from the tavern, their destination on this Saturday evening. Kirsty inhaled the crisp night air, drawing it through her nostrils to enhance the taste, exhaling a little cloud foretelling a frosty dawn, a silver spectacle to anticipate in the morn.

Warmth rushed to welcome them as they pushed open the tavern door, Liam deferring to his sister as he closed the door behind them. Crackle and spit called the voice of the log fire as it bade them sit close by.

Fingers dancing, puckered lips blowing as Eoin set the

tempo, his pipe music had Kirsty on her feet almost as soon as she sat down. A melancholy air was sung 'til Shaun beat out a faster tempo with his drum. Jim's feet flashed as he joined Kirsty in the dance, an unusual sense of excitement invading his chest. Seamus clucked his teeth, winked and nodded at no one in particular, took a pull on his tankard of ale, then reached for his fiddle and stick. Seated once more, Kirsty's face felt warm and flushed as she held her cheeks in her hands to cool them. Yomi smiled, increasing the heat under Kirsty's fingers.

A man burst through the door of the tavern and left it ajar behind him, chill dry air following him in to the warmth. His face, suffused in misery, held back the calls to close the door. Kirsty recognised the newcomer though, without his long black coat, he appeared more skeletal than she recalled from her mother's funeral. Addressing all and none, his haunted eyes swept back and forth as he told his tragic tale. "They've killed my son. My boy is dead. No more he'll see the sunshine... They came this evening, O'Sullivan and his henchmen, claiming I owed... they've killed my only boy, just ten he was... they took all I had, emptied the cottage... he died. I cradled him in my arms as the light fell from his eyes."

Liam led the undertaker to a seat and sat him down, all gathering round to hear his words. "His face is scarred. He's worse than ever... my boy tried to stop them. I held him back... they loaded all upon my cart, took the horse to pull it... my boy slipped from my grasp, ran to stop them. O'Sullivan hit him with his whip... he fell. The wheels, they struck his head. I tried to stem the bleeding ... now he's gone to join his mother; she's not seen him since he was born." Silence stilled the room as he finished.

Jim was first to recover from the news. "O'Sullivan must be brought to justice. We should go to Fitzpatrick and demand the arrest of his tax-collector. We've felt the heel of his boot too often; now he's killed a child." Murmurs of assent responded to Jim's call.

"There was no need to kill my boy... he was no threat to O'Sullivan," murmured the grieving father, his head shaking as he spoke.

The entire tavern emptied onto the road outside, others from the village joining the throng as they exited their cottages to understand the commotion. Jim, despite his youth, was at the front with the undertaker as they went to Fitzpatrick's house.

# Chapter 35

THE villagers returned to the Inn, unsuccessful in their pleas to the gibbering Fitzpatrick.

"We must stop O'Sullivan from collecting old tithes," stated Liam.

"Perhaps he should meet with an accident. That'd stop him," called Shaun, the drummer, his words measured to carry the intended menace.

"Why not just kill him!" roared another who had not understood Shaun's words.

"When killing starts, good men die, same as bad," interjected Kirsty, fearful of the consequences to those that she held dear. Many of the women present in the tavern murmured their assent at Kirsty's prophecy.

Jim spoke for the first time since their return to the tavern. "We've appealed to Fitzpatrick for justice. He's in thrall to O'Sullivan. You've just witnessed his response. He is with the fairies. He had no interest in the death of the boy. If we destroy the records, they'll have no chance to collect past tithes."

"How is that to come about?" enquired Seamus, his interest stirred by the notion.

"We'll take a group of men and burn the building that houses the records," replied Jim.

"Troopers with muskets guard the building. There's never a time, day or night, that O'Sullivan allows it unguarded," said Seamus.

"We'll go in the dead of night, whilst the moon is small in the sky. We'll place dry bundles of twigs close by, a few bales of hay too, during the day. When the troopers are close to the end of their watch is when they seem most at ease. I've watched them for many nights now, noted their routines. We'll set a fire close by and, when they are distracted, we can

175

move the tinder against the building, set the blaze all round." Jim finished, having outlined the plan that had built in his head these past weeks.

"It should work," nodded Seamus.

"How many men will you need?" asked Shaun.

"Four or five, no more," replied Jim.

"You'll all be shot, for what good? There'll still be tithes to pay and, more's the pity, yourselves to bury," said Kirsty as she stood to leave. The conversation and mood of the men had filled her head with foreboding.

# Chapter 36

A sliver of pale yellow marked the moon's position in the night sky as Liam's eyes scanned the heavens. Points of silver light were testimony to the absence of the hoped-for clouds. He prayed the stars would shine kindly on the task that lay before them. He had left his bed as quietly as his concentration and the darkness allowed. His clothes under his arm, he had eased the latch on the door with great care to avoid the usual clack. Once outside, Liam closed the door. His heart increased it's pounding as the latch fell into place, the sound amplified by the stillness of the night. By the well, behind the cottage, he dressed, grateful for the dark though it hampered his movement.

Liam walked down the track, his clothes being the darkest ones he possessed.

Jim crouched in the wood overlooking the building that housed Fitzpatrick's records. He had watched as the guards changed shift some hours before. Now, well past midnight, all that he had observed matched his earlier solitary reconnaissance. Alone he waited, mentally replaying his plan yet again. The kindling was all in place no more than thirty yards from the building. Bales of hay for the diversion had been loosened in the woods to the west of where he crouched, on the far side of the Records Office. He had the flints, dry grass stuffed within his dark tunic, to hasten the flames, to fire the hay and sticks. If the two guards were not drawn to the diversion, a pair of blackthorn cudgels rested beside his leg. If the need arose to use them, the unconscious guards must be dragged well clear of the burning building as it was no part of his plan to kill them.

Despite the completeness of his preparations, a grain of doubt scratched away at his confidence. Jim regretted now the public exposure of his thoughts. Would all present in the tavern last evening keep the secret of what was intended? Would his accomplices in the implementation be stopped, apprehended by O'Sullivan's men? There was no sign before him to increase his doubt but where were those who had pledged to help; surely they should be here now? As if in answer to the question, the sound of footfall on dry leaves carried to his ears. Jim kept himself hidden until he recognised Shaun and another youth from the village beside him. A soft call brought them to the spot.

Perhaps an hour had passed and still there was no sign of Liam. Jim felt sure his friend would not desert him but the chosen time to strike was not far off. A tap upon his shoulder spun him around. "Sorry, I'd no wish to startle you," whispered Liam as he crouched down.

The four men remained silent, studying the compound of buildings to the side of Fitzpatrick's house. A horse neighed in the stables drawing a response from another. The two guards sat, backs propped against the Records Office wall beside the entrance door, muskets resting in the crooks of their right arms. Jim could hear that they were talking but was unable to distinguish their words.

"Right, time to move," Jim whispered.

"You all know what to do," he proclaimed as he shook hands with each man.

"When we're done, disperse and make your own way home," he finished.

Liam picked his way through the trees, arcing round the Records Office to the place where the bales of hay for the diversionary fire had been set. The attack on the office would begin once his fire had taken hold. Darkness, his friend until now, hampered his search for the bales. What if he couldn't find them? His mind raced. He could feel the loss of rationale as the stormy fingers of panic reached for his brain and a thundering pulse beat in his ears. The sight of the bales cast off the panic though the pulsing drumbeat in his ears stayed. He stood the bales on end to create a V-shape with the tops resting against each other and then drew some of the straw from the bales to create a loose heap under the peak. Dried grass, carried in his shirt, was placed beside the loose straw. The flint was struck. A curl of smoke rose as a blade of grass blackened. Orange-yellow flame consumed the dried grass in a moment, taking hold on the loose straw, climbing and licking at the bales. As the glow from the fire lighted his presence, Liam made away, crouching as he hurried off. Away from the light of his fire, unable to re-adjust his eyes to the darkness, he stumbled as his left foot caught in the tangled undergrowth. The fall squashed the air out of his lungs as his chest hit the ground.

Jim watched the flames from Liam's fire grow, watched as his friend departed. The flames had now attracted the attention of the seated guards who jumped to their feet. They ran to investigate, muskets slung over their shoulders. Jim's team of four hurriedly moved the kindling to the Records Office, each setting fires at a different wall. Flames quickly engulfed the building, its blazing, thatched roof lighting the area for some distance. Yells from the guards brought out the next watch who had been readying themselves. Four muskets were pointed as the fire-raisers fled the scene, their fleeing forms lit up by the conflagration they had caused.

Liam had regained his breath but the pain from his now swollen left ankle slowed his escape. As he ran, Jim saw his friend fall even as the sound of the musket fire reached his ears. He crashed through the undergrowth towards the wounded Liam. He scooped his friend from the ground, carrying him away from the light into the safety of the darkness. More musket shots spat out. Twigs cracked, smashed by the small lead balls. Jim paused for an instant, then continued into the darkness.

Lungs seared as the sounds of the perpetrators gasping for more air seemed to fill the woods. Jim tried to steady his breathing as he looked down on the dark form of Liam at his feet. The need for air overcame the need for silence – anyone close by would hear the panting, the hunted at bay, worn down by the chase. Time passed and no hunter came. Jim, his breathing now controlled, helped Liam to his feet.

"It's the ankle hurts the most," Liam said as he rose. "We'd best be away from here. I'm fine to carry on," he continued.

They made their way along the path through the woods.

Jim reasoned that the noise they made stumbling through the undergrowth was a greater danger than being discovered up on the track. There was a fair chance they would hear the approach of any aggressors and slip off to the side to conceal themselves until the danger passed.

Clear of the woods now, the open track seemed too perilous as there was little cover at its edges. Around the fields, keeping to the banks and hedgerows, they zig-zagged towards the Macken cottage. A ditch lay in front of the young men, no more than four feet wide. With two good feet, it was an easy leap but, constrained by Liam's ankle, they had to wade through the icy water. It clasped their calves, tightened the skin. Once up the far bank, Liam found the cold embrace of the water had eased his damaged ankle.

"How's the leg?" asked Jim as they rested, their backs against an earth bank.

"Still bleeding but your bandage has surely slowed it," replied Liam with a friendly pat of the back with his left hand to Jim's right shoulder.

"You're hurt; you're bleeding yourself," exclaimed Liam as his friend flinched beside him from the gentle pat.

Liam could feel the sticky wetness of blood on the palm of his left hand.

"It's nothing. I'm fine," responded Jim. "You're not to make a fuss of this to Kirsty when you're home," panicked words flowed from Jim's mouth.

"I'll not say a thing", cried Liam, his hand raised in mock surrender.

"The Record's Office should be destroyed. 'Tis worth a few scratches for what we've accomplished this night," said Jim. "We'd best be on our way. I hope the others are home safe now," he concluded.

Once more upon their feet, the two friends made faster progress as they neared the end of their journey.

'Clack,' the latch on the cottage door raised, no need of quiet now. Liam and Jim entered the cottage, lit a candle. Their entry had roused Kirsty; she sat upright in her bed. Candlelight revealed the bloody bandage, a strip from Jim's shirt which bound Liam's thigh. Out of bed, Kirsty removed the bloodied bandage, removed Liam's breeches and bathed the wound beneath.

"The two of you have no more sense than the animals of the field!" Her words lashed the ears, smote the egos of the two men. "You'd best be off before further trouble comes," she said, dismissing Jim.

Jim left, head heavy from her words. As he passed by the side of the cottage, a faintness added confusion to his heavy head. Lest he fall, he sat upon the ground, blood seeping from the wound in his right shoulder.

Kirsty's hard words bit deep within. He could not fault her for their uttering. His plan had indeed almost gone awry. His friend lay shot; good luck that the ball struck where it did; good luck that his friend did not lie dead. Of all the heads to heap further trouble upon, Kirsty's would be the last he'd choose. Now he'd vexed her. She held him in such low esteem; an animal from the field meant more to her!

Jim's chest ached. He couldn't stop his thoughts though they were the cause of the discomfort. Throat constricted, pressure building in his breast, squashing, rending – he needed not a remedy for now he had lost the love, lost the love of Kirsty. This notion slightly eased his condition. He had never before admitted to himself that he was in love with her. Fondness, admiration, respect, a need to be near, he recognised these feelings but now it was out, he was in love with Kirsty.

Jim's pulse quickened; he could feel the blood pumping out through the hole in his shoulder. Though his eyelids drooped, covering his eyes, still a mist descended within. How should he repair the damage, change Kirsty's opinion of him? What might he do to show the love he felt for her? No, no, he could not be so forward. What if... what if his love was rejected? Better to love her in secret. The shame he'd endure, that he could not endure if, if... the mist in his eyes was darkening, a lightness came to his body. He felt himself float, floating free of the earth beneath.

Liam's wound had been dressed and he lay sleeping in his bed. Kirsty, close to sleep, heard the noise from outside the cottage, a thud, not a natural sound of the night. She turned, drew the blanket closer to her and tried to sleep. Her efforts thwarted by the strangeness of the noise, she rose, lighting a candle from the glowing embers of the fire.

Outside, the still air gently chilled her body through her shift as she walked around the cottage, past the well and then back to the front. No sign of anything amiss, she re-entered through the door. It was Jim's misfortune that the only wall she'd not walked by was the one beside which he lay.

Kirsty's gentle warm breath blew upon the flame. Light extinguished, she climbed back into her bed. The warmth from her earlier possession was a comfort to her now and, as she snuggled beneath her blankets, sleep rushed in.

Liam was the first to wake, his night's sleep brought to an end by the throb from his left ankle. It was with the utmost care that he placed his weight upon it. Though it ached, the pain was dull, not a serious inhibition. Peeling back the bandage on his thigh, daylight from the window showed the wound not to have gone deep. The musket shot had cut his leg as it passed.

Kirsty wakened to see Liam seated at the table, inspecting his injury.

"How is it?" she asked. "In the candlelight it seemed none too bad once the blood was washed away," she said.

"It's fine, not much more than a scratch," replied Liam.

"What a pair you are!" Kirsty exclaimed, having ascertained her brother's wellbeing. "You could both have been killed and where's the benefit in that?" she asked.

"Don't blame Jim. 'Twas my own fault. I fell. My ankle twisted. It was after that the ball clipped me. Jim came rushing over and pulled me from harm's way. He's shot in the shoulder himself."

"Why'd you not say last night? I would have dressed his wound," interrupted Kirsty. "If he doesn't clean it right away, all manner of problems can result," she admonished.

"Just don't be hard on him Kirsty. He asked me not to trouble you, not to mention it. He's a high regard for you. Completely smitten, I'd say," revealed Liam, a mischievous twinkle in his eye. "Any cross words from you would be as a hundred arrows piercing his skin, as boiling water scalding his arms, as a swarm of bees stinging together, as a..." Liam's poetic efforts were interrupted.

"Alright, alright, I'm sorry. My words last night were so flinty. I'll be kindness itself when next we meet. I might go over to see him, check that his shoulder is properly dressed." Kirsty tried to hide the concern she now felt both for the wound by shot and any caused by her words. She'd felt the heat rise in her face when Liam talked of Jim's regard for her. She understood well the cause of her blush.

## Chapter 37

CONNOR lay in blackness. He could hear waves crashing upon rocks, their sound amplified by the walls of a cavern, relentless battering, throbbing, pounding in his head. He tried to remember, a mistaken endeavour as the roar of the waves increased in his head. Connor opened his eyes carefully, fearing in his heart that he was dead. Nothing had changed. Still there was blackness and still a pain beat in his head. Beating and throbbing, the pain rose and ebbed rhythmically. What was the rhythm? Was it the pulse of the ocean? He had no sense of wetness. He eased the questions into his thoughts gingerly and, anxious not to press, pain was the cane that beat him for enquiring too deep. His heart, his heart set the rhythm he could feel. Realisation, excitement at being alive called down massive blows from the cane. Connor blanked his mind, aware now of the rules. The pounding eased, subsided.

Where was the seat of the pain? Left temple seemed to be the cause. He thought slowly, obeyed the rules. But, . . . but, . . . the back of his head, right side, spasms of pain rippled through his head, confirming his over-eager analysis. His left temple and the back of his head were the damaged areas. He raised his left hand to feel around the swelling. The fingers on his right hand confirmed the lump at the back of his head, it's contours less easy to define through his hair, sticky with congealed blood.

His hands again at his sides, Connor's fingers, unbidden, rolled the links in the chain. Alarm struck, the pain came too, ignored this time as Connor pressed his mind, demanded of his memory. Why? – How? – The chains were gone forever. He was going home to Kathleen, to Liam, to Corryann. He raised his hands, stretching them apart 'til the bite of iron bracelets on his wrists confirmed he was once more a

184

prisoner. Tears poured, wetted his cheeks, aching head unnoticed now as the greater pain ripped at his heart, tore it through his ribs, constricted the back of his throat.

Torment was a dish he would not eat, Connor determined. He'd had taste enough of it in the past eighteen years. He swallowed the tightness in his throat and bade his heart be still. Apart from the blackness and the chains, he had no knowledge of his predicament, of its scale.

Connor felt the wall behind his back and used it to help raise himself onto his feet. He could stand. His hands were shackled together by a chain that was free. Blackness turned to darkness, his eyes adjusting to the grey light from a window close by. He could not yet discern the size of his cell, apart from the notion that he was in a large room. His cheeks chilled to the touch of the breeze blowing through the window, his nostrils detecting the essence of salt-water. He must be close to the sea. Connor heard movement about him, sounds of others in his prison, sounds of the sleeping. Grey light becoming brighter, Connor moved to the window shuffling his feet so as not to step on the sleepers he could sense, hear, about him. A crossed iron lattice, four bars horizontal and four bars vertical, blocked the window as a means of escape. The grey light was now dispersed by the onrush of dawn. Sunlight burnt off the darkness. Connor could now make out the forms of people spread across the floor as he turned from the window. Marks of the window bars criss-crossed bodies with light and shadow. There were perhaps twenty souls enclosed within the room. A heavy iron door was now visible on the wall opposite the windows. Connor's window was one of a pair, the other some ten paces from where he stood.

"We thought you was dead," the words startled Connor as he turned to their source, a shipmate he recognised as the pipe player from the night before.

"I thought as much meself," he replied. "How'd we come to be here? What's happened to our ship?"

The pipe playing sailor sat up, drew in his breath, "Pirates – we was boarded two days ago at night. Yu've been out cold all that time – 'tis why we thought you was dead!" he explained.

"There's no more than half of us left now," he continued, shaking his head slowly. "Many was killed in the fighting, Captain Davy, the first mate too." Connor flinched as the words were spoken. "They threw the badly injured into the sea alongside the dead," his voice quietened as he recalled the fate of his crewmates, his best friend, the drummer, amongst them. "We killed a few of them too. They didn't take us easy," he added, a semblance of pride in his voice. "You must've fallen early yurself?" he enquired.

Connor's memory stirred.

"Aye, I can remember a sound at the stern. As I looked over, a dark face, something in his hand, then nothing," he replied.

"You must've seen them coming. You're lucky you was hit rather than knifed." The pipe player nodded to himself in agreement with his own analysis.

"Where are we now?" asked Connor.

"Barbary pirates took us, took the ship. We've been landed in this town. The ship's gone, I don't know where," replied the pipe player. "There's blacks, Arabs, yellows, browns, all manner of people's here but I've seen no free white people; we's all locked in chains," he concluded.

"Do you know what they want from us?" asked Connor.

"No one's sure for certain but they didn't kill us, only killed the badly injured. There's none with injuries still lying in here. The best guess we've got between us is they'll sell us, sell us as slaves, bound and chained to work forever, least ways 'til the good Lord ends our suffering." The pipe player saw the dismay his last words had caused, noticed the sag in Connor's demeanour.

"Others hold a brighter view; they say we'll be kept so," he raised his hands clanking the chain between them. "Then, when we agree to join them as pirates, they'll take the chains off, not lock us up no more," he finished, trying to sound as cheery as he could.

Connor considered the two alternatives. The second was better than the first as it held more hope for eventual escape.

They heard the clank of an iron key turning in the lock, freeing the door to swing open on its hinges. Two dark-skinned men wearing only cotton breeches that billowed around their upper legs and buttocks, entered carrying a great iron pot. Each held one end of a wooden pole supporting the handle of the pot. Behind the food carriers, four armed men crowded the open doorway, their dark eyes mirroring the menace held in their hands. The iron key clanked as it turned, the lock holding fast in the metal door. There was no great rush for the food, a grainy substance dribbled with the gravy of lamb or goat. A routine had been established in the two days since their capture. The food was more palatable than their rations aboard ship. They were fed twice daily in such abundance that all could eat their fill; the contents of one great iron pot took most of the day to consume, the second, the evening. Fresh water was poured through a hole in the wall the size of a grown man's foot, into a trough some three paces long.

Connor, having eaten and drank beyond comfort, sat beneath the window, back propped to the wall. His captors' treatment of the prisoners did not match with the ferocity that had subdued them. There was plenty to eat and drink, space enough to wander about, fresh air from the windows, light of day, lack of brutality. Barbary pirates, their name and reputation feared, children went to sleep in dread of their presence. Connor's confusion at their treatment collided with a sense of comfort, a sense that their position was familiar.

A group of sailors gathered about Connor's feet, most possessed of more youth than himself, keen to obtain his views on their situation.

"We're well fed," said one young lad, the tilt of his head, left eyebrow drawn down, right eyebrow raised, questioning Connor as to the possible reason for their less than barbaric treatment. Connor's silence as he mulled the implied question drew another to speak.

"We've been treated well since the fight for the ship was lost," he stated. "No beatings," he continued, seeking reinforcement for his view.

"There's badness about somewhere," an older man now spoke. "They've not gained their reputation in church," he finished.

Connor's furrowed brow disappeared in an instant as

clarity opened his eyes to their fullest. He had recognised the familiarity, then his eyebrows sank once more, pressed down by the importance of his discovery.

"We're being treated in the way we look after the cows and goats at home," Connor spoke.

"You mean we're to be eaten?" interrupted the young lad who had spoken first.

"I've not heard that they eat people themselves," Connor replied, "but it's likely we're to be sold on as some form of livestock either to be eaten or, more likely, as beasts of burden," he concluded, his mind easier for solving the familiarity question which had troubled him.

"They'll want us in the prime for the market then," confirmed a sailor who had worked the land before he went to sea.

The group at Connor's feet dispersed throughout the room to impart their newly found knowledge as to their probable fate.

Connor determined that he had only one fate and that was to be reunited with Kathleen, to see again the young son who would, by now, be grown to manhood, to grow his crops and till the fields of Corryann. No man, Barbary pirate or not, would hold him for long from his own land.

Days passed, routine was established, fed, watered, exercised, rested, fed, watered, exercised, rested. Connor's head was mending, the lumps subsiding. He ate well and exercised most of his waking hours. He would have the physical strength to make his escape as soon as an opportunity arose.

Ten nights had passed since Connor had awakened to find his wrists in irons, the dawn spilling its light through the windows of his prison. *Clank*, the key turned in the lock, no iron pot of food this morning as guards poured through the open door, curved knives slashing at the slumbering prisoners. Connor raised his shackled hands, intending that the chain between would ward off the arcing blow. In a few minutes, their task complete, the guards sheathed their knives and exited the door. *Clank*, the key again turned in the lock.

Connor lay curled in a foetal position, his naked body cold

upon the stone floor. There was no mark of knife upon his flesh.

All of the men had had their clothes cut from them.

"What does this mean? Why have they left us so?" wailed a young seaman.

Silence followed, no man willing to talk of the fear they had felt as their clothes were slashed from them, of the foreboding that now gripped them as they lay defenceless, chained, naked, waiting.

*Clank*, the key turned. The door was pushed open until it met the wall inside the room. A guard waved his hand, beckoning the prisoners to exit. Impatient with the response, he raised his musket and fired, the explosion bouncing off the walls causing chips of stone to fly from the ceiling and then the side wall as the ball ricocheted. Prisoners got to their feet and, self-consciously, walked through the door, hands drooped in front to afford some discretion to their privates.

Connor emerged into a courtyard, bright sunlight causing his eyelids to drop, then raise a little, enough to see the way his feet should tread. His hand chain was now linked by rope to three others in line, one behind the other, following an armed guard that led them. Connor, at the rear of the queue, felt the jab of a musket in his back and then, a few paces on, a further jab. Having established his armed presence, the guard at the rear left Connor's back in peace.

Between white-walled alleys they walked, sometimes in shade but, at other times, with sunshine caressing their shoulders. Occasionally wider routes were traversed, squares crossed. Few people were about. Those they passed, all men, took little note of their passage. Now, walking down a broader street, they were led into a large square. Fifty or so iron rings hung from the south wall, spaced one pace apart. Eight had Connor's shipmates already attached, a small length of rope securing the hand chains to the ring. Connor's group was unroped from each other, then roped individually to a ring set at chest height. Connor watched as the survivors from his crew arrived to be roped in similar fashion 'til all twenty, ten to his left, nine to his right, were tethered in the manner of donkeys in a market, the strengthening sun burning their bare buttocks. Connor turned his eyes toward the sun, still low in the sky, and settled his gaze on the distant mountains, gold-capped as the sun's colour reflected upon the snowy peaks. For all the peril of his current situation, he dwelt upon the view. Turning to the west, his eyes picked out the masts of boats standing above the rooftops of the low buildings. That would be the direction of his escape when the time came.

Activity increased about Connor. Camels were driven into the square and tethered to hooks in the wall. A clatter of horses' hooves announced the arrival of strangely attired warriors as they galloped in and then reined in their mounts to an abrupt halt. Goats and sheep joined the gathering throng, dung and urine from all the animals enriching the air. Tethered sailors too, unable to withstand the ache in their bladders, relieved themselves, splattering their own feet. A few, out of nervousness at their plight, defecated. Guards sluiced their legs with buckets of water, eager to present the goods in best condition for sale. Buyers walked amongst the prisoners, forming their own impressions as to the worth of each one, the price they would bid to, if at all. Connor looked into the eyes of the tall black man that held his chin betwixt his thumb and forefinger. The next potential buyer was an old man, his body enclosed in a great cloak which also covered his head. Leathery hands stroked Connor's buttocks and, ignoring the flinch, explored his privates before moving on.

All the tribes of the world seemed to be present, all colours, all modes of dress, all kinds of faces, the biggest stew of people Connor had ever encountered. The tumult of noise subsided. The bray of the mule and the bleat of goat were the only interruption to the quietness. Six naked white girls were led, trussed, from a building adjoining the square, flesh pinched by eager fingers, to a platform in the middle of the square. Once upon the dais, the tumult of noise returned, a crescendo as the bidding started, then falling as buyers quit the bidding.

This established pattern continued through the morning. Connor was untied, led to the platform and paraded, his nakedness no longer troubling him – escape was all that he sought. A crescendo of noise now falling off, he could see the old man with the leathery hands gesticulating to the auctioneer. Connor was led from the platform, his chain passed to another who led him from the square. Salt-water, the taste in his nostrils was unmistakable. Connor's mind was set. He slowed his pace. Caught unawares by the change, his guard collided with him. Connor knocked the guard's musket from his hands and pinned his arms to his side – no chance to reach for his knife now! With no other weapon to use, Connor nodded his forehead with all the power he could gain from his neck muscles. He felt the cartilage of the guard's nose give way, felt the weight of his body as he lost consciousness. Released from Connor's grip, the guard slid to the ground.

Connor stooped to pick up the musket holding it by the barrel in his right hand. With his left, he sought the knife carried about the guard's waist. A musket nozzle prodded his head behind his right ear as a hand reached round from behind, taking the fallen guard's musket from Connor. The gunman pointed the musket at the guard's head and pulled the trigger. The unconscious guard would have no further need of his discharged musket, the contents of his head spread upon the ground by the lead ball's impact. Connor waited, anticipating blows at the very least, in no doubt as to the cruelty of the man behind him. A sharp prod to the base of his spine was all that followed. He walked immediately, his direction determined by a musket prod to either his left or right shoulder. A prod to his spine increased his pace in the direction he faced.

A gangplank pressed on the soles of Connor's feet as he was prodded again in the spine; a soreness had developed from prodding the same spot. Once aboard the single-sailed boat, he was pushed into a small hold below decks. It was then that he realised that his captor led another slave. He held her neck chain in his hand, a cloak draping her body. She too, was pushed into the hold.

In time, three further slaves arrived and they were all stowed together. Two were Connor's shipmates, all three delighting in the reunion. The third was another girl who spoke the same tongue as the first, a language beyond

Connor's comprehension. One of his shipmates was able to converse in a fashion with short, jerky sentences; they appeared to respond to Hollander. The boat put to sea not long after the arrival of the last three slaves. A pot of sweet fruits was passed into the hold, welcome sustenance as they had not been fed that day. The gentle rocking motion of the craft lulled Connor to sleep, thoughts of escape now waiting 'til morning. Dawn had not yet risen when the slaves were awakened, their boat now berthed in a different port. Three armed men drove the five slaves through the streets and alleys as the grey light before the dawn lit their way. Driven into a courtyard, the other four slaves were taken off. Connor was tied to a ring set in a stone bench that surrounded a fountain in the centre of the courtyard. He took the opportunity to drink from the trickling water.

As the dawn light rose from the east, Connor saw again the gold-capped mountains. Within the courtyard, each corner was possessed of a small tree, its branches laden with blossoms in such profusion it seemed they bent under the weight. Birds flitted from tree to tree, crimson breasts, yellow crowns and coats of black. A long-legged bird walked across the courtyard, unconcerned by Connor's presence. Purest white, with long, curved beak, it drank from the fountain's pool, then strode off in regal gait.

Connor chastised his mind for allowing this distraction; its task was clear, urgent; he needed an escape plan. Before his thoughts had settled upon the task, a guard appeared, walking from behind a blossom tree across the courtyard. As he drew close, Connor could detect no weapons about his person. Closer still, Connor felt familiarity with the face, with the eyes.

"Where did you come by that necklace?" asked the tall, black man. Connor stared, confused both by the ability of his questioner to speak his tongue and by the nature of the question. "Where did you come by that necklace?" repeated his interrogator, a hint of menace in his voice indicating his unhappiness at Connor's seeming reluctance to answer.

"It was a wedding present; I've had it twenty years," replied Connor, marshalling his wits.

"Who gave it to you?" the tall man's irritation evident in his voice.

"A good friend, a very good friend. Her name is Yomi. She made it with her own hands. It contains a lock of my wife's hair," Connor tried to appease his questioner.

"What can you tell me of your friend Yomi's history?" asked the tall man with a gentler tone to his question.

"Yomi came to our village some ... " Connor paused to calculate the passage of time since he had first met Yomi, "perhaps twenty-five, maybe twenty-six years ago. She came with a sailor who lived in the village – O'Rourke's his name. He rescued her from a slave ship bound for America." Connor looked at the tall man, seeking a sign that he had answered his enquiry.

"Go on. Do you know more?" encouraged the tall man.

Connor paused to recall Yomi's history as it was many years since he'd last heard the tale. Confident that he could recount most of it, he continued.

"Yomi was but a young girl, fifteen years I think, when strangers from another tribe took her, eight other girls too, gathered at the water ... " The tall man interrupted,

"What of her family? Did she talk of them?" His eyes burrowed into Connor, their intensity squeezing his soul.

"Yomi has two sisters and five brothers. The youngest brother was named Choma. She missed ... " Connor ceased speaking, his mouth crushed against the tall man's chest.

"I am Choma," the tall man stated proudly, squeezing Connor's head between his arms and chest with such force that, despite the joyous nature of this outburst, Connor became unsure as to whether or not he intended to kill him.

"I am Choma. You are Yomi's friend so I shall be your friend," said Choma, releasing Connor's head, clapping his hands upon the prisoner's shoulders. "Now you must come with me. We have much to talk of," said Choma untying Connor's chain from the ring. He led the manacled prisoner across the courtyard into a room where carpets and rugs were strewn across the stone floor, many layers of them.

A servant appeared unbidden. "Bring me some clothes for my new friend," ordered Choma. "Bring food also," his voice arresting the servant's progress in pursuit of the first command. A bow of ascent and he was gone to fulfil his master's wishes.

"When did you last see Yomi? Was she well?" Choma enquired, signalling Connor to sit close by his own seat.

"I've been away for eighteen years. I've not seen Yomi since the day the judge transported me," replied Connor. Choma's smiling face darkened at this news.

"Do you know if she still lives in your village?" A note of urgency strained Choma's voice.

"No, no. I've had no news from home in all the time I've been away – not even of my own family," added Connor, sensing the disappointment of Yomi's brother.

"I must hope, now that I have found her, that she will be well in your village," concluded Choma as his servant returned leading two others, one laden with clothes, the second carrying a tray stacked with food.

Connor's appetite dealt well with the provisions, his hunger sated on succulent sweet fruits he had never experienced before. Clothing his body added to his comfort.

"Why am I still shackled?" he asked, dropping the cloth with which he had wiped the juices from about his mouth, from between his fingers.

"You tried to escape once before. It was I who stopped you," replied Choma.

"I need you to lead me to my sister," he finished, though Connor did not hear these last words for his mind was replaying the fate of the fallen guard. He decided not to press the matter of his hand irons further.

"Why did you buy me at the market? It's a strange coincidence that I know of your sister?" asked Connor, curious for the answer.

"The necklace you wear is similar to one Yomi made for me when I was but a small boy." Choma held his wrist forward. "Now I wear it about my arm as my neck has grown. I have looked for Yomi these past sixteen dry seasons. I left my village to trace her journey, leaving my older brothers to look after our family. They bade me go because our mother wished to know of Yomi's fate. I found the tribe who had captured our maidens, came across the men responsible. I ate with them in the night knowing my likely fate at sunrise. They had taken many people over time. They boasted of their wealth from this trade. They told me I could join them but I was not to be trapped by their snare. I had a pouch of potion, my mother's medicine, which I mixed with their food. It made them sleep so that I could bind each one. Then I bound them all together.

"I did not kill them but followed their own path. I took them to the sea and sold them as slaves for gold coins. On the first day I made them walk all day without food or water so their strength was sapped. That evening, when I tied them to a tree, I took my knife, pulled back the head of their leader and slit his throat like a goat. His blood flowed from his throat 'til he lay dead. The other men grew quiet, then obeyed me without murmur.

"At the town, alongside the sea, I was told the slaves were sent to the white man's land, many weeks' journey across the great sea. I took advice and was told that my colour would prevent me being free if I went there and so I stayed in Africa, trading slaves and other goods. I am a wealthy merchant now. My servants tell me each time there will be white people to be bought in the markets along this coast. I have bought many but none before has known of my sister so I move them far from the markets of the sea to other markets where the price is always higher. When I saw the necklace you wore, my heart told me I had moved closer to knowing Yomi's fate. Your price was much too high; an old man bid against me. If not for the thong about your neck, you would be his slave now," Choma ended his story.

"The slaves I came here with, what . . ." Choma's raised right hand, palm toward him, stopped Connor's question. "They have gone from here now; it is of no consequence to you." Choma's words were delivered with immutability.

Morning passed and became afternoon. Connor continued to answer the questions from Choma, questions about Yomi, questions about Connor's transportation, about the land from whence Connor came. At the end of the questioning, Connor felt that all the juice had been squeezed from him.

"I will not sell you. You may come with me to find Yomi." Choma delivered his judgement at the end of his day of questioning. Connor had noticed no gesture but the servant reappeared, took him away and, when he had struck the shackles from Connor's wrists, led him to a windowless room with a bed. Connor was left to sleep as the key clanked in the lock.

The now familiar voice of this land woke Connor at dawn, a prolonged chant which reverberated over rooftops and infiltrated all the streets between, a chant which took place five times a day. A key clanked in the door and a tray of food was brought in. The door was left open.

Having eaten, Connor was escorted to the courtyard where four horses were tethered. A clap on his back from an open hand and Connor turned on his right heel to meet the smiling face of Choma.

"We ride to the sea. There is a city where ships sail to your land. I have bought a cargo of wool and leather to sell. The captain awaits my commands." Choma's words delighted, confused and impressed Connor. He was on his way to Kathleen. How had the cargo and the ship been procured in the time since the questioning finished only yesterday afternoon? How had prepar . . .

"You can ride a horse?" Choma enquired, interrupting Connor's thoughts.

"Yes, after a fashion," replied Connor, "You'll have to go steady as I've no great ability on horseback," he said, lest his skill be overrated.

Choma mounted and led the others through the arch from the courtyard. The horses galloped along narrow alleys, the fall of their hooves on the hard-packed earth, the only warning for any on foot to clear the way.

Outside the town, the track at first ran close by the seashore but soon turned in, away from the ocean, towards the snow-capped mountains. Exhilaration filled Connor's whole body and being as the rush of air swept his hair from the speed of his horse as it loped along. Once again, he was on his way back to Kathleen. A boat was waiting and, after perhaps a week or two at sea, he would be able to bury his face in her hair and gently squeeze her body 'til it moulded to his own.

The land they crossed was dry and covered in small

bushes. From time to time, shallow rivers were forded, water spraying from the horses' legs a welcome relief from the dust. Mountains to the right had lost their snowy mantle, seemed further away, of less magnitude...

Connor's nostrils tasted the salt-water before the sea came into view. Now their route took them once more along the ocean's side. As moonlight, shining from the water, replaced the light of day, the tired contingent cantered into a town. Masts of ships towered over their heads as Choma led Connor up a gangplank and two servants led the horses away. Lines were cast off. The rolling motion and flap of sails, within minutes of coming aboard, signified they were underway.

# Chapter 38

FITZPATRICK stood weeping, his shoulders jerking with every sob. Watery eyes criss-crossed half-burned timbers, his head, shaking from side to side, showed no comprehension there. Thin trails of smoke rose from charcoal debris scenting the air, nostrils confirming that which eyes refused to see.

"This cannot be, it cannot be," wailed his Reverence to none and all about him. Eyes downcast, ashamed to witness this outpouring, each man went about his task, save only for O'Sullivan.

"Fortune abandoned me long, long ago," sobbed Fitzpatrick. O'Sullivan's arms crossed his chest, his hands reaching and clasping his sides as the self-pitying words spilled from his Reverence's tongue.

"Did you not hear what I've just told you?" barked O'Sullivan, slapping the face of the pathetic body before him.

"How shall I pay my bills, I've a wife and children to feed?" said Fitzpatrick cowering.

"You've completely lost your senses now!" snarled O'Sullivan, "You've no wife; never have had. As for children, there's none as knows they're your'n."

"Help me, help me," pleaded the confused churchman.

O'Sullivan led Fitzpatrick from the scene that had so antagonised him. He would need to sit his Reverence down with pen and paper before the loss of his wits was publicly acknowledged. Proof would be required of their new arrangements. Seated in O'Sullivan's study, quill in hand, clean parchment upon the desk, the churchman waited for instructions.

"You're to write that all overdue tithes to be collected shall be the property of Desmond O'Sullivan Esquire," instructed O'Sullivan. "Then you're to sign it, with your seal too," he concluded.

The document signed, sealed, wafted to dry the ink, was now in the hands of the gleeful tax-collector.

"Why did you want that?" enquired Fitzpatrick. "There's no past tithes to collect. All the records are gone, burned. My wife, what will she say?" babbled the churchman, passing in and out of sanity as he spoke.

"We'll say I have a copy," replied the tax-collector, ignoring the reference to an imagined wife. "Who's to say otherwise with armed men to back my demands."

"You'll save me. You'll get the money for my bills?" pleaded the churchman, pulling at the lapels of O'Sullivan's coat.

"I will, if you do as I say," replied the tax-collector, freeing his lapels from the clutching fingers. "Now, get me some food and a drink."

Food eaten, thirst slaked, O'Sullivan plotted his next move, how to use his new written authority. Swift action need be taken. If the madness persisted, the authorities would come to hear of it, remove his Reverence and put another in his place. Tithes must be collected quickly. First though, the people must be subdued to reduce resistance to his demands.

"I'll need to take strong action, punish those who set the fire," he concluded. "The constable and troopers should bring all the young men to the prison for interrogation. You should issue the order now," stated O'Sullivan.

"Is the girl in blue coming today?" replied Fitzpatrick.

"What girl? Will you listen to me! You're to bring all the young men in. It's not likely a girl was involved," said the frustrated O'Sullivan.

"You promised to arrange for the girl to come for the sewing," continued his Reverence.

"There'll be no more girls for you. Now sign the order," concluded O'Sullivan, raising his hand as if to strike.

O'Sullivan realised it was the Macken girl Fitzpatrick craved. He fingered his scarred cheeks and determined he himself would definitely have her now. O'Sullivan left with the order. He was keen to collect his prisoners before Sunday morning church. The impact, the warning would then be transmitted at the congregation. All would be in fear of his power by midday.

Two troopers, muskets carried over their shoulders, walked behind O'Sullivan as he strode down the track to the Macken cottage. As they approached, the tax-collector was the first to see the body lying at the side of the cottage.

# Chapter 39

KIRSTY felt the warmth of her blush subside. She was greatly concerned for Jim's wellbeing. She would go to him as soon as breakfast was done. Liam smiled to see the colour in his sister's cheeks at the mention of Jim. He hobbled over to his sister whilst she prepared their meal.

'*Smack!*' the wooden door of the cottage hit the inside wall. O'Sullivan marched into the room.

"Where were you last night?" he demanded, glaring at Liam.

"He was here with me," replied Kirsty, stepping forward.

"And him too?" O'Sullivan's voice trailed as he turned signalling for two troopers to enter.

Jim's body was cast on the floor.

"Were you with him too?" sneered O'Sullivan, thrilling at the blood drained countenance of his recent tormentor.

Liam's brimming eyes could hold his tears no longer.

"Take him!" growled O'Sullivan to the troopers. Fresh misery contorted Kirsty's face to O'Sullivan's further delight. He was scarcely able to conceal his glee; the girl was in torment and he was in control.

"If you want to see your brother in health again, you had better change your ways toward me when I return," he smirked as he left the cottage to follow the troopers with their prisoner.

Kirsty sat down on the floor and cradled Jim's head upon her knee. Her fingertips caressed his cheek, brushed the dark locks from his forehead. Her tears fell as she gently rocked. Gently she rocked, back and forth, holding his head, aching within her breast. If only she had let him know, told him of her feelings but now it was too late; he was gone. Why hadn't she seen he was wounded? Perhaps she could have saved him. The noise, the crash, she had gone to look outside.

How was it that she did not see him? He could be alive now, if only, if only she had taken more care in her search.

As Kirsty sat cradling Jim's body, winter sun cast light upon the tragic pair, secret lovers, neither knowing of the other's love. For the first time, Kirsty told him of her feelings. "My love for you surged through my body with every pulse my heart did make, stronger than the waves of the ocean, sturdier than the greatest tree. I feared not tell you; now, too late, I wonder why. Your deep, brown eyes, gypsy locks, your smile, your teeth, to watch the words spill from your mouth, all precious to me then, more precious still the memory now. Darkness when you were cross, laughter, gaiety, all your emotions endeared your face to me. The crack in your eyebrow when you were puzzled, the way you danced and sang, now they are my memories, for I'll ne'er see them again. Rise of your chest, strength of your back, buttocks to be admired from afar, the trail of hairs on your stomach, the long line of your leg, toes on your feet, all of these I admired, now to wither and crumble, the fate of all that are dead. Can I hold all the memories clear today in my mind or will the movement of time cause them to fade or disappear like footprints upon the water?"

Kirsty started to rock gently backward, forward, backward, and forward. "Maybe if I'd known how you felt towards me, I'd have had the courage to be more open about my own feelings. It was only this morning Liam told me. Now he's taken." Kirsty stopped rocking as the tears spilled from her eyes. Time passed. Kirsty bent her head, kissed the violet eyelids on her lap and deep, brown eyes appeared.

"Am I dead and gone t'heav'n?" whispered Jim.

Kirsty covered his face in tears, "And how much of what I've said did you hear?" she asked.

"I've loved you since the first day I could say the word," murmured Jim in reply.

"You've bled a lot by the looks of you," her joy sharing her emotions with concern. "Lie still whilst I clean and dress the wound," instructed Kirsty.

She boiled water, took out clean strips of an old sheet, and helped Jim to make his way unsteadily to the table. She laid him down and bared his chest to begin work on the dried blood which covered a good part of the right side of his chest.

A knock on the door startled both nurse and patient. Seamus walked in.

"I've heard o' the trouble," he stated. "All the young men have been taken." He looked at Jim, squinting to align his vision. "We was told as how you were gone from us forever!" he challenged.

"Not yet," Jim replied feebly, wincing from Kirsty's ministrations.

"Where's Liam?" asked Kirsty, turning from her patient.

"Along with th' others," replied Seamus. "We sent for th' authorities from town," he continued. "They've not the law to do what they've done; he's overstretched himself this time has Fitzpatrick," he concluded.

"O'Sullivan seemed to be the master when he was here earlier," Kirsty responded.

"Well, no matter who, Fitzpatrick or O'Sullivan, they've overstretched themselves and the judge should order a release for all before nightfall," Seamus nodded, confirming this opinion to himself, shaking away the doubts he had.

"Could you call on Yomi, ask her to come?" said Kirsty. "I've some broth for Jim to build him up but I'd value her opinion on the wound." Seamus nodded as he opened the door.

# Chapter 40

YOMI pushed on the unlatched door of the cottage. Kirsty was sitting on the bed by Jim's head, her eyes closed, her fingers intertwined in his hair. Jim lay sleeping, his cheek against her thigh.

Kirsty woke with a start as she sensed movement in the room.

"It's only me. Sorry to startle you," apologised Yomi. "What's happened? Seamus told me Jim had been shot and the authorities think him dead. He told me you needed me to come quickly," said Yomi.

"Jim and Liam were involved in burning the Records Office. Jim's been shot in the shoulder. He lay outside all night and lost a lot of blood. He brought Liam back last night; Liam was shot too, in the leg. I was so cross with them. I turned Jim out. I'd no idea he was hurt at all. This morning, O'Sullivan came with troopers. They'd dragged Jim from outside and threw him on the floor, thinking he was dead. We all thought he was dead but maybe the cold, maybe the loss of blood... anyway, he's revived and he's eaten well but I'm not happy with the wound. Liam's been taken," Kirsty concluded her brief history of the day's events.

"How's Liam's leg?" asked Yomi.

"Oh, oh, that's fine, just a graze but I'll be pleased to see him home," said Kirsty, anxiety straining her voice. "Seamus said they'd release him and the others they've taken so I hope I'll see him this evening," she said, squeezing her left hand with her right.

"Let's have a look at Jim then," said Yomi as she bent to undo the dressing covering his right shoulder. As her fingers explored the wound, Jim awoke, his eyes immediately re-shutting, clenched.

Yomi stood up. Jim's eyes opened. "You will need to boil some water. The ball is still inside and will have to come out." Jim's eyes clenched shut again at Yomi's words.

Removal of the lead ball took little time though Jim might disagree. Yomi smoothed a paste over the injury, then re-bandaged the shoulder. Kirsty exercised the fingers of her left hand to relieve the crush as Jim had squeezed the life out of them during the operation.

Dusk was settling, darkening the cottage. Kirsty lit two candles. As she did so, an inrush of air fanned by the sweep of the door opening, caused the flames to flutter, fight for their survival and regain their balance. Liam's face was a welcome sight for Kirsty, Jim's face a shocking but welcome sight to Liam.

"I thought you were gone," the words were almost a whisper as Liam advanced towards his friend.

"Not for a while yet, I hope!" grinned Jim, "How's your leg now?" he asked.

"Fine, fine. It was hardly a scratch really but O'Sullivan is mightily suspicious. He says it's a musket ball that caused it. I told him to go away with his balls; it was the corner of the table I banged into during the night," said Liam, feigning to make light of it. "He'll be back after me though. His mistake was in collecting everyone, rather than the few he suspected. His face was as full and scarlet as a boil fit to burst when they were told to release all of us," he concluded. His brow creased, considering the seriousness of his position. Kirsty took note of his frown.

"Do you think he'll come back for yourself and Jim then?" she queried, his anxiety infecting her.

"To be sure, if he knew Jim was alive, he'd be back in a moment for him. He'll maybe wait a day or two for me," he answered as he weighed the likely outcomes.

"He's busy collecting taxes," said Yomi.

"But the records have been burnt," Liam responded.

"Well, burnt or not, O'Sullivan's been collecting tithes, worse even than those he took from the poor undertaker," replied Yomi.

"I don't see how..." Liam spoke as he thought. "He doesn't need records. He pays no attention to the truth, that man. He caused the death of the young boy, now his father too," interrupted Yomi.

"What's happened to the undertaker?" asked Kirsty, alarm increasing the beat of her heart, thumping inside her breast.

"This morning they found the undertaker, not a breath in his body, no coat, frost on his shirt. He was lain across the graves of his wife and son – probably been there all through the night. Now all three are together for the first time," Yomi finished, looking at her friends, sharing the sadness that ached in their chests.

The long silence was ended by Liam. "If the devil has two horns, then it must be that O'Sullivan and Fitzpatrick are the shape of them. They're the worst evil I have ever known," he said, his voice even, slow, quiet.

"What further torment can these horns cause?" asked Kirsty of herself and the others in the room.

"Well, Jim must go into hiding. They must never know that he's survived," said Liam with conviction.

"But he cannot go away; I need him near; he's injured," words, reasons leapt from Kirsty's mouth. She'd thought him dead, realised how she felt; to lose him now would be beyond all enduring.

"Yomi, you've seen the wound. It would be a grave risk for Jim to go away unattended," she beseeched her friend to support her.

Liam walked to his sister, held her shoulders cupped in his hands.

"Kirsty, all that I know of your feelings for Jim and his for you, you've a choice to make as has he. You can love him dead here or love him alive from afar."

"How long? How long must he be away?" asked Kirsty, her eyes focused on her brother's.

"For as long as the horns of the devil live here amongst us," replied Liam, his mouth confirming the torture that his eyes transmitted.

"It may be that I should leave for a while myself, 'til the embers of O'Sullivan's fury burn out," he continued, not wishing to draw out the pain for his sister.

"Maybe we should all leave together," Kirsty could think

of no other answer to losing the two men she loved. "How would I talk to Mother? What of our father? How will he find us?" Her words tumbled out, matching the speed of her thoughts.

Liam, alarmed at the distress he was causing his sister, tried to calm her.

"We'll hide Jim in the cave on the other side of the bay – it's no more than an hour's walk. He should be safe there. You could tend to him there. I'll not leave yet but I'll try to measure the mood of the devil's horns; I'll only go if the risks look high." Liam's words soothed Kirsty's despair, easing it from her mind.

# Chapter 41

O'SULLIVAN grasped the stem of the glass in his fist and drank from the bowl, red trickles running from the edge of his mouth, wine rolling down his throat, helped on it's way by his slurping tongue. He was not sure that ale might have been more to his taste but wine was drunk by those who had substance, those with a position. The bottle tipped in salute to the tax-collector as he refilled the glass grasped in his hand. Empty, pushed to the side to join two others, a second cork pulled.

A third cork was pulled. O'Sullivan had slowed his drinking, having reached a conclusion to his earlier question. He was sure he did prefer ale to wine. His thoughts meandered forwards as he watched his Reverence quaff his wine. He needed a plan. He had been humiliated by having to free all the young men. This had the opposite effect to that he had intended. He needed to establish his authority and power over those who must pay him that which he demanded. Lessons must be taught, not with soft words but with hard actions, unforgettable lessons that would be entwined in Corryann folklore. He would be a man to be feared by all.

"We must catch and punish those as burned the Records Office," he said to himself.

"But we don't know who they are. How's it to be done?" said Fitzpatrick in a lucid moment.

"We knows a lot. The guards say they saw four or five men. We knows that Cassidy was one. Pity he died or else we'd have forced the names of the others from him. We knows most likely, in fact, for sure, that young Macken was one; turned out just like his father, a criminal that one. The mother was no better; the daughter's took after her I'd say," he paused.' The fingers of his right hand pawed his left cheek, feeling the scars.

O'Sullivan continued, "We need to make an example of the Macken's; they're troublemakers. We've to show the rest we won't put up with the likes of them," he paused again.

"Yes . . . you're right," slurred Fitzpatrick.

"They've buried their mother on the headland where she jumped. It's a secret grave but I've been told where it is. She shouldn't be there; we should throw her carcass in the pit where the dead livestock rot. That's the proper place for her. When it's done, we'll take young Macken for questioning. I'm sure, in time, he'll admit to the fire, tell us of the others too," he finished, the combined excitement and wine flushing his cheeks.

"One other thing we should do . . . " pressed O'Sullivan.

"Wass thatt?" slurred his Reverence.

"That undertaker as died this morning in the graveyard. It was very suspicious as to how. We should throw his carcass into the animal pit as well," said O'Sullivan, his eyes sparkling in the candlelight, in danger of popping out of his head. Fitzpatrick's head lay on the table, eyes closed and his hand atop the fourth uncorked bottle which glugged out its contents as it lay on its side.

O'Sullivan rose, spat on the sleeping churchman's head and went to his quarters.

# *Chapter 42*

KIRSTY climbed up the cliffside track. Small stones, fragments of rock rolled past her, rolling over her bare feet, dislodged by Yomi's progress four paces above her. Atop the cliff, Kirsty's torn feet were grateful for the softness of the grass now beneath them. She turned. Way down below, a tiny figure at the entrance to a cave held a small arm aloft in a gesture of goodbye. Kirsty waved back and stood for some time matching semaphore with her love below until Yomi drew her away lest Jim's presence be detected by the waving from above.

"'Tis cold and damp down in the cave," she voiced her thoughts to Yomi.

"He can't have a fire to warm him because the smoke would be his undoing," Kirsty continued, talking both to herself and Yomi as they walked away towards their own firesides.

The pale yellow sun, it's day's work starting, melted the silver crusty dew from tree, from grass, from earth, the silver mantle slowly leaving the land. Kirsty noticed it not at all, her mind consumed with thoughts of Jim.

"Am I putting him in harm's way?" she asked herself. "Should I send him away, both for his better safety and his health? The wound'll be slow to mend in present circumstances," she posed her questions holding onto Yomi's arm, bidding her to stop. "What's your view? What is it I should do that'd be best for Jim?"

"He'd be best in your cottage. Warmth from your fire, warmth from your heart is the best medicine for him," replied Yomi.

"But O'Sullivan'll take him," Kirsty responded.

"You're right, he will. So even if the warmth from your heart has to travel a distance, he'd still be best in another cottage with the warmth of a fire giving heat and dryness to mend him," concluded Yomi.

Kirsty's breast rose as a mighty pull of air filled her lungs 'til they could take no more. Her chest fell, the air rushing out at speed through the confines of her mouth and nose, creating a soft whistle.

"I'll send him away this evening. If he won't go, I'll tell him he's nothing but trouble to me". Kirsty started to sob, "That he's nothing but trouble and I wish to be rid of him."

Yomi took her young friend in her arms and gently squeezed the sobbing body, holding it close to her own.

# Chapter 43

TWO weeks had passed since Connor had boarded the ship. Now he stood on the quayside but a few miles from his home, from his wife Kathleen, his son Liam. The clack of horses' hooves sounded on the cobbles as Choma passed the reins of the bay to Connor and mounted his own steed, a dapple-grey. Choma had given orders to the captain that he was to keep the crew aboard and be ready to sail by the evening; they still had a cargo of wool and leather to sell in a city port, two days' sailing from where they lay.

They were soon clear of the town, passing bare fields to the right, woodland on their left. Save seagulls above, there were few creatures about, all resting from the winter. Connor sucked in the air, drawing it through his nostrils to enhance its taste. To smell again his own homeland, the moment of his wanting now so close at hand, was bliss.

On Choma's instructions, they rode first to the home of O'Rourke so that he might finish his quest to be reunited with his sister. There were none to greet them so they travelled on in the hope that perhaps Yomi was with Kathleen. Connor's tears flowed unabated as the horses drew near to his home. He leapt down from his saddle and rushed through the door in anticipation of surprising his wife and son but, alas, he found the cottage empty.

"Where to now?" asked Choma, disappointed for the second time.

"We'll try the headland; that was always our favoured spot," said Connor, re-inflating his eagerness. "If not there, we'll try the village," he said, once more upon his steed.

As they rode past Corryann, past his land cultivated with his sweat and toil and now bedecked with frosty lace, Connor's mood, his exultation changed as the seagulls called her name. As they swooped and swirled above him, he recalled gulls calling, a message on the breeze. He had cried, not knowing why when Warden Gavin had brought his release papers. Connor rode in quiet contemplation, foreboding seeping into his soul and then, ahead, he saw a man kneeling.

Sweeney rose as the two horsemen approached. "Connor?" he said, questioning his own eyes. "Connor, it is you?" Recognition was now complete. Sweeney's smile swept across his face, disappearing almost as it formed. "I'm solly, solly Connor," said Sweeney, pointing to the ground at his feet. Connor dismounted and walked towards him.

"Why are you sorry?" Connor asked.

"Kathleen." said the simple man, his head downcast, his right index finger pointing to the ground beside him.

Connor looked but could see nothing on the ground. "Where is Kathleen? Have you seen her?" he asked quietly.

"Connor, she's died. She's here, lying beneath the ground," Sweeney raised his head, red-rimmed eyes a constant feature now.

Connor knew not what to think. As he drew closer, he could see that the land was disturbed; it did look as if a grave were there but he could not bring himself to believe.

"How, when?" he asked.

"She fell from the cliff over there," Sweeney pointed toward the ocean. "It was some months ago." He tried to think, "September, it was September," he concluded, casting his head down toward his toes once more.

The blow struck Connor full force in the chest, splitting his breastbone, spilling his insides. September, the message on the breeze, now he understood. Kathleen, Kathleen, she was gone from him. "No! No! No!" he shrieked, now on his knees, fingernails piercing the fleshy heel of his hands, hands beating upon the ground.

"I'm sorry Kathleen. I'm so sorry. I left you for too long. I should have been here. I should have been here to stroke your hair, to keep you from harm," he wailed.

Liam hurried along the track past Corryann. Seamus, having heard of the horseriders, had found Liam reading a letter for one of the villagers. Both of them headed for the cottage, then, seeing the marks from the horses' feet, followed towards the headland. Liam arrived to see his distraught father beating the ground. He knelt beside him, clasping him to his chest.

Connor's distress calmed and, as he drew away, he looked into the eyes of the young man and saw Kathleen's eyes.

"Liam. Is it you? My son, Liam."

"Father, it is I. We have waited for you for so long – Mother waited but she was unwell and then..."

"I know Liam," Connor said gently. "Sweeney has told me what happened but how should it be? She knew this place so well; she would never have fallen."

"No one knows, father. Some wonder if it was her illness but we don't believe that. Mother would never have left us for any reason."

"Us? You say us?"

"Father, I have a sister Kirsty. She's your daughter born just months after you were taken. It was Kirsty who found Mother at the base of the cliffs."

The thought that he and Kathleen had a daughter filled Connor with excitement and delight but the horror of what his daughter must have felt, finding her mother, broke his heart. He sobbed again, grieving for the woman he had left so long ago, the woman whose memory had given him hope and the will to live for the past eighteen years and the daughter he wished he could have protected as a father should. He clung to his son, holding tight lest he too might slip away.

"Kathleen, why ever did I deserve one such as you? Why did I not make it back to you in time?" A salt-water stream ran down his face as Connor's emotions, once more unable to be contained, tore through his chest, his throat, his mouth, ripping and squeezing his bones, his flesh. "Kirsty," he repeated. "The name's somehow familiar. All manner of thoughts have come to my head, unbidden on the breeze from the ocean, the call of the gulls," he mused to himself. "Kathleen, for all we've been so far apart, there've been times I've felt your presence alongside of me," Connor said, stroking the grass atop her grave, his fingers as tender as they had once been upon her neck.

"Where is she? Where's Kirsty now?" asked Connor, the

tumult of his emotions swinging wildly between rapture and despair.

"She'll likely be along soon enough; she visits our mother every day. She went with Yomi to see a friend early this morning," said Liam.

Connor felt his emotions coming back under his control. He slowly stood up and looked at his son. Placing his hands on his son's shoulders, he smiled and said, "Liam, Liam. My son. You've grown to be a fine, strong man. Now, I need to introduce you to Yomi's brother, Choma."

Connor waved his right hand in the direction of the tall man who advanced towards Liam, taking Liam's right hand, holding it with both hands.

"Please, tell me where I might find my sister; tell me where Yomi is. Can you take me to her?"

"She'll be with Kirsty. It's best we wait," Liam responded.

Kirsty stopped beside their land. In the distance, she could see the group of people, horses too, on the headland. Good sense bade her turn back, to come again later when she might be alone to talk with Kathleen. As she made her way back to the cottage, bad sense pushed her to ignore good. Once more, she turned, her need to investigate was stronger than her fear.

As she neared, she looked towards the group and saw the tall, unknown, dark man with Seamus and Sweeney. Then beyond, she looked past the horses to the two men beside her mother's grave. The first she knew for certain, the second also; her intuition left her in no doubt that he was her father, returned at last.

She flew the ground between them, casting herself upon her father, knocking her brother to the ground, laughing and crying, a maelstrom of emotions releasing. Connor's vision, blurred by tears, saw much of the young Kathleen he'd left but this, this was his daughter, his daughter Kirsty.

"Kirsty, oh Kirsty. My daughter." He held her tight and then looked at her at arm's length, tears welling as he quietly spoke aloud, "Kathleen, why did you go? Why can't you share this moment with me?" He worked his jaw from right to left, left to right, right to left in an effort to control his emotion as he spoke.

215

"She loved you so . . . she didn't go. It was O'Sullivan who struck her, tore her dress, sent her to the rocks below," said Kirsty, anxious that her mother's alleged wrong be righted. "O'Sullivan told Fitzpatrick she had jumped. 'Tis the reason she's buried here and not on consecrated ground." Kirsty finished, words shared, never spoken, ones she had kept to herself since she learned the truth from the lustful O'Sullivan before she scarred him. Her father was here now, someone to look after her, someone with whom she felt she could confide her dangerous secret.

The impact of her words on those about her brought O'Sullivan's future life into jeopardy. Fury added to the tumult in Connor's breast as he fought to find a fitting means of ending the life of the tax-collector which lacked the mercy of swiftness. Sweeney shook his head slowly from side to side; the inherent badness in his old employer wrought malice in his kindly head. Seamus, already ridden with shame for bending to Fitzpatrick's will at the graveyard, looked like the dead himself, all blood having departed from his face. Liam, grateful to have his inner feelings confirmed (he had never thought his mother had taken her own life), now worried that his father's freedom might be forfeited again if he wrought the vengeance signalled by his tortured eyes.

"Who is this man?" asked Kirsty, eager to change direction.

"He's Choma, Yomi's youngest brother," replied Connor.

"Do you know where Yomi is?" asked Choma, who had, 'til then, stood away from the grief and joy of those about him.

"I was just with her. She'll be coming here soon to meet me again," said Kirsty. "She'll be that pleased to see you; they'll hear the shriek in Africa itself!" Kirsty continued. "She never thought to see you again. Hope in her had all but faded for she knew not how to find the land from whence she came once she learned of O'Rourke's death – he was her only link with her homeland." Kirsty, having pleased Choma, turned to her father and squeezed his head as hard as she was able, crushing him against her flattened breast.

"'Tis the happiest day since the sky and the oceans were born, since birds took wing, since..."

"And there was me thinking I was the family's poet!" rejoined Liam.

Kirsty grinned and winked her right eye at her brother. The trough of despondence had been lifted and the mood changed to one of quiet joy and then to one of celebration.

Seamus cried, "Look!" right arm raised, index finger straight, directing everyone's attention towards a group of men, advancing from the left.

O'Sullivan walked in front of two lackeys, Hanrahan and another pushing a handcart. Two spades bounced upon the bed of the cart as the wheels crunched over stones on the track. At the rear, six armed militiamen followed the handcart. Pale yellow sun warmed the blades of grass beside the path and freed them of the weight of frozen dew. As the tears of dew rolled down, blades of grass reached up towards the warming sun.

Hanrahan was the first to notice the group standing on the headland as they walked towards it.

"What now?" he asked O'Sullivan.

"What we have come to do should be a lesson to all as lives in these parts. The more that knows of it, the better for us," said the tax-collector.

"It's O'Sullivan, troopers and a cart," said Liam, turning to his father.

"What business do they have here? I'll kill that wretched man!" Connor's face, contorted by the strength of his feelings, put all about him in fear of the nearing consequences.

O'Sullivan stopped, his toes sliding into the cap of his boots, stubbed by the sudden halt. The handcart hit him gently behind the knees, it's pushers caught unawares. Hanrahan flinched, his ears ready for the curses though none came. The only sound was a soft hiss as the tax-collector sucked air across his life-stained teeth.

"It's Macken himself." Limbs and lips quivered beyond his control as O'Sullivan stood in fear of the man he had so badly wronged.

"Perhaps we should return another day," said Hanrahan.

"There's no need to inflame the situation now," he continued, seeking to avoid a confrontation, knowledgeable too of the wrong that had been done to Macken. He had been a part of it. Hanrahan's words had the opposite effect to that which he intended. O'Sullivan regained control of his trembling lip and shaking limbs. This was the test. If they left now, without creating the unforgettable lesson, then his authority would never hold. Tithes could only be wrung from a people who had been crushed, ground down to accept his word for fear of the consequence. Macken was but a convict. O'Sullivan stood with a force of arms behind, six muskets at his command.

"Muskets at the ready lads!" O'Sullivan shouted so that those behind would obey and those in front were less likely to resist. As he walked forward, he called for the militia to advance alongside. Seven men in a line fronted Connor, six with loaded muskets. O'Sullivan cleared his throat.

"You've carried out an illegal burial. Kathleen Macken's remains are to be taken from here to be cast in the pit with the other dead animals. She forfeited a Christian burial by taking her own life."

Connor flinched as the tax-collector's words struck, splinters of wood piercing his chest, rough edges tearing his flesh.

"You killed my mother. She never took her own life," Kirsty fired her words at O'Sullivan. "You attacked her here, on this very spot, tore her dress, struck her face and sent her to the rocks below." She now addressed the militia whose shuffling feet and downcast faces reflected the portent that her words had struck.

"Lies! Lies! Lies!" shrieked O'Sullivan, turning to the men whose muskets protected his life. "She's a lying whore, her mother before her too. The father's a convict. The son was one who fired the Records Office, the whole of them a nest of whores and criminals." He spat the words, globs of spittle spraying those about him and running down his chin. Unease amongst the troopers was not steadied by his words. O'Sullivan addressed the wavering militia.

"Kathleen Macken took her own life!" His judgement filled the air as thunder from above.

"Bring the spades," yelled O'Sullivan to Hanrahan who furtively cast around before meekly obeying the command. Connor moved to block access to the grave.

"Move away, move away or you'll be back to Botany Bay, never to return this time!" screamed O'Sullivan.

Liam stepped forward, standing by his father's right hand. Kirsty stepped forward to stand by her father's left hand. Sweeney stepped up beside Kirsty and Seamus, beside Liam. Choma moved forward, the two horses at his side.

"Dig!" screeched O'Sullivan, froth spilling from his mouth as he addressed Hanrahan.

Hanrahan looked at his employer then turned to Connor, "Sorry." He dropped the spade and walked away.

O'Sullivan snatched the spade from the ground, "Raise your muskets!" he screamed.

The troopers looked to their captain for confirmation. He nodded. The muskets raised, pointed chest high.

Choma analysed his position. He had no reason to die for this family. It was not his own. He turned his head and saw the form of a dark-skinned woman some two hundred paces from where he stood. Yomi was coming. In his heart, he knew it to be her. Should they be reunited after all this time only for his lifeblood to ebb from him, staining the earth of this foreign land? The injustice to Connor, a man he had come to admire in the short time they'd travelled together, the debt he owed to the Macken family for their friendship to his sister, it was not enough to die on this spot for. He turned and ran toward his sister.

Seamus stared into the barrel, a dark black hole aimed at his chest. He felt the shame of the churchyard, his brother's daughter now buried on non-consecrated ground. Kirsty's words had soothed him somewhat for her grave looked o'er the sea, o'er Corryann. O'Sullivan it was that murdered her. How could he excuse his thoughts that believed she'd quit life on her own? Seamus eyed the evil taxman. Could he bring him down, kill the evil before the musket ball stopped him dead?

Sweeney's eyes cast down upon the grave. He would gladly fall and die to lie close by Kathleen. How to save her family? That's what she'd want. Could he make the ground to O'Sullivan and carry him over the cliff but a few paces beyond?

Liam brushed his left arm against his father's right hand. He'd die to protect his mother's grave, die alongside his father, the father he'd missed for most of his life, die beside Kirsty and her young life dark before the light took hold. All would be dead. Then, then what, their mother disinterred? All lost, nothing gained... he could see no solution.

Kirsty gripped her father's hand tightly within her own. Her fingers were not able to encircle his, the soft palm of her right hand pressing against callused flesh in his left. She wanted to live. Her father was home and as much the man she'd dreamed he'd be. Now she'd listen to his tales, be able to catch up lost time, learn his history. Stories of Kathleen he'd know, of when she was but a girl. She'd tell all that he might wish of that which happened in his absence, of Kathleen, Liam, herself, if he'd a mind to know. She'd talk of Jim, the love she felt, his problems with the law. Yes, yes, she was sure her life was not ready to be ended. Yet, she would stand beside her father. If shots were fired, she would fall to die with those she loved. In silent prayer, she bade farewell to Jim.

Connor felt the pressure from his daughter's hand and Liam's closeness as his arm brushed his right hand. The emotions of the past hour had exploded within his body, blasting it asunder but still each organ remained in its place. The blasts had caused pain and ache to all of his being. Now he had a son and daughter to protect and his wife's body lay close by. Her murderer was a few feet hence, death for his whole family beyond. His heart pleaded forgiveness from Kathleen for that which he must do. His muscles, body as a whole, refused to obey; he could not abandon Kathleen even as in death she lay.

"Dear God, is there no way my suffering you can end? I must protect my children but I can't abandon my beloved wife," he implored, his eyes raised to the sky.

Sweeney stepped forward towards O'Sullivan. 'Click, click, click, click, click, click,' six muskets cocked, "No! No!" cried Kirsty.

Sweeney dropped to his knees, his face turned to the sky.

All present looked up at the sky, pale blue with small patches of light, grey cloud, wisps of white, gulls swooping, swirling above the ocean. Seagulls scattered abstractly across the sky began to form a pattern in line now, a scythe formation descending, accelerating. O'Sullivan dropped his spade as the swooping birds appeared to be directed toward him. His arms went up to protect his face. Gulls swooped over his head, formation dispersing to return to their abstract dance. O'Sullivan's feet became entangled in the spade as he stumbled backward, desperate to regain his balance. Falling, falling... still there was no ground to stop his progress until the rock bit into his head, releasing all the evil. The ocean crashed onto the rocks and swept the evil far from shore.

Troopers, abashed, put down their muskets and walked away.

Kirsty held her father's hand as they gazed at the rocks below. "He was a truly wicked man," she said.

"Yes," Connor agreed "but he loved your mother. He loved Kathleen. We both did."

## THE END

*Coming Next*

## "Footprints on the Water"

By Larry Tracey

Read the prologue

# Footprints on the Water

## Dresden – Germany, August 1992

Katya struggled to raise her body from the ground. Yesterday's news... offers for old cars, new washing machines, tumbled from her clothing as her legs pushed her upward through the tangle of yellowing newsprint.

Struggling to balance, first on her right foot, then on her left, she stood erect clutching a brown paper bag to her chest. As her weight continued to shift from one foot to the other, Katya pushed the bag higher between her breasts until the neck of the bottle within touched her lips. She gulped fumes from the bottle. Casting it aside, she stumbled through the detritus around her feet.

The clothes that hung on her fleshless frame oozed stale urine and alcohol vomit, a cocktail of filth, the odour of decay. Katya stooped to pick up the front page of the newspaper which lay at her feet.

'BARCELONA OLYMPIC GLORY,' her lips silently mimed the last two words of the banner headline. Her fingers opened letting the paper slip past her stomach, past her knees, sliding over her ankles and feet.

Katya walked towards the sound of the approaching train. "Olympic Glory – Olympic Glory," she whispered as she stepped over the rails. Her feet, loose in old laceless trainers, slipped on the rocks between the wooden sleepers. Katya Schmidt, twenty-eight years old, looked at the pale light coming towards her in the dawn. Her eyelids blocked out the light. She fell, her knees seeping blood on the crushed rocks, her head bouncing lightly on the silver rail.

Pain shrieked from metal wheels, the bite of the brakes on the inner rim at one with the muscles of the train driver, in spasm, strangling his bones. He had seen the figure step over the rail, turn towards him and fall. Now he waited, emergency brakes applied, tightness in his throat and chest, his legs braced. The distance between the figure and himself closed now more slowly and then became constant. His left foot slipped on the step as he raced from his cab. He picked himself up and ran to the body lying five metres in front of his engine.

. . . . . . . . . . . . . .

Katya could see the light through her eyelids. She opened her eyes. A nurse was talking to her, smiling. "Brother," she heard. Then Katya closed her eyes, lost consciousness.